The Christmas Diary
Lost and Found

Book 2

Elyse Douglas

COPYRIGHT

The Christmas Diary Lost and Found
Copyright © 2020 by Elyse Douglas
All rights reserved

This is a work of fiction. Names, characters, places and incidents are either the product of the author's imagination or are used fictitiously. Any resemblance to actual persons, living or dead, events, or locales is entirely coincidental. The copying, reproduction and distribution of this book via any means, without permission of the author, is illegal and punishable by law.

ISBN: 9798693375529

Broadback Books USA

"Memory… is the diary that we all carry about with us."

—Oscar Wilde

***

"Love's not Time's fool."

—William Shakespeare

Sonnet 116

.

To Mom… and her Christmas fruitcake.

The Christmas Diary

Lost and Found

CHAPTER 1

Alice and Jack Landis were lying in their queen-size bed, as early morning light leaked in from under the lacey blue curtains. She was asleep, he awake, dreamily remembering their early morning tangle of love and his sleepy contentment afterwards. He made a little sigh of pleasure, feeling his wife's breath soft and humid against his neck.

Outside, Jack heard birdsong, and the wind sighing around the house. In the distance, he heard the comfortable drone of a single-engine airplane slowly fading into the silence. In the house, there were sounds of life: running water in the pipes; the whisper of the heat kicking on, and muffled footsteps above as the couple in the upstairs room stirred.

It was December second, and from his digital clock he saw that it was 6:42 and the temperature was thirty-eight degrees.

His mind was active and worried. He stared at his sleeping wife, Alice, for a time, and a warm smile hung on his lips as he watched her fluttering eyes. What was she dreaming?

As if she'd heard his thoughts, she began to stir. Minutes later she awoke, put the back of a hand to a yawn, and glanced at her husband, squinting with sticky, sleepy eyes. "Good morning."

"And a good morning to you," Jack said.

Alice stretched both arms and yawned again. "Have you been awake long?"

"Ten minutes or so."

"You look wide awake, and I hear your brain working."

"Yeah... I guess I can't shake off last Thursday's City Council meeting. Those developers will choke off the peacefulness and beauty of this place," Jack said, soberly, his hands laced behind his head as he stared up at the ceiling. "They'll cut down that grove of trees near the pond, and put a road across the back meadow where the wildflowers bloom in spring, and where we have picnics in summer."

Alice rolled onto her side to face him. "Is there anything else we can do? Have we done enough? There's got to be some way to stop them."

"I don't know. I've seen this kind of thing play out in other areas. More often than not, by the time people like us find out about a real estate project like the one we're up against, and we identify all the issues we don't like, the basic decisions have already been made. Just like at the City Council meeting last Thursday when we all protested."

"We got a lot of media attention," Alice said.

"But I don't think it will change anything because, as my father used to say, the horse has already left the barn."

Alice ran a hand across Jack's mass of black chest hair, her eyes taking him in with pleasure. She loved his thick, black, wavy hair, his flat stomach, his muscled arms and lantern jaw. She loved gazing into his clear, steady eyes that startled her with unexpected excitement, like the first time she'd seen him three years before, standing tall and handsome in that ski lodge.

Besides being head-over-heels in love with her husband, Alice also admired and respected him. Jack owned his own construction business, and because he was skilled, honorable and dependable, he was in persistent demand, having more work offers than he could accept. As a result, the leaders of the neighborhood had come to him for guidance when the news about Morningside Developers' intentions first became known.

Alice lifted on an elbow, fixing Jack with a stare. "We have to find a way to fight this. Our house and others like it have been here for a hundred or more years. It's the reason we bought this place and turned it into a B&B. And guests love it here because it's historical, quiet and beautiful."

Jack turned his head toward her. "So you've said many times, and so you said at the meeting on Thursday. But Mr. Allister Caldor thinks otherwise."

Alice screwed up her lips in distaste, speaking his name as if it were a virus. "Allister Caldor. I don't like him or his name."

"Like him or not, he's the spokesman for the Morningside Developers. And you heard what he said standing on that high school stage. 'Folks, don't be afraid of change. Change is good. Change is the lifeblood of this country.'"

Alice blew out a sigh, rolled onto her back and folded her arms. "And you know what I say to that?" she said, hotly.

"Yes. I think it has something to do with a big animal, with big horns, who defecates. You whispered your angry response into my ear during Allister's presentation, or maybe you didn't whisper. I saw Margret Stern glance over and give you an approving nod."

"They're using the word 'change' to manipulate, and I don't like anybody thinking I'm stupid. Those developers want to convince us all that everything's going to be just dandy, as long as we agree to let them knock down the neighborhood and chop down the trees, and who knows what else, so they can build condos and those cookie-cutter houses that will fall apart in twenty years."

"You're preaching to the choir, Alice. How many times have we been through this?"

She sat up, turning to face him. "And it really irks me that he offered you some of the construction work, worth more than three-hundred thousand dollars. It's nothing more than a bribe. He knows if he gets you in on it, he'll get everyone else in the area."

"Yes, and since then, he's upped it a hundred thousand."

Alice's eyes fully opened. "You didn't tell me that."

"I'm telling you now. Allister called last night. It's called business and politics."

"Well, it just makes me crazy, and we've got to find a way to stop them."

"They want this area to be like the one over in Green Leaf," Jack said. "Those apartments got built because of the developer's slick deal-making with the town. Have you seen those apartments?"

"No, I haven't."

"I did a lot of work over there a while back, before the construction. It was a simple and quiet little neighbor-hood. Anyway, the same developers slapped up those apartments a little over a year ago. Now seventy percent of them are vacant, and they displaced more than twenty people who had been living in older, but more reasonable apartments for years."

"And won't it raise property taxes, which will force lifelong residents out?"

"Yes. That's the kind of change they don't talk about."

"But property around here is worth more than in Green Leaf, isn't it?" Alice asked.

Jack looked at his pretty wife, Alice Ferrell Landis, and just looking at her helped release some of his anxiety and frustration. He loved her, her strong opinions and determination, and he loved her fighting spirit.

"Yes, property is worth more around here, but some of the houses are showing signs of wear, and you know that retirees are watching their money, and some have health issues. Lou and Mable Baxter and the Campbells need money, so they're ready to sell their homes."

"Well, I hope you talk them out of it. Change for us means preserving what we have, remodeling our neighborhood's historic homes, which is one of your specialties, and then throwing out Morningside Developers. That's the kind of change I want. You'll come up with something, Jack. You always do."

Jack sighed, audibly. "Morningside already has so much money tied up in this thing."

"We have to fight them. We just have to. We've worked so hard to make this place appealing and comfortable. We have to preserve it."

Jack smiled at his wife.

She drew back. "Why are you grinning?"

He took in her pure white skin and her appealing beauty mark, just above the left side of her mouth. Her tousled, thick, auburn hair looked sexy, and her chocolate brown eyes held intelligence and resolve.

"So what are you smiling at?" she repeated, her eyes probing him.

"You…"

She changed her mood, recognizing his flirtation. "Really? Me? What about me? And, yes, I'm fishing for a morning compliment, so be very careful what you say about my bedhead."

"All right. How about this? You look so darn sexy in the morning."

She winked. "Perfect, and you ain't looking so bad yourself, you with that dark, shadowy beard that's going to scratch my chin. Right?"

"Right."

He reached for her, drawing her down into a tender kiss. A moment later, she rolled on top of him, her busy mind still spinning.

"If Morningside convinces our neighbors to sell out, will you want to sell?"

"Not necessarily."

"I won't be able to watch the bulldozers and the cement trucks and the destruction. It will break my heart."

Jack lifted his head and kissed her nose. "We're going to fight this. We're in it together."

Alice kissed him deeply and warmly and then held him in her eyes. "I'm so glad I found that diary three years ago, Jack. I'm so glad I went off on that journey, like a crazy woman, and found you."

Jack traced her lips with a finger. "And you, Mrs. Alice Landis, have a way about you that makes me feel like a seventeen-year-old kid falling in love for the first time."

"Well, aren't you the romantic," Alice said, moving her face close to his, feeling his breath on her.

"Only when you look at me like that," Jack said. "Come here."

"I'm here."

"Closer…"   .

CHAPTER 2

An hour later, Jack sat at the kitchen island, scooping up the last of his scrambled eggs. Alice was seated on a stool opposite him staring into a laptop, a blue coffee mug beside her, along with a plate of sliced cheese, fruit, and a half-eaten bagel. It had clouded up and the landscaper, thirty-year-old Robbie Crawford, was visible outside the glass sliding kitchen doors, busy removing fallen tree limbs that had snapped in the last ice storm.

Alice's hair was damp from a shower and tied into a ponytail by a scrunchie. She wore designer jeans, a white blouse and a burgundy sweater, items she'd purchased at a local shop she frequented to help keep the woman in business. Jack's flannel shirt was black and red, his jeans faded, his boots, Timberland steel toe.

"How's the new ad coming?" Jack asked, reaching for his mug of coffee.

"Almost there. Here's what I've got so far. See what you think.

Beautiful bed and breakfast in a six-bedroom, turn-of-the-century Queen Anne Victorian house in Meadow Green,

Pennsylvania. Manicured landscaping, lovely views, a duck pond and friendly hosts, Alice and Jack Landis.

'Rooms by the night starting at $165, and $725 for the week. A suite with bedroom, sitting room and private bath is $210 per night. Great Wi-Fi, plenty of parking, and a delicious, custom prepared breakfast. Perfect location for large outdoor weddings and small indoor weddings in our quaint Victorian parlor. Complimentary wine and cheese served at 5 p.m. Weekly tea parties. Hope to see you soon!'"

Alice looked up. "What do you think?"

"Good. I like it. Have we gotten any new reviews?"

"Yep. I'll read you a couple," Alice said, leaning forward. "Oh, this is a good one. 'Every detail to pamper us was taken care of, from chocolates in the rooms to plush robes to wear. Alice and Jack are the best. Their pretty daughter, Kristie, entertained us one night during wine hour, playing her guitar, singing and reading some of her poems. Their teenage son, Andrew, helped us repair our flat tire. We've already made a reservation for next spring, and we can't wait to sit by the great stone fireplace and drink wine."

"Well, three cheers for Kristie," Jack said. "And those plush bath robes aren't cheap."

"Don't worry. I found some cheaper ones on eBay. Here's another review that just came in two days ago.

'Wonderful, six-bedroom house on a wide, curving, tree-lined street with other Victorian homes nearby. Quiet and relaxing, since the owners rent out only three bedrooms (they use the other three themselves).

'Be ready to share public space, the driveway, and upstairs bathroom. Jack, one of the owners, said he is installing a new

bathroom, but it won't be ready for a few months. Limited places to "plug in," but there is Wi-Fi.'"

Alice frowned. "She gave us four stars."

"She should have rented the suite," Jack said, "Then she would have had a private bathroom and many outlets. And I still need at least a month to finish that bathroom. Okay, read one more, a good one."

Alice sat up, energized. "You'll like this one. This is from that older couple from Pittsburg, Ralph and Tippy. He's a retired architect, and she's a retired schoolteacher. Okay, here goes.

We had a great time at the Meadow Green Bed and Breakfast. The owners/hosts, Alice and Jack, were friendly and did things with excellence! The beautiful, red brick house has a fine architectural design with an octagonal extension on the right, balanced on the left by a three-story octagonal tower. You'll love the wraparound porch and the two porch swings. You'll also love the quiet beauty of the surrounding trees and duck pond. This is a rare find, and my husband and I will definitely return. Thank you, Alice and Jack, for a memorable autumn vacation.'"

"You can tell Ralph was an architect. I couldn't have described the house any better," Jack said. "And you said both rooms and the suite are booked for Christmas?"

"No, I've taken only one couple for the suite and a single for the Rose Room. We'll leave the Blue Room vacant so we don't have to work so hard. We want to have fun, too. And you know what I've been thinking? Maybe Kristie should sing and read her poems during wine hour every week-end."

"She seems in a bad mood this morning," Jack said, draining the last of his coffee. "She grunted at me when I said, 'Good morning.'"

"You know she's not a morning person," Alice said, not looking up. "And it was her turn to get up at 5:30 and start breakfast. Then she has to make up the beds and wash the bathrooms. Not her favorite things."

"No," Jack said, "but she certainly loves the money you pay her."

"She asked me for a raise."

Jack licked his lips, wrinkling his forehead in new worry. "She's been moping around a lot lately. Have you talked to her? I don't like it when she mopes around. I feel like she's plotting something."

Alice glanced over. "I haven't talked to her all that much lately. We've both been so busy. But she's the temperamental, artistic type, and after three years, I've learned to let her have her... well, attitudes. She's probably working on a short story or a poem or something."

Jack slid his plate away. "I know I've said this a hundred times, but she's more like her mother every day. She worries me. Has she said anything more about her boyfriend? What's his name, Josh?"

"Just that he's going with his family to Florida for Christmas."

"Does she want to go with him and his family?"

"No. She doesn't like his mother, and from what she's told me, Josh's mother doesn't like Kristie all that much either."

"We all know that Kristie has a direct, sharp tongue. God knows I can't talk to her about anything personal without her biting my head off."

Alice said, "Do you want some more coffee?"

"No, thanks. I've already had too much."

Alice took a drink of her coffee. "Jack, Kristie wants to break up with Josh."

"Okay… And why?"

"She's been seeing another boy."

Jack shut his eyes and lowered his head. "Why doesn't Kristie ever talk to me about these things?"

Alice considered her words carefully. "She loves you, Jack, you know that. It's just that eighteen-year-old girls don't often talk to their fathers about their boyfriends. I never did."

Jack opened his eyes. "And who is this guy? I mean, Kristie goes through so many boyfriends I can't keep up with them."

"His name is Taylor. Taylor Barnes."

"Is that why she's been so moody?"

"Partly. She dreads breaking up with Josh. He's the angry type."

"Well, she's the angry type too. Should I be worried?"

"No, I don't think so."

"Have you met this new, other boy? What's his name, Taylor?"

"Yes. Twice. Kristie wanted my opinion. He's tall and handsome, and a little remote and moody, like her. He's older, a sophomore at the college, and he plays guitar in some rock band."

"They sound a lot alike. Aren't opposites supposed to attract?"

"Not in this case. Kristie and Taylor are a lot alike, and from what she's told me, they both write gloomy poems, listen to gloomy music, and watch gloomy, dystopian movies. They also want to transfer to Penn State next year."

Jack stood up. "The only reason she's going to that community college is because of Josh, right? I mean, that's why she didn't go to Penn State in the first place. I tried to convince her to go. She was accepted."

He shook his head. "Well, okay, whatever. I came to the conclusion some time ago that Kristie and I are never going to have a meeting of the minds."

"Don't say that. She's still just a girl, Jack. Kids have a lot on their shoulders these days. It's not easy for them."

Jack softened, lifting his hands in surrender. "All right. Enough said. It's Saturday, and since I've put all my clients on hold, today's the day I'm going to tackle that basement storage room I've put off remodeling ever since we moved here. I can't believe it's been nearly a year already. There's always one room in every house that I don't get to for months."

"Don't forget about the upstairs bathroom."

"Oh, yeah, right. I already did. Okay, I'll work on the shower this afternoon and ask Andrew to help me install the sink."

"You're a good man, Charlie Brown."

Jack placed his hands on his hips. "Do you know that I work harder on my days off than on workdays."

"Just be careful down there in that back room. It's so dark and dusty, it gives me the creeps. Is Andrew going to help you?"

"I checked on him before I came down. He's sleeping in. He worked on his app till after two in the morning. He said he's in the testing phase."

"I'm proud of him," Alice said, "He is so smart; a real computer whizz. One day he was going to be a professional snowboarder, and the next a computer programmer. I can't keep up with him. I told him I want to test out that app."

"So let me get this. He said it's a scan-to-shop app, right?"

"Yes."

Jack pushed his hands into his pockets. "Like I know what that is and how it works, even though he's explained it to me twice now, and I'm starting to feel stupid."

"I love it when I get to feel superior," Alice said, with a playful grin. "Okay, here it is one more time. Think like a woman, Jack. What do women love to do?"

"Shop?"

Alice clapped her hands together. "Yes! Women will use Andrew's app to scan items they want to purchase: clothes, shoes, makeup, whatever. Then the app searches for those items, or for their closest match on various online shops. Viola! His app will then shoot back the name of the shops with the lowest prices, and the shopper can instantly purchase the items. Clever, isn't it?"

Jack nodded. "Yes… I have no idea how he came up with it, or how he programs it but, yes, it's very clever. Let's hope he makes enough money to help pay some of his college tuition."

"Face it, Jack. Your sixteen-year-old son may wind up being a millionaire before he's twenty."

Jack considered it. "Good, a son should give his old man something to brag about when he's getting his hair cut at the local barbershop. Not that any of those jugheads will know what I'm talking about, any more than I knew what Andrew was talking about."

Alice laughed. "All right, I'm going to clean up and go help Kristie."

Jack turned to leave, then stopped and glanced toward the dining room. "How are our guests? I came down the backstairs."

"They were in the dining room having breakfast when I came down. They're happy. The Carters are hoping for snow so they can build a snowman. They're from Fort Lauderdale, Florida."

Jack lowered his voice. "We're supposed to get a dusting tonight, but not enough for a snowman. How's Mrs. Bundy?"

Alice whispered. "She's very nice, but very talky."

"Yeah, I know. That's why I came down the back-stairs."

"I'll go out and see how things are going. Good luck down in the basement. If you find anything interesting, let me know."

"Even if it's a skeleton?"

"Don't even joke about that... but I wouldn't be surprised."

CHAPTER 3

At the dining room table, 75-year-old Mrs. Edith Bundy was reading a paperback novel, spooning in the last of her oatmeal. She was thin, with a helmet of white hair and small, alert eyes, and she possessed the quick, active mind of a thirty-year-old.

When she glanced up to see Alice approaching, she closed her book, as if caught in the act of doing something naughty. Her perky grin suggested she was grateful for another person to talk to. "Hello again, Alice."

"Hello, Edith. How was your breakfast?"

"Delicious. Kristie told me she puts a little apple cider in the oatmeal and I just love it."

Alice looked about. "Did the Carters leave for their morning walk?"

"Yes… They're very nice people, but they don't eat much breakfast. Nancy Carter eats like a bird, and she's not a small woman. I don't understand people who don't have a hardy breakfast. They each had a piece of dry toast, no butter, a thin piece of cheese, some coffee and an apple, unpeeled. Imagine that? An unpeeled apple. And Don Carter is a big man. How can he face his day with a breakfast like that?"

Alice lowered her voice. "I think Mrs. Carter has her husband on a diet."

"Well, God love him, he's on vacation. He should have a man's meal, pancakes and sausage. Kristie said she'd make them for him."

"Kristie makes the best pancakes. She learned from her father."

"I bet your husband doesn't eat like a bird, and he's a good-sized man too."

"No, Jack likes a good breakfast."

"And when Don Carter stood up to leave, well he burped, and it was like a burped-bad-note from a tuba. It startled me. He was so embarrassed."

Alice added, "Maybe it was that unpeeled apple."

"Well, there's no doubt about it. That would make me burp."

Alice sought to change the subject, and her eyes fell on Mrs. Bundy's paperback. "Is it a good book?"

Edith Bundy shoved the paperback aside, dismissing it with a flick of her hand. "It's a silly murder mystery I bought at the airport, Murder in the Bed and Breakfast."

Alice's eyes widened. She didn't know what to say.

Edith continued. "I don't know why I read them. Not a single person in that book, except the detective, is somebody I'd like to know, and I'm starting to dislike him. He's snooty or something. And, anyway, I already know who killed the unfaithful wife. It was the unfaithful husband of the rich, invalid wife."

Alice made a move toward the staircase, pointing at it. "Well... I'd better get to work."

Alice started for the stairs on her way to help Kristie clean the rooms, but ever the talker, Edith's voice stopped her.

"Now, how did you say you met your husband? Did you say it had something to do with a diary?"

Alice lingered. "Yes, I just happened to find an old diary in a bed and breakfast. It turned out that it was Jack's diary that he had written fifteen years before."

Mrs. Bundy's eyes glittered with new interest. "That is so romantic. Imagine a man writing a diary. Now that is unusual, isn't it? That shows sensitivity and a bit of the literary."

"Yes... His first wife had given it to him and asked him to write in it. She was a writer herself."

"And how long have you two been married?"

"Almost three years."

"Well, isn't that just the nicest story? And when did you start this business?"

"About a year ago. I used to have a gift shop in New York, but I sold it when Jack and I married. I had intended to open another shop here in Meadow Green, but brick-and-mortar retail suffered when internet shopping took off. So, Jack and I came up with the idea that we'd start a bed and breakfast and I'd mostly run it, while he continued with his construction business. It's worked out well."

Edith put her hands together, her face filled with happiness. "And what a wonderful place it is. I hope you'll keep it just as it is, so quiet and wonderfully historic. I bet this house could tell stories that would keep us listening for hours. Just think of all the people who have lived here and the lives they've lived. I'm so happy I found it. And you are the perfect hostess."

"Thank you, Edith, that's very kind of you."

Just then, Kristie descended the stairs, her expression bored, dark, and brooding.

Alice excused herself and met Kristie at the bottom of the stairs. "Is everything all right?"

Kristie was a tall, moody beauty, with high cheek bones, short blonde hair styled in a messy bob, and a little diamond stud in the side of her nose. She favored her mother with her steady, penetrating, blue eyes, pouty mouth, and smooth, creamy skin.

"I hate this," Kristie said, in a harsh whisper. "I hate making up other people's beds. I hate cleaning their bathrooms and vacuuming. I don't even like cleaning my own room."

Alice leveled her steady eyes on her. "We pay you, Kristie. You agreed on a price and we pay you every week."

Kristie folded her arms. "Okay, fine, so I don't want to do this anymore. It's not me, okay?"

"Okay... So you can find another job."

"I don't want another job right now. I want to go somewhere. I want to do something fun. I don't want to be stuck here on Christmas, cleaning other people's rooms."

Alice's voice deepened, as she summoned patience. This had not been the first time they'd had this conversation. Kristie had never been easy to deal with, her mood swings being a definite challenge.

"We've already discussed this, Kristie. You don't have to clean rooms anymore if you don't want to. I'll do it, or I'll hire Brenda back."

Kristie wouldn't meet Alice's gaze. "Well that makes me a whiny, selfish bitch, doesn't it?"

"No, but I wish you would have come to me earlier, so I could have made plans."

"Well, it makes me feel shitty. I don't want you to be mad at me."

"I'm not mad at you," Alice said, glancing back over her shoulder to see Edith Bundy again engrossed in her murder mystery.

Kristie looked away, fingering a strand of hair. "Josh is like, well you know, driving me crazy. He keeps texting me and I keep ignoring him."

"Don't ignore him. Tell him you want to break up. Get it over with."

"He gets all, I don't know…" She shrugged.

"He gets all what?"

"He gets all hurt and angry. I told him I didn't want to see him again."

"Have you told him about Taylor?"

"No…"

"Kristie, just tell him it's over and tell him not to contact you."

"Yeah, well… I just sent him a text and said that. Anyway, I just want to get out of here for a while. I need a different experience. I want to get some new material for a novel and nothing here inspires me. It's just the same old thing every day. Boring."

"Where do you want to go?"

"I don't know. Wherever. I want to like, get on a train or plane or something, and go anywhere and get off someplace I've never been before."

"Have you talked to your father about it?"

"Of course not. No way. He'll get all mad at me because I don't want to do this work anymore. He'll say I'm not being responsible. You know he will. I want to go to New York or, I don't know, maybe skiing in Colorado or something."

"With who, or should I say, with whom?"

"I don't know. Maybe a girlfriend."

"Okay, but talk to your father. He might surprise you. He knows a lot of people and he might be able to suggest some places you could go."

Kristie made a sour face. "That's not going to happen and you know it."

Kristie was in one of her grumpy moods, and Alice knew there was nothing she could say that was going to shake her out of it.

Alice breathed in and out, twice. "All right, I've got to finish cleaning the rooms before the Carters come back, so…"

Kristie cut her off. "… Everything's done. I did them. Now I just want to go out somewhere and be alone."

Alice's shoulders settled. "All right, then go. I'll clean up the breakfast dishes. If you stay out long, just text me, okay?"

"Yeah, sure. No problem."

After Kristie bounded up the stairs to her room to change clothes, Alice started for the parlor. It was designed in Victorian burgundy colors with a generous fireplace, an upright piano, a loveseat, a couch and three plush chairs.

She was tidying up the gray-and cream-colored pillows when she looked up to see Jack approach, his face tense with a foreboding expression. His shirt sleeves were rolled up to the elbow, and a white construction mask rested below his chin. He drew up to her, stopped, then shoved his hands into his back pockets.

"Yes?" Alice said. "What an expression… Did you find a skeleton down there?"

He didn't smile, and he didn't speak.

"Okay, Jack, talk to me. What is it? What's happened?"

Jack's voice was low and thoughtful. "When we moved in, we shoved a bunch of old trunks and boxes into a back corner of that room."

Alice nodded. "Yes, I know."

"When we did, we blocked a door. An old door. A door that was locked. Remember? I couldn't find a key, so we moved on to other things. We had so many other things to do."

"Yes, I remember," Alice said, waiting, her eyes moving across his face. "Go on."

"I just moved the trunks and the boxes and, after a few attempts, I managed to shoulder the old door open. I shined my flashlight inside. There were more old trunks, a typewriter, some hat boxes and a couple boxes with old photos tossed inside. There were two dusty dolls, an old red wagon, and a stack of old magazines from the 1940s and 1950s."

Alice felt her pulse rise. "Jack... What is it? Just tell me."

"I found an old, wooden, lost-and-found bin with things inside. Do you remember that the real estate agent said this house had been a boarding house back in the 1950s?"

"Yes."

Jack ran a hand through his hair. "Okay, well, you're not going to believe this, but when I shuffled through the objects in that bin, I found an old diary."

Alice narrowed her unbelieving eyes on him. "A diary? You mean... a diary?"

He nodded. "Yep. I took it out and wiped off the dust. It has an embossed red leather cover, with water spots and stains on it. It also has a protective strap and a brass lock."

"Did you open it?"

"Since the lock is broken, it was easy. Yes."

"And?"

"Alice, I don't know what to think about this."

"So just tell me already, Jack. You're being so dramatic, and it's not like you."

He gave her a frank stare. "I took the diary out into the other room, into the light. I released the strap and opened it. On the first yellow-lined page, the owner wrote the address, her name and date."

"And?"

"She wrote the diary in this house, 298 Chestnut Street, Meadow Green, Pennsylvania. Her name was Alice Ferrell and the first entry is dated December 2, 1944."

"What?" Alice said, searching his face for any hint of a joke. There was none.

"It's true. Her name was Alice Ferrell, and that's F e r r e l l, spelled just like yours."

They stood staring, thinking, breathing.

CHAPTER 4

Jack led Alice into the back room and pointed to the lost and found bin where he'd found the diary. She cast her eyes about the shadowy space, illuminated by a 60-watt bulb hanging from an old, pull-chain ceiling fixture.

"It smells moldy and damp in here, like a tomb," Alice said.

"Well, I did find a lot of small bones. Probably from mice."

Alice cringed and whirled around. "I'm out of here."

She exited the storage room to the main basement area, walked past the boiler and over to Jack's seven-foot work bench. She stood under the florescent light and stared down at the diary. It looked deliciously old and mysterious, and it seemed to beckon to her, to speak to her, to dare her.

With care, she picked it up as if it were fragile, and turned it over, gently running a hand across the back and front. With an intake of breath, she opened it as Jack drifted over, peering over her shoulder.

Alice read the author's name repeatedly, swallowing away a dry throat, feeling a chill run up her spine. She turned to Jack with a little shake of her perplexed head.

"I don't understand... It's so, I don't know, strange. What are the chances of this happening? What are the chances of this woman and me having the same name?"

"I don't know, but you do seem to have a way of sniffing out old diaries."

"But *you* found this one."

"It's the same thing. What's mine is yours, till death us do part."

Alice closed the diary, and again, she ran her hand over the embossed surface as if trying to make some mystical connection with the writer. "I wonder how it got down here and in that dark room."

Jack scratched his cheek. "Apparently, somebody tossed it into the lost-and-found bin a long time ago, and it's sat there gathering dust ever since."

"I've got goose bumps," Alice said. "Maybe the woman and I are related somehow."

"It's possible. Are you going to read it?"

She gave him a tense smile. "Of course. Did you read any of it before you went upstairs?"

Jack shook his head. "No, I stopped when I saw the name and date. That sort of took the wind out of me. Why don't you read a page or two now, and maybe we'll learn who she was."

Alice hesitated. "Do you think Debbie and James knew about that room?"

"Obviously not. Or, if they did, they didn't bother to clean it out. That door hadn't been opened for a long time, and they owned this house for ten years. I have no idea who owned it before them."

"We should find out."

"Yeah, why not? We could search property records and deeds and see what comes up."

"How would that work, and how far back could we search?"

Jack tilted his head in thought. "We could go to the county records facility and look it up. If that doesn't work, we could probably check the U.S. Census Bureau to find copies of property records from sixty or seventy years ago. I don't know the laws so you might have to check that out. We could also hire a title agent to do a search for us."

Alice's eyes remained focused on the diary. "Let me do some searching first. It'll be fun. I wonder how old this Alice Ferrell was in 1944, when she started the diary."

"Go ahead and read the thing. You've got me curious. Whatever she wrote, she must have written it during World War Two."

Alice's hand lingered over the diary, her eyes entranced. "All right... Should I start at the beginning?"

"Sure. Let's get the whole story, front to back."

Alice opened the diary, examined the woman's name, the date and address, and then slowly and carefully turned the yellowed page. Her eyes were clear and focused as she studied the handwriting. "Oh, wow, Jack. Look at this," Alice said, holding up the diary so he could see it. "Her handwriting is so artistic and legible, a bit slanted back, but filled with lovely flourishes. They actually taught cursive writing in those days."

"Do you remember the excuse Andrew's school used when they stopped teaching cursive writing?" Jack asked.

"Yeah, I remember the letter. Something about writing being less legible than print, and it creates confusion. And they used some example about tax returns getting lost or something."

"Ninety five million tax refunds weren't delivered because they were unreadable."

"Well, I don't care. People just got lazy. Look how beautiful her writing is."

Jack squinted. "Some of the ink has faded, and a few words are smeared."

"Probably from leaking pipes in that foul-smelling old room," Alice said, scanning the page.

Jack waited patiently, surprised at how anxious he was for Alice to begin.

Alice passed her fingers over the page, as if to time travel and touch the person who had written the words. She began to read, allowing one of her fingers to trace the words. Her voice was deliberate and measured, breathy at the start, but gaining strength as she progressed.

Saturday, December 2, 1944 12:03 a.m.

I bought this diary the other day in town at McCrory's Five and Dime, as a kind of early Christmas present. I'm calling it my Christmas Diary, because I intend to put all of my thoughts and emotions in it during this Christmas season.

I haven't been able to sleep, and Aunt Sally said I should buy a diary and write things down until I get sleepy. So that's what I'll do. That's what she did when Cousin John was killed in 1943 flying his bomber in the Pacific. She still won't talk about it, and she's bitter about losing her only son. Uncle Fred only talks about John when he gets drunk. I miss John, too. He was like an older brother to me, so kind and thoughtful. He taught me how to drive and, sometimes, we snuck away from the house and smoked cigarettes together, laughing like naughty kids. I used to pray for him every night.

We all miss Ruth-Ann, who's working in a war plant in Michigan. She and Sally never got along too well, a mother/daughter problem, I guess. Ruth-Ann and I got along okay, but she always kept me at arm's length. She's not warm-hearted like John was. But now Sally has regrets about Ruth-Ann. Well, who doesn't have those these days, with the world upside down.

Aunt Sally and Uncle Fred have left for Philadelphia to take care of his sick father. Sally said they'd probably use up most of their four gallons of rationed gas and might have to stay for a while. So this big house is empty and so quiet. Sally wants to move because she says the house has too many memories. Fred says he doesn't want to move. He says John's ghost roams the place at night. I think the ghost is in Fred's head. I've never seen a ghost, only Fred's shadow wandering the place when he can't sleep.

I can't sleep either, so that's why I'm making my first entry. I like the look of the diary and the lined pages. I don't like to write on blank white paper. I like the support of the lines. They're like a foundation for my pen; an invitation for my thoughts.

Charles' mother called me on August fifth and told me he was killed in action somewhere in the Pacific. Since she's been following the battles in the newspapers, she's sure he was killed on Guam in the Mariana Islands. She'd been crying, and she didn't stay on the telephone very long. She told me, 'Charles spoke so highly of you, Alice. He wrote to me that he was in love with you and wanted to marry you when he got back. I'm so sorry I have to give you this sad news.'

So many boys have been killed on those South Pacific islands and in Europe, and so many families are suffering. Betty, who lives down the street, lost her husband last month. He was killed somewhere in Europe after D-Day. Aunt Sally said the poor woman hasn't left her house. Sally took over a casserole and used most of her sugar ration to bake her a cake. Sally's a good soul, but she can bite your head off, too. And is she ever opinionated. I've learned to watch what I say around her.

I'm hurting tonight. I miss Charles so much, but I've got to be strong and brave. I have to remember all the good times, and that's what I'm trying to do. What a swell time Charles and I had together just doing simple things, like roller skating, having sodas at the drug store and going to the movies. He could always make me laugh. I wrote him a letter almost every day, and once I even sent him a box of cookies.

I can't forget his last letter and, yes, it makes me so sad and, yes, it keeps me awake at night. I've got his last letter lying next to me on the bed as I write this. I'm going to enter some of it in this diary, so if I lose the letter, at least I'll have a record of it.

"Just before we shipped out, I got your box of cookies, and they sure were appreciated. But, Alice, geez, when I opened the box, there was nothing in there but crumbs and a few chocolate chips! Somebody else got to them first. But that's okay, because me and some of the guys finished off what was left. The U.S. Marines took care of it, just like we're going to take care of those Japs!

"My best pal, Tom Lawson, was wounded. A piece of shrapnel struck his right thigh between the knee and the hip, but it didn't break the leg. Another piece hit his back, on the left side, but didn't go in very far. I guess he'll be shipped back to the States, the lucky dog! I'll miss him though. Do you know that he was right next to me when he got hit? Lucky me, not a scratch!

"I know we'll be together soon, dear Alice. I'd give anything to get back to you. I know I'm coming back to you after this terrible war is over. I know I'm going to make it. I keep dreaming about the way you love ice cream with Baby Ruth bars! Memories like that keep me going. Guess what? I've hand-carved three cigarette boxes in the last few weeks and I sold two of them. I'll bring the other one home for you. Until

then, don't sit under the apple tree with anyone else but me. Haha. I know you like the Andrews Sisters."

Okay, diary, my eyes are all blurry from tears. It's late, and I have to try to sleep. I'll write more, maybe tomorrow.

1:45 a.m.

Still can't sleep. I loved Charles Morgan and he loved me. Why didn't we get married before he shipped out? Maybe I could have had his baby.

I lie awake thinking, I bet all soldiers think they're going to come back. God forgive me, but I wish it were Charles who had been wounded and sent back to the States, and not his best friend, Tom Lawson. Dear God, forgive me for thinking that.

Alice Landis lifted her eyes from the page and stared at nothing. "Well, that was sad, wasn't it?"

Jack spoke at a near whisper. "Yeah…"

A minute later, Jack said, "Is the diary full? Did our 1944 Alice fill all the pages?"

Alice gingerly leafed through the diary, observing that every page was full, front and back, including the last one. "Yes, she filled it."

"Are you going to read all of it?"

Alice turned to him. "Of course I am. Maybe I'll find names and addresses of people she knew. Maybe I'll be able to find Alice's descendants. I'm sure they'd want the diary."

"Read it first. You never know what might be in there that certain people wouldn't want others to know. Remember my diary? If anyone but you had found it, I would not have been a happy man."

"You weren't a very happy man when I told you about it."

"No, not at first."

He leaned and gave her a peck on the lips. "But it all worked out in the end. We're living happily ever after, aren't we?"

Alice stroked his cheek with two fingers and winked. "So far."

Jack arched an eyebrow. "Is there something I should know?"

"Yes, but not right now. I'd better get back upstairs in case one of our guests needs something. Are you going to keep working down here?"

"Oh, yes, I'm determined to clean out that room."

Alice started to the basement stairs, had a thought, and pivoted. "Jack, didn't you say you saw a box of old photos in that room?"

"Yes."

"Bring it upstairs later, okay? If we go through them, we might find my historical namesake's photo. Wouldn't it be fun to see what she looked like?"

Jack appraised his wife. "I see it in your eyes."

"What?"

"That obsessive quality."

"What do you mean?"

"Alice, you're going to dive into this diary like a deep-sea explorer, and you won't come up for air until you've uncovered every little secret."

"Is that a bad thing?"

He pursed his lips. "We'll see. You never know where these kinds of things might end up."

Alice looked at the diary she held in her hand. "That first entry moved me, Jack. I want to know who Alice Ferrell was, and what happened to her."

CHAPTER 5

Back upstairs, Alice found Nancy and Don Carter seated on the parlor couch, she reading a book and he, the thin local newspaper.

"Did you have a good walk?" Alice asked, smiling.

Nancy Carter, a robust woman with short gray hair and ruler-straight posture, glanced up. Her serious expression suggested a person who liked control, and her proper uplifted chin suggested a love of discipline.

"Oh, yes, quite pleasant, Alice," she said. "I see that just down the street you have a bakery. Don and I just had to go in and sniff about. We couldn't help ourselves. We shared one of those blueberry scones."

Don's head periscoped up from his newspaper. He had white, bushy eyebrows, a fringe of white hair circling a bald dome, and bold eyes staring out from black-rimmed glasses. "I wanted to eat the whole thing, but Nan wouldn't hear of it. We each could have had one... but no. I live with a drill sergeant," he said, crisply, going back to his paper.

"You didn't need the whole thing, Don. If I hadn't taken charge, you would have stuffed that entire scone into your mouth and swallowed it down like some wild, hungry animal."

Don grunted something under his breath, but Alice didn't understand it.

Nancy laughed a little, looking a bit girlish, the serious glare vanishing. "Don still thinks he's playing college football, when he could eat the half side of a barn and not gain an ounce."

"I'm still in good shape," Don said, the newspaper muffling his voice.

"I'm glad you're enjoying yourselves," Alice said, wanting to move on. "Let me know if there's anything you need."

"Well, there is something," Nancy said. "This room is just screaming out for a Christmas tree. I know it's only December the second, but why not start early? The season always goes by so fast. When will you be getting one?"

"Today, actually. Yes, Andrew is going to pick one up at the tree stand in town. We'll decorate it tonight."

Nancy bobbed some nods. "Well, that's just fine, isn't it, Don?"

"Yep," he said, not looking up. "But that tree will dry out before Christmas, make no mistake about it. That's the downside. You start Christmas too early and the next thing you know, you're sick of it when the day comes. Anyway, that's what I always say."

"Stop being so negative, Don. Stop being Ebenezer Scrooge. I'm sure Jack knows how to keep a Christmas tree from drying out. Look what he's done to this place. He's a master craftsman, isn't he, Don?"

"Yep."

"I'll leave you to your reading," Alice said, turning to leave the room, but stopped by Nancy's voice.

"Is that a book you're reading?" Nancy said, noticing the diary Alice held in her left hand.

"No… It's…" Alice didn't want to explain the diary, so she told a little lie. "I use it for bookkeeping, and speaking of bookkeeping, I'd better get to work."

Alice was on her way to the back office to do some ordering and banking when she thought about Andrew. Would he remember to buy the Christmas tree? Crossing under the staircase and turning left down the short hallway, she poked her head into the kitchen and saw Andrew seated at the kitchen island, eating some cereal, a banana lying beside his bowl.

"Good morning," Alice said, entering.

"Hey," Andrew said, slumped over the bowl.

"Your father said you were up late working on your app code."

"Yeah…"

"How's it going?"

He shrugged a shoulder.

"Does that mean okay, good, not so bad or… what?"

"Okay, I guess. It's not working quite right."

"You'll get it."

"I should have got it by now."

"Maybe you should take a day off. Do you have a lot of homework?"

"Yeah…Waste of time stuff. History. Who cares?"

"It's good to know some history, Andrew."

He stayed silent, not interested in pursuing the conversation.

Andrew looked older than sixteen, and girls both younger and older had eyes for him. He was tall and broad like his father, but his handsome face was softer than Jack's.

Andrew's hair was stylish, thanks to Kristie, who had insisted on accompanying her brother to the barbershop the week before. She'd been in one of her art moods and had given the barber a clear description of how Andrew's hair should look. While he snipped, Kristie circled the chair, pointing and directing, ignoring the barber's growing irritation.

But the final result was a good one. Andrew's raven black hair was short on the sides, long on top, and spiked with gel, giving him a smooth, "I don't care, I'm cool" look, or so Kristie had declared. Andrew liked the cut, and Kristie beamed with triumphant pride, and when she handed the middle-aged barber a generous tip, their chilly relationship thawed.

Alice had spent almost three years adapting to and getting to know Jack Landis and his two children, and she had fallen in love with them. It hadn't been easy. There were times when she was caught in the middle and times when she felt like an outsider. But she'd persisted, and they'd persisted, until they'd bonded in predictable and unpredictable ways, eventually becoming a family through good times, challenging times, and growing pains.

In her head, Alice had defined them. Jack was forthright, concise, and loving; Andrew secretive, evasive, and thoughtful; Kristie moody, unpredictable, and affectionate. Of them all, surprisingly, Andrew was the most challenging to understand, still remaining somewhat of a mystery to her. Of course, he was at the age when the boy was changing into a man, and contradictions abounded.

Andrew had many practical skills, thanks to his father, but he also possessed a quick, probing mind that enjoyed word games, crossword puzzles and computer code. And he delighted in his secrets.

Alice watched Andrew peel back the banana and bite off a piece. "Will you be able to pick up a Christmas tree for the parlor this afternoon?" she asked.

"Yeah, sure. No problem. I need to go into town anyway. Should I get one for the dining room?"

"No, let's wait a week or so. We could put up the artificial tree in the meantime. What do you think?"

"Cool. It's easier."

"Okay, I'll be in the office if you need anything."

"Is Dad downstairs in that back room?" Andrew asked.

"Yes... You should go down and take a look." She held up the diary. "He found this old diary and some photographs."

Andrew lifted with awakened interest. "A diary? Another diary?"

Alice read his expression. "Yes, I know. It's very bizarre, and that's not all. It was written by a woman in 1944, and we share the same name... the exact same name."

Andrew scrunched up his eyes and straightened his back. "You mean her name was Alice Ferrell—spelled just like yours?"

"Yes."

"That's awesome. Does Kristie know? She'll freak out."

Alice lowered the diary to her side. "Not yet. It freaks *me* out."

"She's going to want to find out all about that woman," Andrew said. "I mean, you might be related or something."

"Yes, I know. I want to find out too."

Andrew shook his head. "What are the odds of something like this happening? I mean, to find a diary in your house, written by a woman with your name, back in 1944. That's like... totally unreal. I read the other day that the chance of winning the lottery is something like one in two-hundred ninety million. That's what this is. What did Dad say about it?"

"Like you, he's surprised, and like you, he's perplexed by the odds."

"Did you read any of it?"

"A few pages. She's young, and her boyfriend was killed in World War Two and she couldn't sleep. That's why she bought the diary, to write herself to sleep."

"I'd love to read it," Andrew said.

"I thought you didn't like history."

"This kind of history I like. I could bring it to school and show it to Mr. Harmon, our history teacher. Maybe he'd give me an A instead of the C I know I'm going to get."

"No, Andrew. Not now anyway. I want to read it first. It's personal and I think we should respect that. Besides, your father and I want to try to find her relatives, which could possibly be my relatives too. One of them might want the diary."

Andrew grew thoughtful. "Maybe she's still alive."

"I doubt that. She'd be a very old woman."

"But it's possible, isn't it?"

"Yeah, I suppose so."

"How old was she when she wrote the diary?" Andrew asked.

"I don't know yet."

Andrew did some quick calculations in his head. "Let's say she was twenty-four. This is 2016, so that would make her... Let's see, seventy-two years since 1944; add twenty-four and she'd be ninety-six. But maybe she was younger. It's possible she's still alive."

"I'm going to read more tonight. I'll let you know what I learn. Right now, I've got to get back to the office and put in a grocery and cleaning supplies order. We've also been getting a lot of reservations after the New Year that I have to fit into slots."

Andrew got up and took his bowl to the dishwasher. "I'll go downstairs and see if I can help Dad. I've got to see that old room. It's going to be fun remodeling it."

"Better you than me," Alice said. "See you."

Andrew reached for the banana and left.

Back in the office, Alice sat at the antique mahogany desk that Jack had refinished for her and tried to work, but she was distracted by the diary. It sat next to her, waiting, beckoning. She stared out the bay windows toward the duck pond, her eyes searching the cloud-heavy sky, following a flock of geese as they drifted over an island of trees.

Unable to contain her curiosity, Alice opened the diary and turned to the next entry.

Sunday, December 3, 1944.

10:15 p.m.

He's asleep in the back, first-floor bedroom—the man I helped out of the car after he crashed it into that tree. What else could I do? It was snowing so hard and so fast. And here I am, alone in the house with a strange man who says he knows me. But he doesn't know me. How could he? Then he fell into a deep sleep.

CHAPTER 6

December 1944

Twenty-one-year-old Alice Ferrell awoke on Sunday morning, December 3, with the heavy memory of that glorious, late February day less than a year before. It was one of the last times she'd seen Charles.

He had already enlisted and was waiting to be shipped overseas. He'd come by that morning, kissed Aunt Sally on the cheek, presented her with flowers, and handed Uncle Fred some cigars. Finally, he'd grabbed Alice's hand and said, "Let's have a picnic and a row on the duck pond." He held up a brown paper bag. "See? I brought a couple sandwiches and two Baby Ruth bars."

Since it was unseasonably warm that day, she quickly agreed.

They picnicked on the back meadow, where white and yellow crocuses blossomed in the sparkling sun. Afterwards, they rowed across the duck pond in an old skiff, while Charles tossed out one bad joke after the other. She sat opposite him, dressed in a red and blue floral headscarf tied under her chin, a blue woolen coat with flannel lining, and saddle shoes.

"Hey, Alice, here's one you'll love. Why did the golfer change his socks?"

She folded her arms and screwed up her lips, pretending to ponder the answer. "I have no idea."

"Because he got a hole in one."

Her face twisted in mock pain. "That was dreadful, Charles."

"Here's another one. I heard it in bootcamp. How do you make holy water?"

Alice shrugged.

"Come on. Guess."

"I don't know. Say a prayer over it?"

"No. You boil the hell out of it."

Alice sat up. "That's terrible. Lightning's going to strike us dead."

Two mallard ducks paddled by, one quacking up a storm, as if yelling at them to get off the pond. Even though the air was cool and the trees bare, the sun was warm, and so Alice unbuttoned her coat and lifted her face toward the sun.

"Nice day, huh?" Charles asked.

She shut her eyes, smiling into the glory of the sky. "Yes. It's like a May day."

"Okay, one more joke," Charles said. "Hold on now, with both hands. This one is really going to hurt. There are three fish in a tank. One asks the others, 'How do you drive this thing?'"

Alice opened her eyes and rolled them. "Oh, brother. That's the worst one of the bunch."

"Do you get it? Tank. You know, like a Sherman Tank."

"Yes, Charles, I got it. I know what a tank is."

Charles dipped his oars into the water and pulled on them, winking at her. "How's Alice Ferrell, the prettiest girl in town? Your autumn hair shines like reddish gold, even with the scarf on. And those deep, chocolatey eyes always seem to be searching for something, always filled with a mischievous curiosity."

Alice looked away, self-conscious. "My eyes are not mischievous, Charles. And where do you come up with all those words? And you don't even read that many books."

"Do you know who you look like?"

Alice lifted her chin with a smile, enjoying the attention. "Who?"

"You look like a young version of Greer Garson."

Her eyes twinkled with delight. She loved Greer Garson. Her favorite movies were *Mrs. Miniver* and *Random Harvest,* both starring Greer Garson. Alice was thrilled but suspicious. "No... Really?"

"Yes, except you're even prettier."

Alice made a face of doubt. "Now I don't believe you. You're such a flatterer, Charles."

"I'm a Marine, Alice. I always tell the truth as I see it."

She grinned playfully, taking in his closely cropped sandy hair, his twinkling gray/green eyes and his pressed Marine Corps uniform, his cap lying beside him on the wooden seat. The uniform consisted of a long-sleeved midnight blue coat with a standing collar, seven gilt buttons, and red trim, worn with a white web belt.

As Charles drew on the oars, Alice noticed his taut arms and swelling neck muscles, and it gave her a tickle of passion as her eyes grew vague, her body tensing with desire.

She quickly snapped out of it, batting her eyes flirtatiously. "Well... Alice is certainly flattered that you think she's the prettiest girl in town. Thank you. Did I say I love your uniform?"

"Yes, you did, but the real question is, do you love the guy wearing the uniform?"

Alice averted her eyes. "You know how I feel, Charles, and you're especially handsome in your uniform."

"These are my dress blues, supposed to be worn for formal occasions. Today, I'm making an exception."

"Then I should have worn my black evening gown."

"There's still time for that, my lady. We're going out on the town tonight."

In the bright sun, her eyes sparked with excitement. "Are we?"

"Yes, ma'am. To the good old Victor's Café and, because he's a friend, and because I'm shipping out, he said he won't take my money or ration coupons for our meals. I'm only sharing this very crass fact so you'll be more impressed with me, because you'll know that I have friends in all the right places."

"And so I am impressed."

"Okay, Alice, now that we're almost to the dock, here's my last joke of the day. Are you ready?"

Alice sat still, hands folded, alert. "Yes, I'm ready. Go ahead."

"A guy went to buy some camouflage trousers, but guess what? He couldn't find any."

He laughed out loud at his own joke. Alice didn't laugh.

"Come on, Alice. Don't you get it? He couldn't find the trousers because they're camouflaged. Don't you think it's funny?"

"No, I think it's sad."

"Why sad?"

"Because it brings the war back, and you're leaving in a few days."

"Let's not think about that, Alice. We have the entire rest of the day and a big chunk of the night to be together. Now, let's dock this boat and ask Sally to take some photos of us."

The sound of the winter wind howling around the house shook Alice from her memory and brought her back to the present. With a little sigh of grief, her head dropped back into the pillow.

It began snowing while Alice was sitting at the kitchen table sipping coffee. She gazed out the window, watching the heavy snowfall blanket the meadow, sugarcoat the trees, and obscure the pond. She would not be attending the Methodist church today, even if it *was* only four blocks away.

She fought the urge to re-read Charles's letters. Instead, she asked God's forgiveness as she performed minor housecleaning tasks on a Sunday, needing the distraction.

She dusted the upstairs bedrooms, the downstairs parlor and the dining room. After a short break sitting by the window and watching the snow fall, she mopped the kitchen floor and cleaned the upstairs and downstairs bathrooms.

In early afternoon, Alice returned to the parlor and switched on the Philco console radio. She swung the dial until Jimmy Dorsey and his orchestra, playing *Julia,* burst from the speakers and filled the house. It was a peppy, swing band ditty with a jumping rhythm, a smooth clarinet and a jazzy sax. It gave her just the lift she needed. Inspired by the beat, her feet started to shuffle; her shoulder and hips started to sway. With her arms extended and her hands floating, she sailed across the floor, allowing the music to take her back to the dance at the high school gym, the last night she and Charles were together before he left for war.

What a magical and romantic scene it had been. The lights were dimmed, and the dance floor was packed with couples dipping and swaying to big band swing music. There was a mirror ball suspended from the ceiling, and tiny, glistening circles of light floated around, little specks sliding across their faces, the ceiling and the walls.

With wide grins and damp faces, Alice and Charles twirled and shuffled. They surged left and right, dodging other couples who cut in and out, arms raised, hands wiggling, faces young and animated. They danced in a delightful frenzy, aware that in a few inevitable hours, many of those dancing boys would be sent off to war and many would never return. Charles would never return.

When a deep-voiced radio announcer broke the spell, advertising Carter's Little Liver Pills, Alice sagged to a stop near the sofa, winded, her smile waning, the happy memory fading. She shut her eyes and, on the screen of her mind, she saw Charles laughing. As Charles kept laughing, she wasn't entirely sure what she felt inside. It felt like rage. It felt like sorrow. It felt like hopelessness.

Minutes later, Alice sat slumped in a parlor chair, staring glumly out the window at the swirling snow as it sailed on a wild, circling wind. She had the crazy impulse to burst out of that house and charge into the thick of the storm; to be blown off into other realms, somewhere, anywhere. She wanted to escape, to explore, to do something different.

Sometime later, after she'd nodded off, the snow dwindled to flurries, but the blustery wind roared through the trees, blowing snow into little tornados. From where she sat, Alice had a good view of the street, and when she saw a car approach, moving much too fast, she stood up, concerned. She stared anxiously as the car came skidding and fishtailing, just missing two parked cars across the street. As the speeding car neared the house, she watched in alarm as the front tires jumped the sidewalk, and the car shot across the lawn, plowing hood first into the trunk of a thick, oak tree.

In utter shock, Alice put a hand to her opened mouth. On reflex, she scampered to the front hallway and yanked the closet door open. She ignored her boots, but grabbed her gloves, hat and winter coat, and then rushed to the front door. Outside on the porch, a gust of wind shoved her backwards. The blizzard of snow had returned, swirling in chaos.

Determined, she ducked her head and gingerly descended the front stairs, in a direct confrontation with the storm. Snow bit into her face and the wind whipped up the color in her cheeks. She squinted at the wrecked car; the front windshield wasn't shattered, but the driver was slumped over the steering wheel. Steam boiled from the car's hood, but was swiftly dispersed in the driving wind.

Tramping through six inches of drifting snow, Alice felt the cold shock on her feet, and she wished she'd stopped to pull on her boots. Near the car, with her pulse drumming, she grabbed at the door handle. Even with gloved hands, it was cold. Sucking in a bracing breath, Alice tugged on the stubborn handle with both hands until it opened about two feet.

Vapor fled from her mouth as she peered inside. A soldier was sagged over the steering wheel. Was he dead? Injured? He wore a heavy overcoat, his peaked cap on the seat beside him. His eyes were squeezed shut, he moaned in pain, and a trickle of blood oozed from his nose.

"Are you all right?" she shouted, as the wind squealed around her. "Can you move?"

He struggled to lift his head, and when he looked at her, his eyes held wildness and confusion.

"Are you hurt?" Alice asked.

The man tried to speak but failed. His face was as white as the snow, his lips blue.

"I'll help you out," Alice said. "You can't stay out here. It's too cold. I've got to get you into the house."

Alice wasn't a big woman, but she'd worked hard all her life and was strong. With a straining effort and fighting the snow, she screwed in her heels and forced the door open another few feet. She knew she could tug him free and get him inside if he had the strength to turn his body around and help her. She reached for him.

"Come on now. Turn toward me."

It took several attempts but, with Alice's help, the soldier managed to swing his legs and body around to face the open door. He scooted forward, rested his feet on the broad running board and paused, breathing heavily.

"Good. Now take both my hands."

The soldier obeyed. With all her strength, Alice locked her hands in his and leaned back, trying to pull him out of the car. Gulping in cold air, she rocked back and forth, gaining momentum until, finally, she hauled him out and onto his feet.

He was a big man, and she was terrified that if he collapsed before she got him into the house, she'd never get him up.

Did any of the neighbors see her? Probably not. It was time for Sunday dinner and the roaring wind must have masked the sound of the car's impact.

Thankfully, the man didn't fall, and as they progressed toward the house in clumsy steps, he seemed to recover some of his strength. He leaned against Alice for support as they slowly mounted the stairs, taking slow, careful steps not to go sliding away. On the porch, the soldier stopped, grimacing with pain. Alice struggled to hold him up.

"What happened?" he asked, in a strained voice. "What the hell happened? I blanked out."

The frigid wind pushed at them, punishing their faces.

"Let's get inside," Alice hollered over the attacking wind, "before we freeze to death."

She steered him toward the front door. With her hand braced against the doorframe, Alice forced the door open and they blundered inside into the welcoming warmth of the hallway.

Alice slammed the door and stood fighting for breath, her legs wobbly, her heart kicking.

The soldier dug into his coat pocket and pulled out a handkerchief, shakily blotting his bleeding nose.

Alice stared at him, the reality of what she'd done expanding into electric anxiety. She'd helped a perfect stranger into the house, a soldier, and she was alone. Completely alone.

His eyes captured and then released hers. His were puzzled and glassy.

Confronting the reality, Alice said, "I'll call for a doctor."

"No!" he said, forcefully. "No damned doctors. I've had enough of doctors and hospitals. No. Please."

He swayed, staggered. Alice reached—caught him, seizing his arm, steadying him, her stamina waning. The soldier shut his eyes, as if to muster strength.

"I'm not so good. Feel dizzy. Got to sit or I'll drop. Help me sit... Please."

CHAPTER 7

December 1944

With a worried face and crossed arms, Alice paced the parlor, the living room, the kitchen, and around the back staircase, pausing in the hallway that led to the spare bedroom. She stared uneasily. That's where he was. That's where the soldier was. She didn't even know his name, and his car was still jammed against the oak tree, covered with two inches of new snow.

She'd managed to guide him to the bedroom and over to the bed. He sat down in a bounce, groaning. She helped him out of his coat and tugged off his boots, then stood back, not wanting to remove any part of his Marine Corps uniform. Frozen to the spot, Alice watched as he collapsed onto his back and fell into instant sleep.

Alice paced the house for long minutes as the wind outside howled, as the snow continued to fall. No one would be out in this weather. Even if the soldier wished her to call Dr. Williams, he was a man in his sixties. He wouldn't drive in this storm.

What about the neighbors? Agnes and Millie Leach lived next door, but they were elderly. How could they help? Morris Stall lived across the street, but he was a widower who'd lost his wife the year before and he was sickly and asthmatic. All the young, strong men had gone to war.

Alice was rattled. She didn't know what to do. If Aunt Sally were here, she'd have a plan. She was practical and efficient, with a cool head and steady manner.

The idea to call her aunt sent Alice to the parlor telephone. She found the number Sally had left in the address book and, using the heavy rotary black phone, Alice sat down and dialed the number. An annoying, pulsing buzz hurt her ear, and she jerked the receiver away.

Nervous minutes later, she tried again, and again she got the same ugly noise. A call to the operator brought a small, pinched, female voice that sounded miles away. Alice asked if she could place a person-to-person call to Philadelphia.

"The lines are down," the voice on the telephone said. "No calls are getting through right now. It could be two or three days before they repair the lines. Please try your call then."

Alice hung up and swallowed away a lump. She jerked a glance toward the back of the house and drummed her fingers on the arm of the sofa. On the edge of fright, she shot up and started pacing again.

At a whisper, she said to herself, "I can't be alone in this house with a strange man."

Alice was in the kitchen when darkness fell and the snow dwindled. She wore a gray floral apron and had her hair tied back with a cream-colored scarf. Her hands quivered as she turned the can of Spam over. She took the "key" attached to the bottom and twisted it around the can until it opened, and with a couple of good shakes, the Spam emerged coated with a jiggly jelly. Alice sliced the meat and placed it in a hot cast iron pan, in some bacon fat she'd scooped from a Mason jar. After sprinkling the slices with a little thyme and pepper, she slowly browned them, turning them frequently.

While she worked, she threw nervous glances about, every sound making her jumpy, every stray thought building the tension in her shoulders, making her headache worse.

Was the soldier still asleep? Had he died? She'd resisted checking on him, although she'd stopped by his door several times, placing her ear against it, listening. Twice she heard snoring. Twice she heard nothing at all.

When the Spam slices were cooked, she scooped them up and slid them onto a blue ceramic plate. From a separate pot, she spooned cooked cauliflower and potatoes and placed them next to the Spam. She was about to sit down at the kitchen table when she heard footsteps approaching from the hallway. They sounded loud and threatening.

She froze, her face hot with fear. The plate was still in her hand when the soldier stepped into the kitchen, his sleepy eyes squinting against the light. He held up a hand to shade them.

Speechless, Alice stared, hovering on terror.

He looked at her, his face still pale, his eyes small and vague from sleep. When he spoke, his voice was rusty and halting. "I... Well... I couldn't help but smell the food."

Alice didn't budge, still unable to find her voice.

As his eyes adjusted, he lowered his hand and then lowered his eyes to the plate of food that was still gripped tightly in her hand. "I don't want to be a bother, but would you have some coffee? Anything, really. I don't think I've eaten in a while."

She didn't look at him or speak for a time. Finally, she eased her plate down on the table and slid it toward him, pointing at the chair. "There," was all she could force out.

He looked at it, hungrily. "No, ma'am. That's your dinner."

Alice spoke timidly. "Sit down. Eat. I'll make another plate for myself."

He hesitated.

"Please, just sit down and eat," Alice repeated. "I'll make some coffee. We don't have any sugar, though. We used up our ration. Uncle Fred took all we had to Philadelphia."

The soldier's hands were restless. "That's okay. I don't need sugar."

Alice stiffened when she realized what she'd said. Should she have told him about Fred being in Philadelphia? Did he know they were alone in the house?

He remained standing. "I'll just wait until you have your plate."

Alice wanted to steal a look at him, but she didn't. She felt too vulnerable, not knowing what kind of man he was; not knowing what he might do if he knew she was alone.

She filled the percolator with coffee and water, set it on the stove, and lit the flame. Then she prepared her own plate and, with two knives and forks in hand, she moved toward the table. Keeping her distance, she placed a knife and fork next to his plate and, still jittery, she lowered herself down in the chair opposite him. Once she was seated, he sat.

Neither reached for their fork; he was waiting for her to begin. Gathering courage, she slowly lifted her eyes.

His eyes were shut, and his mouth moved in little whispers. Was he saying grace?

They ate in silence, with heads down, as a lingering wind wheezed and moaned around the house.

Finally, he said, "Is my car still smashed up against that tree?"

Alice stared into her plate. "Yes."

"I'm sorry... I'm truly sorry that happened."

There was more silence as they ate, he ravenously, she measured.

He looked up, but she would not meet his eyes. "It's good," he said. "Thank you."

In a little whispery voice, Alice said, "You're welcome."

He glanced back over his shoulder. "I cleaned the carpet where my wet boots tracked in snow and mud. I apologize for that, too. The carpet's as good as new."

Again, Alice simply said, "Thank you."

"It was quite a storm," he said.

"Yes..."

"I hope it's over," he said, trying to jumpstart a conversation.

Alice ventured a question, still not lifting her eyes. "Do you have folks around here? I mean, is that where you were going?"

He waited, chewing, swallowing. "No, I don't have any folks nearby. I promised a Marine buddy something. That's why I..." His voice trailed off.

Her eyes finally came to his. The color had returned to his face and, for the first time, she got a good look at him. He had a fine, masculine face with good, handsome features. His black hair was militaristically short, his eyes a deep blue, his jawline clean, his shoulders wide. There was a weariness in his eyes, a deep, wounded fatigue, as if he'd seen the devils in the depths of hell. Those eyes moved her, drawing a sudden compassion.

She stared at him, unable to pull her eyes away. All the months of grieving and pain and loss seemed to rise up in her and get trapped in her heart. And she hurt, and her heart ached, and she felt the start of unwanted, burning tears. They ran freely down her cheeks and she didn't bother to wipe them away.

He looked at her, perplexed. "Did I say something...?"

She interrupted him, looking down and away. "No. I'm sorry, forgive me."

Alice pushed up and ran from the kitchen to the parlor. In a rolltop desk, she found a freshly ironed embroidered hankie, one of several she'd placed there, accessible for whenever the tears came spilling out.

Standing by the window watching snow flurries drift by, she blotted her wet eyes. It had been the pain she'd seen in the soldier's eyes that had overwhelmed her. She'd seen her own pain in them, her own anguish.

A minute later, she sensed the soldier's presence, but she didn't turn to face him.

"Are you all right?"

"I don't know," Alice said. "I should be brave and strong, shouldn't I? Aren't you fighting soldiers brave and strong? So I should be, too, but the truth is, I'm not so brave or so strong."

Alice heard his breathing. "You were strong when you helped me out of that car. You were brave when you brought me into this house and into that bedroom. You were strong, and you were brave."

His kindness touched her, and she turned to him. The parlor lamp was on dim and a plank of yellow light spilled out from the kitchen, bathing him in half light and half-darkness.

"Who are you?" Alice asked.

"I'm Corporal Tom Lawson."

A chill rose in her. She knew that name. She'd read the name in many of Charles' letters. Tom Lawson was Charles' best friend. Tom Lawson had been wounded and sent back to the States.

She tried to speak, but words wouldn't come.

"Are you Alice Ferrell?" Tom asked.

Alice choked back more tears as she covered her face with the hanky. All she could do was nod.

"Charlie and I were the best of pals. He made me swear that if anything happened to him, I'd come see you. He wanted me to tell you that he loved you more than his own life. He wanted me to say that he will always love you."

Alice felt a storm building in her chest, a boiling angry, hurting storm.

In a contrite voice, Tom said, "I'm sorry, Alice. I wish Charlie were standing here before you instead of me."

Alice doubled over, grabbing her stomach, weeping, her body a spasm of anguish."

CHAPTER 8

December 2016

Alice looked up from the diary with reluctance, then closed her eyes and pinched the bridge of her nose. The diary's story was a poignant one, and it felt strange to be living in the same house as young Alice had.

She was about to read more when a text "dinged" in. Alice glanced at her phone. It was from Kristie.

Met a girlfriend at Starbucks. We're going shopping. Be back for dinner.

Alice sat back with a little sigh. She shouldn't doubt Kristie, but she did. Why didn't she mention the name of her girlfriend? It was more likely that Kristie had met Taylor, and they were off to who knew where. Why didn't Kristie just tell her the truth? Alice knew why. Because she and Taylor were going off to do what a lot of young people do. She could only hope that Kristie was being smart and careful.

Forcing herself to ignore the text and the diary, Alice booted up the laptop and went to work.

Around a half hour later, a knock on the office door startled her from her inventory list.

She twisted around. "Yes?"

The door opened and Jack stepped in.

"Well, hello, handsome," she said breezily. "Have you been busy down there in the basement?"

Jack closed the door behind him. "Yes. Andrew's thumbing through old 1950s magazines. I doubt whether either one of us will get much work done. How's it going up here?"

"I read more of the diary. It's quite a story. So far, a sad one. Now I'm working on the holiday inventory: food, Christmas decorations, cleaning supplies, towels, sheets... Well, you know. It never ends. Oh, and I have some charities I want to give to before the end of the year."

He started toward her, holding a manila envelope at his side.

"What's in the envelope?"

He set it down on the desk before her. "Photos from downstairs. I brought the most interesting ones. There are more, and from the look of them, some date all the way back to the 1920s and 1930s. For the life of me, I don't understand why someone didn't take them or just toss them out. And do you know what else I found in that lost-and-found bin?"

"I'm afraid to ask."

"An old stopwatch which doesn't work, but probably wouldn't cost much to repair, some keys, a tarnished gold ring with some kind of cheap stone, and two pairs of glasses."

Alice looked at the envelope, intrigued. "Have you looked at all the photos?"

"Not all. Many."

"And the photos in this envelope are...?"

Jack reached for a wooden chair, drew it toward the desk and sat down next to Alice. "I'm not positive, but there may be photos of the author of the diary, Alice Ferrell. On the back of two such photos is handwritten 'Alice,' and she looks to be quite young, maybe in her early 20s."

Excited, Alice nudged her laptop aside, seized the envelope, pinched the gold pins and opened the flap. She snaked her hand inside and grabbed a handful of the photos, spreading them out before her on the desktop. Her eyes poured over them as she shifted and rearranged them into order, top to bottom.

Alice zeroed in on one particular photo. It was black-and-white, taken outside on what appeared to be a winter day, as the trees behind them were bare. A pretty girl wore a below-the-knee winter coat, saddle shoes and a floral scarf tied around her head. Next to her was a soldier in uniform, his arm wrapped about her shoulder and a big smile on his face.

It was the girl that drew Alice's attention. She had a natural beauty, a lovely, slim figure, a playful smile, and spirited eyes that looked back at the camera candidly. Captivated, Alice could almost hear the young girl speak.

"Turn it over," Jack said.

Alice did. Written on the back of the photo, in a faded blue pen, was *"Alice and Charles, February 1944."*

Alice looked at the photo again. "She was pretty, wasn't she?"

"Yes… There are two more of her and the soldier, similar shots," he said, pointing. "There… that one, where she's looking at Charles and he's backing away from her, playfully, making a scary face."

Alice smiled. "They were cute together. It's tragic that he was killed in World War Two."

"What else have you read in the diary?" Jack asked.

Alice brought him up to date, finishing with, "I'm going to skip movie night and read more."

"You're going to miss *The Shop Around the Corner?*"

"I've seen it three times. Edith Bundy said she hadn't seen it in years. She's excited."

"Oh, I almost forgot." Jack took the envelope, reached inside, felt for something, and then removed a folded yellow piece of paper. "I found this with the photos. I thought you might get a kick out of it."

"What is it?"

"I think young Alice may have written it. It matches the diary handwriting."

Jack handed it to her, and Alice opened it and peered at the faded blue ink.

"Aunt Sally said that women should use their hair to 'fix' any flaws in their face type. If a girl has perfect, shiny hair with a good color, she should use it to frame her face. If she has a full face, she should pile the hair on top of her head to distract from it. If she has a thin face, her hairstyle should be down and over her ears to make it look wider. Sally said I have shiny hair with good color, so we came up with a style to frame my face. She's so bossy sometimes. I'm not going to tell her, but I don't like it all that much."

Alice looked up. "I wonder why she wrote this on a separate piece of paper?"

Jack pointed at the bottom of the page. "It looks like it might have been part of a letter and she tore it off, for some reason."

Alice turned to Jack. "We have to find out what happened to her."

He looked at her laptop and nodded at it. "Haven't you already searched?"

She smiled. "Yes… I found one Alice Ferrell on Legacy.com, and she was about the right age, but she was born in England. Anyway, she died a little over five years ago. Of course, our Alice probably married and there's no way to know what her last name was or is."

There was another knock on the door.

"Come in," Alice said.

The door opened and Andrew poked his head in. "Dad, there's a guy out here who wants to talk to you. He's in the hallway."

Jack stood up. "Who is it?"

"Allister Caldor."

Jack and Alice traded sour glances.

"What's he doing here?" Jack asked. "Why didn't he call?"

"Do you want me to tell him you're busy?"

"No, I'll talk to him."

Alice's eyes heated up. "Don't developers ever take a day off? Do you want me to come? I'll be happy to tell him to go take a flying jump into our duck pond."

"No thanks. Be nice now. I'll make it short and sweet."

Allister Caldor was in his early 40s. He had the sure, practiced expression of a man who was used to winning, and his manner was precise and polished. The smile wasn't flashy; it wasn't calculated to ingratiate, but it was the familiar smile of an old friend. He was a tall man, about Jack's height, and well-dressed, wearing a cashmere overcoat over a tweed sport coat with brown corduroy trousers. His hair was a sandy brown and stylishly short, and his face was round, his eyes small and penetrating.

Allister's anxious hand was outstretched as Jack approached; the smile was there, and the charm was there.

"Hello, again, Jack. Forgive me for dropping in like this without calling. I stopped by to talk to Lou and Mable Baxter, and since I was close, I thought I'd take a chance."

He glanced around with approving nods. "Beautiful home you have here, Jack. Yes, I have heard about your exceptional skills and I can see it in the fine woodwork of that staircase banister. That's your work, isn't it?"

Jack nodded. "Yes. My son, Andrew, helped. Can I take your coat, Allister?"

"No, no, thank you. I won't be staying long. How is Alice?"

"She's well, thank you."

"That's fine. Just fine."

"What can I do for you?" Jack asked.

"As I said, I just had coffee with Lou and Mable Baxter. They think very highly of you, Jack, as I dare say most of the people in this area do. It seems you and your company have done a lot of work around here for nearly everyone. And people say you often give them discounts."

Jack pulled on his left ear. "Old houses need a lot of work, and, these days, everybody needs a discount now and then."

As if on cue, Allister took the idea, grateful for the opening. "Yes, you are right about that, Jack. Old houses do need work, and that takes money. Now I know that you and Alice have no intention of moving away from here, and why should you? You both have thriving businesses and a good place to raise your kids."

Allister took a minute to turn serious and lower his voice. "You know, Jack, Lou and Mable are ready to sell their house and move to Florida."

Jack's mouth firmed up, but he stayed quiet.

"And there are others… Oh, I'd say six or seven others in the immediate area, and three more on this street. They're concerned about the upkeep on their houses and, well, maybe they want a new and different kind of life, away from the endless repairs, the high cost of living and the bitter winters."

Jack let him ramble on, knowing where he was going.

Allister shifted his weight, his face set in a serious devotion to the moment. "What I'm getting at here, Jack, is that Lou and Mable and the others have the highest respect for you. Frankly, they look up to you and Alice, and why shouldn't they? You're a fine and honorable couple, respected citizens. I say that's rare these days. My point, Jack, is this: they, and some others, are rather hesitant to sell if you are against it."

"It's their homes, Allister, and their business. It's their choice, not mine."

"Yes, true… But, how can I put it?" Allister looked up at the ceiling and then down, meeting Jack's eyes. "They're afraid, and that's as frank as I can say it."

Allister let that settle before he moved on. "Dreams, Jack… New dreams and change often frighten people, don't they? Let me just get to it. I came by because I was hoping that maybe you could talk to some of your neighbors and let them know what you just said to me: that it is their homes and their business, and they should make up their own minds."

Jack stood to his full height. "Allister, you and all my neighbors know how I feel. There are no secrets about it. I don't want this land developed, at least not the way you'll do it. Frankly, you don't care about the land, your mind is on your investors and making a buck. Okay, fine, that's the way the world goes sometimes. But I won't sell one acre of my land, and I won't encourage anyone else around here to sell either. There is a rare peace and beauty about this area, and I will fight you any way I can to stop your company from changing one square foot of it. No offense to you personally."

Allister lowered his head, nodding and thinking. He didn't show anger or offense. "All right, Jack. I can appreciate that. It's good to know, once and for all, where you stand. Now I will be just as honest and frank."

He stared Jack hard in the eye. "My company intends to develop this area, and we will do it with the respect and care that it deserves. Now, whether you and your neighbors agree or not, change is coming. Change cannot be stopped, and I, for one, am damn proud to be a part of that change."

Allister extended his hand once more and Jack took it. They shook firmly. "I thank you, Jack, for seeing me and for your honesty. You have a good evening. My best to Alice."

Jack nodded. "Good night, Allister."

After he was gone, Jack returned to Alice's office and told her what had occurred.

Alice sighed. "They have big money and big power, Jack. We won't be able to stop them, will we?"

Jack stood, looking out the window as snow flurries drifted. "The snow is starting. By the way, have you heard from Kristie?"

"Yes, she texted and said she was out with a girlfriend."

He turned to her. "Do you believe her?"

"No."

He dug his hands into his pockets. "That girl…" He stopped, then started again. "I spend so much time worrying about her. I'm going to have to stop, if I can."

Alice got up and went to him, looking him full in the face, and then she wrapped her arms about him, resting her head against his shoulder. "Kristie is just a girl trying to grow up. She has a good heart and she's smart."

Jack sighed. "Smart has nothing to do with it, Alice, and you know it. She has a wildness in her and that has made me a praying man."

CHAPTER 9

December 1944

Alice awoke at dawn, groggy and stiff, startled to find herself on the parlor couch. She sat up, her eyes swollen and sticky from tears. It took a minute for her to reorient herself, to remember the events from the previous night, the emotions, the words, and the soldier. Yes, the soldier!

She tossed back the woolen blanket and looked at herself. She was fully dressed, wearing the same blue print dress and socks she'd worn the night before. Her shoes were carefully placed at the foot of the couch. *Was the soldier still here? Was Tom still here?*

She swung off the couch and pushed to her feet, feeling dizzy. Touching her head with a hand, she staggered and dropped back down on the couch in a little bounce. Why did she feel so strange and disoriented?

Glancing toward the back room, she rose again. *Where was Tom Lawson? Had he gone? What about the car?* She staggered to the window, opened the curtains and peered out, shading her eyes from the new light of day. The snow had stopped, and the sky was clear, a shockingly clear blue sky.

His car was still there, jammed against the tree. Again, she glimpsed a look over her shoulder, anxious. *Was he in the house, asleep in the back bedroom?*

Turning from the window, worried, she strained to remember all the events from the night before. After Tom had explained who he was and why he'd come, she'd had a kind of breakdown. He'd helped her to the couch. He'd brought her some water, but all she could do was sob. Seeing Tom in the flesh, and hearing the truth of his words, had brought fresh anguish over Charles' death, like stabs to her heart. Charles was dead. His best buddy had told her so.

Charles had been her landmark, her anchor, her polestar. Now, they would never marry or have their own home and family; they would never grow old together. Alice had lived that dream for nearly a year. She'd been all plans and excitement, pouring her heart out to Charles in every letter, during every telephone call.

Seeing Tom Lawson and hearing his words had finally, once and for all, killed her hopes and dreams. Her turbulent emotions must have finally exhausted her, and she'd fallen asleep. Tom had removed her shoes, found the woolen blanket in his bedroom closet, and covered her with it.

Alice closed her eyes and massaged her forehead. Her ribs were sore from crying, and she felt a dragging resistance to move, or do anything. As she started for the staircase, she paused again, venturing another tentative glance toward the back bedroom.

An hour later, Alice descended the stairs, having taken a bath and washed her hair, fingering it dry over the steel grill floor register in the corner of the room. She'd applied some light makeup, slipped into an ivory dress with blue polka dots, and put on a pair of black oxfords.

Before entering the kitchen, she stepped to the parlor telephone and called the law office where she worked as a secretary. Wallace Bates, the older of the attorneys at Bates and Parker, answered. She was about to tell him that she was feeling ill and wouldn't be in when he interrupted her. "Don't bother coming in today, Alice. I had one helluva time getting here. The roads are a mess and the buses won't be running until this afternoon. Take the day off and bake an apple pie or something."

When Alice entered the kitchen, she stopped short, astonished to see that Tom had washed last night's dishes and cleaned the kitchen. *It was so generous and considerate*, she thought. How many men would do such a thing? She stood there thinking, evaluating. What should she do now?

She left the kitchen and ambled toward the back bedroom. At the closed door, she lifted a fist to knock, then hesitated. Drawing in a quick breath, she rapped lightly, then stepped back.

Tom's deep voice from inside said, "Yes... Is that you, Alice?"

She was gently startled to hear him say her name. After clearing her throat, she said, "Yes. Do you want some breakfast?"

She heard him stirring. The door opened about a foot, and Tom peered out, unshaven and sleepy, wearing an unbuttoned, long sleeve shirt. He blinked at her. "How are you? Feeling better?"

Alice took another little step back, feeling the moment was too intimate. She touched her neck self-consciously. "I'm... fine..."

"Sorry I overslept. I meant to be up and out by now."

She kept her eyes down. "Would you like some breakfast? I have a few eggs and bread. No bacon. It's hard to get now."

He grinned with pleasure. "Eggs would be swell. Anything, really. I'll just clean up and be right out."

About a half hour later, Tom appeared, dressed in his informal uniform, a green jacket, green trousers, khaki long-sleeve button-up shirt, khaki tie, and glossy black boots. On the left side of the jacket were ribbons and marksmanship badges. Alice wondered what the ribbons were for, but she didn't ask.

"I hope I didn't take too long," Tom said.

"No... not at all. You're wearing a different uniform."

"Yes. I went out last night and pulled my duffle bag from the trunk of the car."

Alice nodded, and their eyes met for a few seconds before she pulled hers away. "Well, sit down, and I'll make the eggs. Is over-easy okay?"

Tom noticed a tender bloom on her cheeks and it froze him. In the light of day and, after a good night's sleep, he got the distinct impression that Alice was a very special person. He could feel it. See it. "Yes... that's fine," he said, still standing. "But do you have enough eggs? Aren't they rationed?"

"I have enough. Please... sit down."

He moved toward the chair. "I have money. I'll pay you for the food."

She turned. "No... I don't want your money. Sit down now."

He obeyed, sitting, folding his hands on the table and glancing about. "It's a nice house, and a big kitchen."

Alice went back to work, not speaking.

"I haven't seen anyone else about. Are you alone in the house?" Tom asked.

Alice tensed up. She had an answer waiting. "My aunt and uncle will be back soon," she said quickly. "Any time now."

"I guess they won't be too happy with me slamming my car into their tree. I looked at it, and I don't think I damaged it much…"

Alice didn't want to talk about it. "The bread's in the oven, and the coffee's almost ready."

"Sounds wonderful," he said, sitting, his back ramrod straight.

Keeping her voice low, Alice said, "I apologize for how I acted last night."

"There's no need for that," Tom said.

"And thanks for cleaning up. That was nice of you. You did a good job. Everything was spic and span."

Tom nodded.

"I never knew a man to clean up a kitchen so well. Most men won't go near one, other than to eat or make a mess."

"I grew up in an orphanage. They worked us pretty hard, and I washed up a lot of dishes. And then I had my fair share of KP in basic training."

Alice turned around. "An orphanage? Did you grow up in an orphanage?"

He didn't look at her. "Mostly… but it wasn't so bad, really."

Alice flipped the three eggs over, the grease jumping and popping in the black skillet. "Where was it?"

"Springfield, Ohio. The Pythian Children's Home."

"When? I mean, how old were you when you entered?"

"About ten years old. My parents were both killed in a car crash. I had an aunt, but she didn't like kids, so…"

Alice thought of Aunt Sally and Uncle Fred, who had taken her in and made her part of their family when her own mother died. She was twelve. "What was the Home like?"

Tom shifted in his seat. "It was a big, castle-like place, and it had girls and boys in separate buildings, of course. There was even a separate cottage for babies. A few months ago I got a letter from one of my buddies who's in the Navy. He went there too, and he said they closed it down earlier this year. Some nuns are going to use it for a home for the elderly."

Alice scooped two eggs into his plate and one into hers. She removed the warm bread from the oven and reached for two coffee cups.

They ate quietly, feeling more at ease than the night before, but Alice couldn't shake her tangled emotions. Having Tom in the house made the war seem closer and Charles' death more final, and the world more volatile. It also expanded her guilt. She'd often wished it were Tom who'd been killed instead of Charles—a selfish, thoughtless wish, and she was ashamed of herself.

"I hope you don't mind, but I used the phone in the bedroom," Tom said. "I found a local garage in the phonebook. In a couple of hours they're going to send a tow truck to pull my car from the tree and haul it off to be repaired. I'll be on my way and out of your hair."

Alice stopped eating, suddenly despondent. When he left, she'd be alone, and she didn't want to be alone. Who knew when Sally and Fred would return.

Tom continued. "I should have found a better way to tell you who I am and why I came. I've never been too good around people, but Charlie and me, well, we just became good pals. And then he wanted me to come here to see you, so..."

His voice fell away, as he took a sip of his coffee. "I don't know, maybe I shouldn't have come."

"No, I'm glad you came," Alice said, much too fast. "I mean… It's what Charles wanted, wasn't it?"

CHAPTER 10

December 1944

Alice and Tom struggled to adjust their moods, uncomfortable by the growing silence. Tom finally spoke up, nudging the conversation back to a safe topic.

"You know, Charlie and me hit it off right from the start. You always wonder why you take to some people and not others, but Charlie could make me laugh, and I'd make him read books."

Alice raised her eyes, surprised. "Books? I never knew Charles to read a book. He said he wanted to live a book, not read it."

Tom smiled. "Yeah, he told me that, too. Do you know what I said? I said, 'Charlie, you can do both, and one will help you do the other even better.'"

Alice gave a little nod as a memory surfaced. "Charles was so funny. I gave him a book for his birthday, and do you know what he said? 'Alice, I've already got a book.'"

They both laughed, and it felt good to laugh, and the laughter helped to dispel some of the sadness.

"Yes, well that sounds like Charlie all right," Tom said.

"What books did you both read?" Alice asked, feeling a little jealous.

"He loved *The Great Gatsby*, once I got him into it, but his favorites were the Zane Grey westerns. He devoured them, and he would reread them until they were dog-eared and moldy. I remember one night in some Jap-held island, we were reading by a dim flashlight under a shelter, even after the air-raid siren had already blown and we should have been in a foxhole."

They lapsed into silence again until they finished their eggs and bread. Sharing those simple stories about Charles had helped to calm Alice, and she was grateful for that.

"You must miss him too," she said. "I'm sorry, I didn't think about that until now."

Tom kept his face under tight control, but Alice saw the sorrow in his eyes.

"Yeah, I miss Charlie. He was like the brother I didn't have. We got to be that close... but then you get close when you face death together every day, don't you?" Tom held his coffee cup to his lips and stared at nothing.

Alice sat still, thankful the tears didn't flow. Had she finally cried them all out?

"You were wounded... Charles wrote me about it. Have you fully recovered?"

Tom faded back into a low mood. "I'm doing just fine." He forced a smile. "All put back together again by good doctors and smiling, pretty nurses. How lucky can a guy get?"

"I'm glad," Alice said. "Charles said you were next to each other when..." She didn't finish the sentence.

"We weren't exactly next to each other but... Well, you know how Charlie used to tell his stories and make them more dramatic than they were. Yeah, Charlie was always smiling, even when things were bad. He was the best of all us guys in the platoon."

Alice sighed, setting her fork down. "This awful war has killed so many men and so many dreams. Do you feel that?"

Tom looked at her honestly. "I've done my duty in this war, Alice, but I guess I'll have to do more of it. I have never run from combat, even the last time, when we were ordered to take that bunker and I knew it was suicide. I charged it anyway and was hit by that mortar. Even now, I feel as though some of the life got kicked out of me. Ever since I was a kid in that orphanage, I've lived for my dreams and imagined better times. Forgive me, Alice, but with so much dying around me, my dreams are dying, too, and I can't seem to stop it."

Alice fought the urge to reach for his hand, to try to comfort him, the way he'd tried to comfort her. "This war will end, Tom. It will, some day."

He didn't look at her. "I'll have to go back to it... We'll have to invade Japan and, who knows, maybe I'll survive, maybe not. But after Charlie was killed, I'm not the same person I was when he and I shipped off all those months ago. No one can go through this war and not be changed by it."

Tom slid his empty plate aside, holding Alice in his somber eyes. He smiled, a thin, wise smile. "We're all casualties, Alice, but we have to go on, don't we? As you say, some way, somehow, this damned war will end. And then maybe we can all start dreaming our new dreams."

"Where will you go when you leave here?" Alice asked, her voice soft, her eyes taking him in.

His unsure, restless eyes moved about. "I don't know. I still have time on my medical leave before I have to report to the West Coast. I guess I'll find a hotel some place while my car's getting repaired. I bought it cheap at a used car lot in Philly."

Tom was rambling, wanting to fill up the empty silence. He was feeling some of the cold unease he often felt around 'nice girls,' a nagging insecurity that made him want to retreat. Although he had been told by more than a few girls that he was handsome, he didn't see himself that way. He saw himself as a loner, an outsider, a kind of outcast who'd been tucked away in that dark castle of an orphanage.

He was comfortable with women he met in dreary bars or honkytonks, and with girls who worked at all-night diners, who seemed as lost and lonely as he was.

Alice Ferrell was different from most 'nice girls'. She was a smart, warm, and sensitive girl; a girl who could mean something to a man; a girl Charlie had loved; a 'special girl' he'd said; a girl he would rattle on about, endlessly, to any soldier who'd listen.

Tom had to admit that under Alice's lovely eyes and girlish smile, his cold unease warmed and softened, and it was a new, unexpected feeling.

"Don't you have any plans, Tom?"

He snapped out of his private thoughts. "Oh, well, I think I'll take my time driving across the States and take in some of the sights. Maybe I'll stop by the orphanage, just for old time sake. And then again, maybe I won't."

"With gas rationing, how are you going to travel across the country?" Alice asked. "You won't get very far."

Tom grinned. "I'm a Class C driver, which means I have the head-nod that's reserved for essential war workers, police, doctors and mail carriers. I figure I earned it, and I don't think most people would mind, since I'm headed back to war. A girl I knew at the orphanage works for the government, and she came to see me at the hospital and fixed me up with the Class C. I have no gas restrictions; that is, unless a brigadier general pulls me over."

A strange, lonely desperation arose in Alice, an impulsive and irrational feeling. She wanted to say something that would change his mind, but when the words came out, they were more direct than she'd wanted them to be. "Why don't you stay here... I mean, just for a day or two, while the car's at the garage? You can save your money. Hotels are expensive, aren't they?"

He gave her a worried, searching look, and then he glanced away toward the window. "I was going to shovel your walkway, driveway and sidewalk. It's the least I can do since you've fed me and given me a place to sleep."

They avoided each other's eyes, not knowing what to look at or what else to say.

.

CHAPTER 11

December 2016

Alice turned to Jack and watched, amused, as he pushed a stick of spearmint chewing gum into his mouth, then chewed vigorously.

"Are we going in?" Alice asked. "You took two hours off from work so we could do this."

They sat in Jack's blue Ford pickup, in midafternoon, looking out at the ranch-style house that was set back from the road into some snowy trees.

Jack chewed for a moment. "Like I said, Sharon Packer only agreed to let us come by and speak to her mother because I gave her a discount on remodeling her kitchen a few years back."

"So you said. Then why aren't we going in?"

Jack continued, chewing the gum, making snapping sounds. "I'm not sure… Maybe I'm not ready to spit out this gum. I like it."

Alice eased back into her seat and held out a hand. "Okay, then, give me a stick and let's have a chewing party."

Three days before, on Monday, Jack had shot off an email to his current and former clients. He asked if anybody remembered Sally and Fred Long, who'd lived in the house Jack and Alice currently owned. He'd received an email back from 61-year-old Sharon Packer, who said her 84-year-old mother remembered Sally and Fred, having visited them several times with her mother when she was twelve or thirteen years old.

Sharon lived about thirty minutes away from the Landises, and she'd reluctantly agreed to allow Jack and Alice to talk to her mother, as long as, "You don't upset her or tire her out," she'd said strongly.

Rolling down his window, Jack surveyed the area. "It's nice to see the snowplows got to this place pretty fast. I bet Sharon keeps the County on its toes. Anyway, my point is, Sharon isn't all that friendly, and neither was her husband, Carthal, when he was alive. He died about a year ago and I've heard Sharon has turned even more sour since his death."

"What does Sharon do for a living?" Alice asked, chewing the gum on the left side of her mouth. "That's a nice home and there's a new car in the driveway, and it looks like the house sits on about three acres."

"Yeah, that's about right. They owned three liquor stores. When Carthal died, Sharon sold two of them."

Alice looked at Jack. "Well, it's a nice thing that Sharon keeps her mother with her and not in some nursing home."

"True enough."

"What's Sharon's mother's name?"

"Ida."

"Did you meet her when you were working here?"

"Only once. She has her own room off to the left there," Jack said, pointing. "See? She was pleasant, more so than her daughter, and she was sipping a glass of scotch, as I recall. And I know it was scotch because she offered me some. You know, I don't like hard booze all that much."

Alice smiled. "Well, good for her that she has a scotch now and then. Okay, let's do this, Jack, and hope that Ida remembers Alice Ferrell."

Jack rolled down his window and blew his gum out the window into a pile of plowed snow. Satisfied at his shot, he nodded.

Alice had watched him, bemused. With a little shake of her head, she said, "What is it about men? You guys just have to spit your gum out, don't you?"

Jack grinned. "Yeah, since I was a boy. It's fun."

Alice emptied her gum into a tissue and dropped it into the waste basket under the dashboard.

As they left the truck and started up the shoveled walkway, Jack said, "It was a long time ago and, even if Ida does remember, I doubt if she'll know what happened to Sally."

"Well, we're here. You never know."

At the door, Alice pressed the lighted doorbell, and the chime rang three times. Seconds later, the door flew open, and Alice and Jack stepped back, startled. A flax-en-haired girl of about nine, with bright, big eyes and a pouty mouth, looked up at the couple, with a challenge.

"Who are you? I'm Matilda."

Alice smiled. "Hello, Matilda. We're Mr. and Mrs. Landis, and we're here to see Sharon."

At that moment, a sturdy woman appeared. She had a tight, square build and tight lips, and she wore tight, orange running pants with a matching sweatshirt. She stood firmly in white sneakers, hands on hips. Her stylishly spiked gray and black hair gave a militaristic look, and her direct, no-nonsense expression reminded Alice of a stern gym teacher she'd had in high school.

"Hey there, Jack," she said, flatly. To Alice, she said, "I'm Sharon. Come in."

Matilda obstinately blocked entry into the house.

"Get out of the door, Matilda!" Sharon barked. "Let these people in. Nobody wants to see you with a smart face like that. Go back into the family room and finish your puzzle."

Matilda's mouth opened—on the verge of firing off words of defiance—but Sharon cut her off with a warning, wagging finger and a fiery stare.

"Don't you even think about sassing me, young lady. Go!"

Matilda galloped off, and Sharon opened the door fully. "That's one of my granddaughters, and she's already a handful. Come on in, folks. It's too cold to linger."

Inside, Jack shut the door behind them and then briefly introduced the two women.

"Thanks for being on time, Jack," Sharon said. "I always appreciated that you were on time. If you said you'd be here, by gosh, you were here. That's more than I can say for those sons-of-bitches I hired to put on a new roof at the store on Freemont Street. They're worthless. They're never on time, and when they do show up, they're all thumbs and excuses. Well, that's spilt milk, isn't it?"

Before Jack could answer, Sharon blabbered on. "All right, so you want to talk to Mom?"

"Yes, that would be great," Jack said. "Like I said on the phone, we'd just like to talk to her about the couple who lived in our house back in the 1940s. You said she remembered them; even met them once or twice."

"Yeah, so she told me. Mom is still as sharp as a tack, so if she met those people, she'll remember. You said on the phone that the couple was Sally and Fred Long, right?"

"Yes," Jack said.

Sharon shook her head. "They don't mean nothing to me, but then, why would they? I was born in 1956 and I was seldom in that neighborhood. Okay, come along, and I'll take you to meet Mom."

At her mother's door, Sharon knocked loudly. "Mom, you've got the visitors I told you about. Can we come in?"

Alice heard a small woman's voice say, "Yes, Sharon, come in."

Sharon opened the door and stood aside to let Alice and Jack enter. "Do you want something to drink, Jack? And... I'm sorry, what was your name?" Sharon asked Alice.

"Alice."

"Yes, Alice. I know it's early afternoon, but would you like a beer or some wine?"

Alice and Jack shook their heads. "No thanks, Sharon, we're fine," Alice said.

"All right, I'll be out in the kitchen if you need anything," she said, then closed the door behind her.

Ida Swearengin sat in a rocking chair near a large picture window that had a grand view of trees and open land. She laid her book aside and pushed herself up with both hands, offering a friendly smile.

To Alice's surprise, Ida was nothing like her daughter. She was thin, with a soft energy, soft speech, and soft, white hair, combed back from her face and tied in the back by a blue ribbon.

"Come and sit down," Ida said, with a warm smile. "I've been looking forward to this little visit. As you can imagine, I don't get many visitors these days."

After introductions, Alice and Jack sat on a firm, brown sofa with plush cushions, opposite an electric fireplace with glowing artificial logs. The living room was well lit by windows, and had modern furnishings, a dark beige-colored carpet, and walls painted in a warm hunter green. Many framed photos of kids and grandkids were displayed on a table near her rocking chair, and a bookshelf was filled with hardback and paperback books. It was a comfortable, lived-in space.

Ida returned to her rocking chair, lowering herself down. She folded her hands in her lap, and the hem of her gray and white patterned dress fell well below her knees. There was a sparkling intelligence in Ida's eyes, and her kind, lined face suggested wisdom. Alice liked her immediately.

Ida leaned a little forward. "So, I have been sitting here reading Shakespeare's Sonnets, recalling those days in the 1940s. Do you know that I was a high school history and drama teacher for thirty-eight years? I required my drama students to memorize at least one Shakespearian Sonnet."

She pointed at her head. "Those sonnets are good for the head and they are good for the soul. My favorite is Sonnet 116 and here is my favorite line from it. 'Love's not Time's fool.'"

Ida held her smile. "So you want to know about Sally and Fred Long, is that so?"

"Yes," Alice said. "Do you remember them?"

"How did you hear about Sally and Fred?"

Alice looked to Jack, with questioning eyes. Should she tell Ida about the diary?

Jack spoke up. "I was working in a back room in the basement, and I found a lost-and-found bin. Inside it was an old diary, written by a young woman who lived in the house with Sally and Fred."

Ida's interest sharpened. "Did you now? What an interesting find. It's like finding a buried treasure, isn't it? Who was the young woman?"

"Alice Ferrell," Alice said.

Ida narrowed her thoughtful eyes, pondering the name, and then she softly repeated it as if to dislodge an old memory.

Alice continued. "Incidentally, Ida, my maiden name is Ferrell, with the same spelling as the diary's author."

Ida shut her eyes, and there was deep thought in the tilt of her head. When she spoke, she kept her eyes closed. "The same exact name. How utterly fascinating. Do either of you know of the German poet, philosopher and physician, Friedrich Schiller?"

Jack looked to Alice. She said, "I've heard of him, but I couldn't tell you anything about him."

Ida opened her eyes. "Friedrich Schiller was far ahead of his time. He died at forty-five years old in 1805, and he left behind a very impressive body of work, including plays and philosophical papers on ethics and aesthetics. He once said, 'There is no such thing as chance; and what seems to us merest accident springs from the deepest source of destiny.'"

Ida stared at them, pointedly, and Alice and Jack waited for more. "Well, this fairly smacks of destiny's intervening hand, doesn't it?"

"Mrs. Swearengin," Jack said, "Alice wants to try to find out what happened to the author. It's possible she's still alive."

Ida nodded, and her eyes twinkled. "Well, I think this calls for a beverage. Coffee perhaps? Or scotch?"

"Coffee is fine," Jack said.

"Yes, coffee," Alice added, "but only if it's no bother."

"It's no bother at all. Sharon is an excellent hostess, despite her gruff manner."

Ida struggled up and started for the door. "I'll have her make some fresh coffee for you, and I'll have scotch on the rocks. I find that scotch does wonders for my memory and overall health and, even if that's just wishful thinking by an old woman, I love the stuff. I'll be right back."

At the door, she stopped, turning back to Alice and Jack with a curious gaze. "It is intriguing that after all these years, Alice's diary turns up, and in the same house. Perhaps it will reveal some long-held secret or a mystery waiting to be solved."

CHAPTER 12

December 2016

Ida Swearengin held a crystal rocks glass, gently swirling the scotch, the ice clinking against the side. Alice and Jack cupped mugs of coffee in their hands, waiting for Ida to continue her story about Sally, Fred and the historical Alice.

While she considered the past, Ida's eyes were filled with a vague, distant quality as she stared out the window at the overcast day and snowy meadow.

"Mother and I visited Sally and Fred after her son, John, was killed in the war. Sally was part of the Methodist congregation, and my mother had become friends with her. It was a sad time, that war. I was just a girl of twelve and rather shy and retiring, but I had big ears and watchful eyes. I learned things about people just by observing. I recall my heavy feeling when I entered Sally's and Fred's house. They appeared so unhappy and forlorn. As they said in those days, Fred was hitting the sauce pretty hard. I guess it helped him cope with his only son's death. Sally seemed to suffer in outbursts of bitterness and then silence. My mother always brought them a cake, or pie, or casserole, something. People did such kind and generous things in those difficult days."

"Did you visit them often?" Alice asked.

"Three or four times, as I recall."

"And do you remember meeting Alice Ferrell?" Jack asked.

Ida needed no time to think about it. "Yes, I remember Alice."

Alice Landis was all ears, feeling a little flutter in her chest, hanging on Ida's every word.

"She was attractive, I remember that, and I remember she had lovely brownish or chestnut hair."

Alice opened her purse and removed the two black-and-white photographs of Alice and Charles. She rose and handed them to Ida, who took them eagerly, adjusting her tortoiseshell glasses for a clear focus.

"Is that the Alice you met, Ida?"

Ida's eyes widened in recognition. "Yes... Yes, that's Alice. I don't know who the man is with her."

"His name was Charles... He was also killed in the war, in the Pacific. I believe he was killed only a few months after John."

Ida took her time viewing the photos, studying them, lost in memory. "This Alice looks so happy. When I saw her, she was so pretty and so sad. I didn't know about Charles being killed. I'm not sure my mother told me. Grownups didn't talk so much to their children in those days."

Ida handed the photos back to Alice, and she returned to the sofa.

"I recall that Alice would always bring mother and me coffee on a tray and then she would sit with us, but not for very long. My watchful eyes saw the restlessness in her; saw a sadness that I took for shyness. She once said to me that I had pretty hair. It was a reddish blonde, and yes, it was quite pretty, and my mother fussed with it whenever we went to church or out socializing. Alice also once said that I'd have many boyfriends when I got older because I was so pretty."

Alice sipped the coffee. "Ida, do you know why Alice was living with Sally and Fred? Was she related to them?"

Ida considered that. "Yes, Sally was Alice's aunt. Mother said Alice's father was a lout. He'd just up and left his wife; left her with nothing, and that was before the war. Unfortunately, soon after, Alice's mother had a kind of mental breakdown. It's unclear to me what happened to her because people in those days didn't talk about mental illness like they do today. Anyway, Sally took custody of Alice."

Jack said, "Do you have any idea what happened to Alice?"

Ida shook her head. "No, I'm afraid not. I recall that sometime after the war, maybe the late 1940s or early 1950s, Fred died and Sally sold the house and moved away, I don't remember where. As far as I know, there was no mention of Alice, whether she'd already left, or if she moved with Sally."

Alice noticed Ida was wilting a little, growing tired. No doubt the scotch had made her sleepy. Alice nodded at Jack and they stood up.

"Thank you, Ida, for letting us fire our fifty questions at you," Alice said. "We appreciate it."

Ida swallowed the last of the scotch and set her glass on a side table, near her book. "I have thoroughly enjoyed it. You have given an old woman a delightful afternoon. I wish I could have been more help. It was so long ago… lifetimes it seems."

Alice reached into the side compartment of her purse and drew out Alice's diary. "Would you like to see the diary, Ida?"

Ida straightened, alert, all the fatigue gone. "The diary? Oh, yes, I certainly would."

Alice walked it over and presented it, and Ida took it with a gentle hand, viewing it with awe, as if it were a religious relic. "It's a connection to my past, isn't it? It's from another world, long gone, most of the people dead and buried."

Her eyes misted with tears as she raised them to Alice. "Have you read it through?"

"I've skimmed all of it, and read some entries several times, but I plan to go back and read all of it again more closely. As you can imagine, I've read the last few pages. Who could resist that?"

"No one, of course," Ida said, running a finger along the spine. "I suspect that Alice would love to have her diary back if she has remained in the land of the living. I do hope you find her, or, at least, find out what happened to her."

Ida opened the diary, carefully, slowly turning the pages, reading randomly. She made a little sound of surprise when an entry seized her attention. "Oh… my. Listen to this.

"I don't want Tom to leave, and I shouldn't write this. It's not right or proper. I'm alone in the house and, when I spoke to Sally on the phone after dinner, she said that Fred wouldn't leave his ailing father, so she would stay with him. She wasn't sure when they'd return. I didn't dare tell her about Tom, afraid she'd scold me for having him in the house, sleeping in the back bedroom. I know how it sounds, but it's not like that. He's such a gentleman and he loved Charles

like a brother. After they towed his car away, he shoveled snow from the sidewalk, driveway and walkway.

At dinner tonight, we didn't talk much. I feel so confused inside myself. I know I've lived a sheltered life, and Charles never forced things the way that some men do. Even on that last night, when I told him he could, because I wanted his baby. But Charles was good. He said, "No, Alice... I want the best for us. I want us to start right and finish right."

I have a confession to make. Maybe because Tom told me he grew up in an orphanage... Well, I guess that's why I told him. Maybe I shouldn't have. I never showed the letter to Sally. How could I? I got the mail first that day, and she didn't know about it.

Anyway, I told Tom about my father, but not my mother. He listened so patiently. I told him that just a few weeks ago, I got a letter from my father, the father I hardly remember. In the letter, he said he had been in the war and was wounded in Europe. He said he was living in Cincinnati, Ohio at a boardinghouse. He wants me to go and see him. He said he was sorry for leaving Mother and me like that.

I asked Tom what I should do, and he was so understanding. Do you know what he said? "I'll take you, Alice. He's your father, isn't he? Yes, I'll take you. It sounds like he needs you. Yes, of course you must go, and I'll drive you."

Ida lifted her eyes from the page, her face filled with wonder. "Had you read this section, Alice? Did you know about it?"

"Yes... And there's another coincidence, Ida, another synchronicity about me and the diary. Alice said her father was living in Cincinnati. My father also lives in Cincinnati."

Ida looked bewildered.

Jack told Ida the story of how he and Alice had met, explaining how she had found his diary three years ago at a bed and breakfast, and that he had written it fifteen years before.

Ida handed the diary back to Alice, and when she spoke, her voice was firm, her eyes steady.

"You must find out what happened to Alice. You must. There are too many peculiar connections for this to be a coincidence. I'm convinced that there is a reason you found that diary, and you found it in that house at this particular time. Please find the Alice Ferrell who wrote that diary and then come back and tell me what happened. Will you do that?"

Alice nodded. "Yes, of course. And even if we don't find her, I'll tell you everything we learned about her."

Ida smiled confidently. "You *will* find her. I know it. I feel it in these old bones of mine."

CHAPTER 13
December 1944

After breakfast, the tow truck came, and Alice and Tom stood on the porch, watching, as a heavy-duty chain and hook was attached to the underside of Tom's car.

"Will you think about it, Alice? He's your father and he's a veteran. Wouldn't you like to see him?"

Alice avoided his eyes. "I don't know..." Then she swiftly changed her mind, not wanting Tom to think badly of her. "Yes, I should go see him. Of course I should."

"Okay then," Tom replied eagerly. "As soon as the car's repaired, we can go. It's not that far."

The truck went to work, belching smoke from its vertical exhaust pipe, the engine growling, the chain taut. With a final roaring effort, the truck tugged the car across the lawn and back onto the road, while curious neighbors peered from windows.

Tom faced Alice. "Think about it. We can leave whenever you're ready."

Tom bounded down the porch steps, hurried down the walkway to the truck, opened the passenger door and pulled himself up into the truck cab, closing the door. He rolled down the window and waved as the truck lumbered away, leaving Alice on the porch, waving back, a sorrowful emptiness in her expression. He'd be back, but how long would he stay? And what should she do? Go to Cincinnati or stay home?

After he'd gone, Alice slipped into her coat, hat and gloves, left the house by the backdoor and went walking. She wandered up the rising snowy meadow toward the grove of trees on her left, with the duck pond in view on her right. There was an icy crackle in the air that invigorated and fully awakened her, and her thoughts. The glistening, spreading meadow and snow-heavy trees reminded her of the cover of the Christmas card she'd received from the law firm. The sentiment, written with a red calligraphy flourish, simply said, "Christmas Greetings."

As she thought about going back to work, her once conscientious spirit vanished. She no longer had the desire to be trapped in that narrow office typing endless letters, law briefs, pleadings and motions; to hear the same, stale jokes from the two partners; to being asked to dinner by male clients, who were too old to enlist in the military. She'd been called "honey" and "doll" and, worst of all, "pretty baby."

Alice's breath puffed clouds of vapor as she ambled and slapped her gloved hands together for warmth. Her shoulders were hunched against the blustery wind, and her face was tilted up into the sun, seeking warmth and guidance from the heavenly blue sky.

Her scattered thoughts were on Sally and Fred and her cousin John, and then they settled on Charles. It seemed years since she'd last seen him, and as the memories of him surfaced, despair was bitter on her tongue. So she walked in an aura of cold loneliness and regret.

Alice rambled, stopping beside the pond, pocketing her hands. The small dock leaned left and the surface of the pond was frozen, dusted by a scrim of snow. It had been less than a year since she and Charles had rowed across it, on that warm February day.

Turning away, she meandered toward the cover of trees and kicked at the snow, remembering what Charles had told her as they'd walked and talked, not wanting the day to end.

"There are some Civil War soldiers buried under those trees," Charles had said. "Did you know that? My grandfather told me when I was a kid, soon after my family moved to this neighborhood. He fought in several Civil War battles, including The Wilderness and Gettysburg."

"Is he buried here?" Alice had asked.

"No, but he knew two men who were. It's hard to find their stones now, even in the spring. You really have to look. Most people don't even remember the graves are here. So life goes. You die and you're forgotten."

Pensive, Alice circled the space. That memory, that haunting February memory, expanded the moment and deepened her melancholy and apprehension: If she left with Tom to see her father, her life would shift in a fundamental way. Did she possess the courage to go through with it? Was it a wise choice, or a foolish one?

She took several steadying breaths, guiltily allowing herself to imagine Tom walking beside her. Within minutes, most of the despair had melted away, being replaced by breaths of hope and a mounting excitement.

She lifted her eyes toward the sky again, whispering a little prayer. She imagined what it would be like to drive away from Sally's and Fred's house; away from the town and away from her life. Alice measured the consequences and agonized over all aspects of her decision. It was a choice that might utterly uproot and alter her life forever. There was still time to back out. No one was forcing her. No one except herself and a troubled, aching heart which cried out for change.

A rustling sound jerked Alice's attention to the left. A spooked deer sprang up, arched over a fallen tree, and went scampering into the cover of pine trees. Alice longed to dash off after it and keep on going, and never return.

Back inside the house, Alice screwed up her courage and called Sally.

"I want to go, Aunt Sally. I can't explain it. I need to go. I need to go see my father."

Sally was stunned and furious. She leapt into the conversation with a sharp voice and harsh words. "Alice, what has gotten into you? Have you lost your mind? I don't know who you are when you talk this way. First of all, why did you let that strange man stay in our house? And *you,* completely alone in the house with him? It's reckless. Shocking and reckless, and I'm at a loss to understand you. And why didn't you tell me your father had sent you a letter? What has happened to you?"

It took a moment before Alice gathered herself, found her quivering voice and struggled to muster a rational defense. "Charles is dead, Sally. I'm scared. I'm lonely. Nothing seems right or safe or stable anymore. I can't sleep and I don't know what to do or where to turn. I have to get away and think about things."

Sally's voice turned cold. "Alice, do you think you're the only woman in this world who has lost someone in this terrible war? Don't you think I want to scream? Or that Betty wants to scream, or thousands of other women who have lost sons, husbands and brothers? It's time for you to get ahold of yourself and grow up, Alice. You're twenty-one years old. Running off with some strange soldier to see your despicable, abusive father is not only irresponsible, it's dangerous. You don't know this guy from the man in the moon. What's his name, anyway?"

"Tom Lawson. I told you, he was Charles' best friend."

"Well, I forbid it, Alice. I utterly forbid it. Do you hear me? Fred and I are leaving the day after tomorrow. I expect to see you at the house when we get there."

Alice braced herself with a hard swallow. "I have to go. I must go. Please understand."

There was a long, hurtful silence before Sally spoke, her voice low and threatening. "If you go off with that strange man to see your nothing of a father, Alice, then you will never be welcome in my house again. Do you understand me? You will not have a home to come back to."

"Don't say that, Sally," Alice pleaded, her voice breaking. "This is my home. You're my family. My only real family."

"Then stop this insanity right now. Tell that soldier to leave this very minute, and then get on with your life, like I and many other women are doing. Don't throw your life away like this. Pull yourself together."

Alice trembled, her throat constricted. "Sally, please understand. Please. I have to go."

She heard the loud, final click of Sally's phone.

CHAPTER 14

December 1944

In the late morning of the following day, Alice and Tom set off for Ohio. Alice had thoroughly cleaned the house from top to bottom, locked all the doors and windows, and then lowered the thermostat. With a trembling hand, she'd jotted down a note.

Dear Aunt Sally and Uncle Fred,
Please try to understand why I had to go. I will call you. I'll write.
Love, Alice

Alice backed away toward the front door, casting her eyes about the place one last time, feeling in her heart of hearts that she was leaving for good, and she would never return. She felt sorrow, but she accepted it—and then left the house.

Tom sat tall behind the steering wheel of his 1937 Oldsmobile coupe, with its deep, comfortable seats and beige mohair interior. Alice sat on the passenger side, as far from him as she could, her shoulder against the door. She was staring ahead into sunlight, noticing that on this bright December day, the car's black paint had a sharp bluish tint.

Her eyes were dull and tired from lack of sleep, and her insides were knotted up with tension and trepidation. With futile effort, her whirling thoughts, once again, tried to understand and rationalize her actions, but there was no sorting them out. Something alien and wild had taken possession of her, yanking her from that house, just as a wild storm rips up the roots of old trees and flings them away into a whirling tempest.

There was no making sense of what she was doing; it was a freak of nature. What was happening to her was as unpredictable and volatile as any sudden storm. She was at the mercy of nature, Tom Lawson, and her father. She was being blown into the unknown, into a foreign land, and she had no idea if she'd survive it. Sally had told her never to return, so where would she go after visiting her father, and after Tom left her? From the moment Tom had piled his car into the trunk of that tree, her life had never been the same.

The day before, while his car was being repaired, Tom had spent the night in the house. Both had kept an uneasy distance, and he had skipped dinner with the excuse that he'd eaten a late lunch at a "greasy spoon" near the garage.

The next morning, Tom's car was ready. He called a taxi, and Alice rode with him into town, exiting at the local bank. When she closed her account and stuffed the cash into her purse, she drew curious glances from the male teller and female clerk, both of whom attended the Methodist church. She made no comment as she walked purposely out of the bank into the cold, sun-heavy day.

After a bus ride back home, she called the law firm, explaining that she was leaving town and apologizing for not giving notice. On the other end of the line, she heard surprise and irritation from Wallace Bates. "What the hell has happened to you, Alice? After all I've done for you, you up and leave me high and dry?"

"I'm so sorry, Mr. Bates. I have to go see my father. He was wounded in the war."

And then she'd packed two suitcases, leaving behind items that provoked painful memories or possessed no personal value. Finally, she placed her diary in her purse. She would record everything that happened to her; all her fears and all her feelings. She would write the unraveling story of her new life.

Back inside the car, Alice flinched when Tom spoke. Neither had talked for long minutes.

"Are you sure you don't mind if we stop in Springfield, Ohio first?" Tom asked, glancing over.

"No... As I said earlier, it's fine... Yes, it's okay."

"We'll only be about two hours from Cincinnati. Strangely enough, I thought about that orphanage a lot when I was in combat. I thought about the kids I knew, and the teachers. I even thought about the name, The Pythian Children's Home. When I was a kid, I thought Pythian meant pathetic."

Alice glanced at him. "But you learned better, didn't you? I mean, you and the others weren't pathetic."

"Oh, yes, we learned better, but a lot of us boys called it that right up to the time we left. I guess that's just the way boys are."

They lapsed into silence again as they traveled a lonely, two-lane road that rose and fell across farmland, white with snow, and through small, sleepy towns. For a time, they drove parallel to a train puffing black smoke as it threaded its way through trees, finally snaking around a hill and out of sight.

"That's a troop train," Tom said. "God only knows where those soldiers are being sent to."

Alice stole a look at Tom. Again, he wore his informal uniform, looking so handsome and so confident. After all, he had fought in battles and survived; fought and been wounded and survived. He'd had to be tough and hard and clever, hadn't he? He'd had to be a killer. And yet, there was something easy and gentle about him; something about him that touched her heart and aroused her.

Alice was puzzled that he had never mentioned a girl-friend. Surely there was one, or had been one. She'd been wanting to ask, and she decided this was the time.

"Tom... I'm sure you have other friends, I mean good friends, like Charles?"

"Not so many. A few of the guys are okay, but none are like Charlie."

"Do you have a girlfriend?" she said, deciding to blurt it out.

Tom had both hands on the steering wheel, and he didn't look over. "I don't have a girl, a steady girl. Not in this war. Maybe someday when I get back and the war's over. Then maybe I'll think about it, but then again, maybe I won't."

Alice kept her voice low, her eyes down. "Did Charles talk about me much?"

"Yes. Much. He was always gabbing on about you. He carried three photos of you, and he would show them around and brag that you were the prettiest girl in the world. I told him once he was a damned fool for kissing your photo every night."

Alice stiffened at the perceived insult.

Tom quickly corrected himself. "No, Alice, I didn't mean it that way. It was just buddies having a go at each other. I didn't mean nothing by it. Hell, I was jealous of him. A lot of the guys were. You know how guys are around other guys."

Tom sought to change the subject. "You never said how long it's been since you last saw your father."

Alice turned to stare out her window. "A long time. Not since I was nine. Twelve years ago."

"... And you said he'd been wounded?"

"Yes. He said it happened in Europe, but he wasn't in combat. His letter wasn't specific—he didn't elaborate. As I said the other night, I don't really know what happened."

"And your mother?"

"She's dead."

Tom looked at her, surprised, then he swung his eyes back onto the road. "I'm sorry, Alice. I had no idea."

"She got sick, that's all. She got sick and died when I was twelve. That's when I moved in with Aunt Sally and Uncle Fred."

Before Tom could respond, Alice changed the subject. "I was thinking I may look for work as a secretary at a war plant. I've been feeling so left out working at that law firm, while other women are out doing things... Doing new things and learning new things... and meeting people. It's time I did something like that."

Alice heard the words. It was the first time she'd not just thought them, but actually spoken them aloud. The sound of them produced a surge of hope and helped lighten her mood.

Tom ran a hand across his jaw and spoke in a quiet voice. "Alice, are you sure you want to do this... I mean, are you sure your aunt and uncle won't be sore at you for being with me?"

Alice turned her full, honest gaze on him. "I don't care if they're sore, Tom. I've made my mind up. It wasn't easy, but I've made up my mind and now I'm moving on."

Now that she'd released her thoughts into words, all the trapped words wanted out, and she didn't stop them. "Tom, something happened to me when you showed up; when you told me Charles had asked you to come. Something happened and I don't know yet what that is. But am I sure I want to do this? Yes, I'm sure. Now that I'm gone and away from that house, I'm more sure about this than I have ever been about anything else in my entire life."

Tom glanced at her, pulling his eyes from the road for a short time. But in that snapshot of time—in that instant—he glimpsed Alice in a new way, and something inside shifted. Her luscious, auburn hair was side swept with pin curls that accented her girlishly pretty face. Her hands were small but elegant, her mouth slightly puckered as she pondered a thought. But to him, her lips were poised, waiting for a kiss.

After Tom's gaze returned to the road, he'd been changed. Just like that—he saw what Charles had seen in Alice: a shy, classy girl, who seemed vulnerable and unsure of herself, like Tom was. And yet, she was leaving her home and her past, tossing the dice and taking a chance on the future, and that took strength and courage. He admired her for that. She had more steel in her than he'd first thought.

In that glancing instant, Tom felt a gathering tenderness toward her; a loosening of shyness. It was a brandnew thing. It was a foreign thing that he'd never fully experienced before. It opened him up, and it scared him a little.

His mouth tightened, and he rebuked himself for the surge of attraction he felt for Alice. After all, they'd only met, and she'd been Charlie's girl.

And then Alice looked at him, and *she* seemed changed, as if she'd pushed through some obstacle into a new light of understanding. Her face held happiness. Her eyes twinkled in the sudden splash of sun that streamed in through the windshield.

She said, "I haven't been on a road trip in so long. Thank you for taking me, Tom."

Distracted by *his* inner shift, he stayed quiet.

"I packed sandwiches and dried fruit for a late lunch. How long will it take us to get to Springfield, Ohio?"

"According to the map, we should be there by three."

Alice leaned back with a comfortable sigh. "I'm going to enjoy every mile," she said in a rich, lyric voice—in a stronger voice than Tom had heard before. She cranked down her window and presented her face to the cold rushing wind. "It feels so good to be moving... It feels so good to be traveling down a road to a new place, and away from an old place."

Alice's buoyant mood was contagious. Tom pushed thoughts of the war away, allowing himself to be hopeful and to enjoy himself being with Alice, on a trip that was leading him into his past, to the orphanage.

When she hummed a song he'd never heard, he asked her what it was.

She shrugged. "I don't know. I make up little tunes sometimes when I feel good."

The sun was cheerful, the snowy land was lovely, and Alice's humming voice was sweet. Tom settled back with a little smile.

As they approached Springfield, Ohio, a mood came over him. He thought, *This kind of living is good. Being with Alice is good, and it's comfortable.* He wanted it to go on for a little bit longer.

But he knew that after he dropped her off at her father's place, that would be the end of it. He'd drive off toward the West coast and he'd never see her again. What waited for him was more combat, and he'd either live or die. Hadn't he lived with that obvious fact for months now? So what had changed? Was it Alice?

His mood thickened, like the grey clouds above that slid over the once blue sky. *That's what happens when you've been away from civilians,"* Tom thought. *That's what happens when you're thrown into combat, wounded, and then confined in a hospital for weeks. You forget feelings and things, and you push your emotions down, and you shut yourself off and hang out a sign that says "CLOSED."*

Death, pain, and loss are too close and too real; the only real. And then you meet a special girl and you think, didn't I want to meet a girl like Alice some day? Don't most guys want to meet an Alice? But then what? Even if she hadn't been Charlie's girl, could he hope for that one chance to beat the odds and make a go of it with her—a true, happy relationship? Who was he kidding? Even if that were a possibility, the odds of surviving the war were against him.

Tom shook his head as if to reset it. *Isn't that what Charlie had said many times when they were about to go into battle? "Hey, buddy, do you think I can beat the odds, survive the war and get back home to Alice?"*

Alice brought Tom out of his thoughts. "What will you do after the war?"

He didn't look at her. He waited, needing time to clear his head. "I don't think that far, Alice. Look what happened to Charlie."

Alice's face fell, and Tom wished he could take the words back.

CHAPTER 15

December 2016

On Wednesday, December 7, Alice found a cream-colored envelope on her bed, addressed to *Mom and Dad,* in Kristie's artistic script. With rising anxiety, Alice eased down on the bed in a slouching posture and opened the envelope. When she read the note, her heart sank.

In frustration and anger, Alice slung the note away. "Why did you do this, Kristie?!" she said in a tense, harsh whisper.

Alice glared at the note, then jerked her glance toward the windows. Jack wouldn't be home for three or four hours.

This is not something I can text him about, she thought. She wasn't going to call him, either. He used power tools, and he climbed ladders, and he met clients.

Alice snatched up the note, shoved it into her left jean pocket, and stuffed her cell phone in the other. She slipped away down the back staircase, grabbed her hat, gloves and coat from the wooden pegs, and pushed outside into the windy day.

Why is Kristie so bright, brittle, and complicated? She thought to herself. *Why is she so selfish?* Alice walked briskly toward the pond, gazing at the trees and the quilted overcast sky that held pockets of snow. Three inches over night was the latest prediction.

As she circled the near-frozen pond, Alice dug Kristie's note from her pocket, feeling her stomach pitch. There was no predicting what Jack would do or what he could do. Alice turned her back against the wind and re-read the note.

Hey you two:

Don't be mad and don't be upset. Taylor and I are jetting off to Colorado to go skiing. We plan to be away a week or so. We'll probably be home by Friday the 16th. Dad, I would have asked but you would have said NO, and I really want to do this. Taylor is a responsible, smart and nice guy. We'll be just fine. He's twenty years old and I'll soon be nineteen. In other words, we're old enough to make some of our own decisions.

Alice, I'm sorry I won't be able to help with the housework. I just have to get away for a while. I'm feeling really trapped.

Anyway, I'll text and I'll call, but don't shout at me over the phone. I'm plenty old enough to do this and I have my own money. Taylor has some friends going too, so we'll split the expenses. Hey, every girl needs an adventure now and then, doesn't she?

Love to you both and don't worry. I'll be just fine. Yell at me when I get back, but remember it will be Christmas, so be nice. Lol!

Love,
Kristie

Alice yanked her cell phone from her pocket and started a text to Kristie. It wouldn't do any good, but she had to try something.

Her thumbs went to work. *Are you sure you want to do this without asking your father?*

Minutes later Kristie shot back. *I'll be home before you know it. Love.*

Alice wandered on, feeling the whistling wind chill her face and Kristie's actions chill her heart. She'd have to call Brenda Ashford to take Kristie's place. Brenda was a single mother who needed extra money, and she wouldn't have to be trained. She'd worked for them last spring and done an excellent job. Alice had reluctantly laid her off when Kristie pleaded for the job to make extra money for school. In many ways, Alice would be happy to have Brenda back; she was a reliable and cheerful hard worker, and the guests liked her.

Brenda answered the phone after the first ring and enthusiastically agreed to start the following day.

After the call, Alice roamed aimlessly, kicking at a fallen tree branch. For all her intelligence and charm, Kristie had a cold, selfish streak that Alice could not understand. Jack didn't understand it either. During their night-time pillow talks, they usually concluded that Kristie was just inexperienced and immature, only a girl, after all, an independent girl who'd lost her real mother.

Alice sighed and kept walking, keeping her eyes focused on the path, stepping around stray limbs and rocks. As an escape from her anxiety, she thought about the diary, the young woman who wrote it, and her aunt, Sally Long. During the last two days, she and Jack had searched the internet, made calls and followed some leads, hoping to learn what had happened to Sally Long after she'd moved away, but they'd come up empty.

"There's something else we could try," Jack had said the previous evening.

"What?" Alice had asked, her chin resting in a palm, her eyes blurry from staring into the computer.

"Hire a private detective. They're used to finding missing persons."

"No... It doesn't feel right. Besides, most of me is enjoying this. I truly believe that if I keep looking, I'll eventually break through to something."

The breakthrough came sooner than they had anticipated, and it was Jack who made it. He arrived home that evening, a little after six o'clock. Alice was in the kitchen, listening to Christmas carols and slicing potatoes. He drifted over, gave her a kiss, and grinned broadly with satisfaction.

Alice laid the paring knife aside and touched his lower lip with a finger. "Hello, there. Why are you grinning like that and how much snow do we have so far?"

"About two inches."

She considered showing him Kristie's note, but decided not to, not wanting to destroy the light mood. And, anyway, she dreaded it. Waiting another minute or two wouldn't change anything.

"Why do you look so happy?" Alice asked.

"Because I have news."

"Okay. I'm all eyes and ears."

Jack clasped his hands together. "I got a phone call today from Sheriff Al Bledso. You remember him, right?"

"Of course I remember him."

"A few days ago, I called to ask if he could help track down Sally Long and/or Alice Ferrell."

"That was smart thinking. And?"

"Well, through some computer database, he was able to track down Sally Long, and where she moved after she left this house."

Elated, Alice wiped her hands on her red and green Christmas apron. "Go on."

"She moved to Woodland, Pennsylvania to live with her sister, and lived there until her death in 1962."

"Wow!" Alice said, in a low tone of awe. "And what about Alice? Any information about her?"

Jack rocked on his heels, showing pride. "Yes, ma'am, this cowboy has the information you've been seeking," Jack said, in a playful southern accent.

"Well, go ahead, tell me."

"Sally's sister had a daughter named Mary, who had a daughter named Judy Barker, who still lives in Woodland. Al gave me her number, in confidence, of course. I thought you'd want to call her."

Jack tapped his phone. "I'll text you her name and number."

"Fantastic!"

After a hug and the peck of a kiss, Alice considered showing him Kristie's note, but again, she resisted, not wanting to break the cheerful spell. She glanced up at the ceiling. "I had a thought today."

"Yes? About?"

"We know that Alice took the diary with her when she left with Tom, right? I mean we've established that?"

"Yes, we have. And we know that the diary ended up back here or we wouldn't have found it. So, what's on your mind?"

Alice lowered her eyes on him. "It's obvious that Alice returned here, isn't it?"

Elyse Douglas

"Not necessarily. She may have shipped back some of her belongings, one being the diary, but never actually returned herself."

"Yes, maybe, but that's a long shot."

"I don't think so. And, for all we know, something may have happened to Alice, and someone else may have mailed the diary to Sally and Fred. It could have been Tom. Or the diary could have been mailed back to this house after Sally left it, and that's why the thing ended up in the lost and found. Remember, this place had become a boarding house in the 1950s. We just don't know."

Alice crossed her arms, sighed, and leaned back against the counter. "I never thought of that."

"So why don't you call Judy Barker right after dinner?"

"I will."

"How are the guests?"

"They're all fine."

"How's Andrew? Is he still at work on his app?"

"Yes, he went out with a friend, Mike Turner; at least I think he's a friend. Andrew was a little mysterious about the guy. He didn't want to talk about him. Anyway, they're going to grab a burger and keep working."

"Okay, and how's Kristie? I texted her. No response. Has she been in touch with you?"

Alice looked away. "Kristie is…" She stopped, reached into her back pocket and tugged out the note. She handed it to Jack who stared, reluctantly, before taking it.

Alice saw the sudden change in his expression, from calm pleasure to spreading despair.

In a low, dragging voice, he said, "I'm not going to like this, am I?"

Her eyes came to his. "No, Jack, you're not."

He reached into his flannel shirt pocket for his reading glasses, slipped them on and stepped under the overhead light. Alice went back to slicing potatoes as he read, keeping her back to him. She heard his breathing deepen; heard an audible sigh when he'd finished reading it.

"Well... all right. I can't say she surprises me anymore. I take it you didn't know anything about this?"

Alice quickly turned. "Of course I didn't know. I saw her this morning at breakfast and she didn't say anything. When I got back from the market, I found the letter on our bed, and she was gone. I didn't call you because I didn't want you distracted and angry while at work."

"Angry?" He slung the pages down on the kitchen island counter top. "Why should I be angry? Like she said, she's all grown up now and she can do whatever she wants, can't she?"

It was a long moment before he started for the back staircase, then stopped. "Do you have someone lined up to do her job tomorrow?"

"Yes. Brenda agreed to come back."

His eyes flared. "Good. As far as I'm concerned, if Kristie ever asks to work in this house again, we say, 'No.'"

Alice nodded. "I agree."

He lowered his head in defeat. "Dammit, Alice. I just never know what she's going to do."

He stood there, his mind turning. "I suppose she's having sex with this Taylor kid?"

Alice dropped her gaze. "Kristie told me she was. I stressed the importance of protecting herself."

Jack's eyes were direct. "Protect herself? Is she even capable of that? Why didn't you tell me she was sleeping with the guy?"

Alice's voice was soft with apology. "I should have. I'm sorry."

"Yes, you should have, Alice. I am her father."

Alice hesitated. "... She told me not to tell you. I don't know. I feel caught in the middle sometimes."

Jack glanced away, hurt. "Yes, well, I always feel like I'm on the outside looking in."

They stood staring, lingering.

"Did you call this Taylor kid's parents?"

"No... I don't have the number. Kristie said his parents are divorced. He lives with his mother and he's an only child. I guess I didn't want to call her."

Jack pushed his hands into his back pockets, his head down. "Have you met her?"

"No."

"We should call her. Maybe *Google* her number or something. Do you know her name?"

"It's Connie... Connie Barnes. Do you want me to?"

"It might be better coming from you. In my current bad mood, I might intimidate her."

"All right. I will."

Jack turned, hesitated, and pulled his hands from his pockets. "I'll go wash up."

And then he was gone.

Alice's shoulders sagged. "I should have told him," she said, at a whisper.

She grabbed her cell phone and, using an online website, Alice searched Connie's phone number, finding it in minutes. She dialed the number and left the counter, pacing. On the fourth ring, a light female voice answered.

"This is Connie. Who is this?"

"Hi, Connie, I'm Alice Landis, Kristie's stepmother."

Alice heard a whooshing sigh. "Yes, Alice. I know why you're calling. I was going to call you but, frankly, I put it off. I'll make this simple. Taylor left me a note. He didn't ask me. He said he called his father and he told him, 'Go ahead. You're twenty years old. Make your own decisions.' I'm livid, of course. I've called and texted Taylor. He hasn't taken my calls and he's only returned one text, which basically said, 'I'm fine. Don't worry. I'll be in touch.'"

Alice closed her eyes and switched her phone from her right ear to her left. "Okay... Can you track him through his phone or laptop?"

"I could have if he hadn't disabled the GPS and deleted the history on his laptop."

Alice said, "Yeah, Kristie did too. I had hoped to see what airline they were flying on at least."

Connie's voice softened. "I've met Kristie... She seems like a sensible girl, and smart. Taylor's smart too. But why didn't he at least ask me, or just tell me he was going? What can we do?"

Alice stared ahead. "I don't know. Just keep calling and texting, I guess."

CHAPTER 16
December 1944

"All us kids had to learn the history of this place," Tom said. They were strolling the grounds of the former Pythian Children's Home, now The Knights of Pythias Nursing Home.

"It's so big," Alice said, staring in amazement. "There must be ten buildings and, you're right, it does look like a fortress."

Tom pointed to an impressive Victorian home with turrets, steeply pitched roofs, pointed arches and front-facing gables. "See that home over there? It was built between 1880 and 1882, and it was modeled after some castle in Italy. When I was here, they used it as the main administration building and for any VIPs that might be staying the night."

They walked to where the playground had been, passing several closed and shuttered buildings.

"It's so quiet," Tom said. "It was never this quiet with all the kids moving around." He kicked at the brown weeds poking up through the snow. "The place had a playful noise about it, a kind of rough energy."

He gazed reflectively. "Nothing stays the same, does it? I guess that's a good thing… and it must be a good place for the elderly. I betcha the trees and shrubs are still full in spring and summer; and the flower gardens still bloom."

They strolled a winding concrete pathway with a good view of the extensive snow-covered lawn, the misty faraway hills, and the stone-field walls. The sun played hide and seek in gray-heavy clouds, and Alice pinched the collar of her coat tightly about her throat as the wind came in chilly bursts.

"How long were you here?" Alice asked.

"About eight years, until I was eighteen. After I left, I worked with a carpenter for a while and then enlisted in the Marines."

He pointed to a rectangular, ornate building on their left. "That's where I lived."

"How many other children lived there?"

"If I remember right, about a hundred. But not all the kids were orphans. There were others, like Gus and Amos. Gus was fifteen and Amos was twelve when I met them."

"If they weren't orphans, why were they here?" Alice asked.

"It was a sad story. Their father died and left them with nothing. Their mother was going to move in with her sister, but there was no room for the boys. And, anyway, when people from the State checked up on her, they discovered she had a serious drinking problem and often left the boys alone."

Tom's stare was inward, as he remembered the past, recalling the smell of the rooms, hearing the echo of voices. Alice gazed out toward the line of trees where a flock of birds scattered and screeched.

"Gus told me all this later," Tom continued. "He said his mother died about a year after they were brought here. He was older than me and he left when he was eighteen. He's in the Army, fighting in Europe someplace. I don't know what happened to Amos."

Feeling nostalgic, Tom gestured vaguely. "It all seems so long ago. And, like I said, it's real quiet. It's funny, isn't it? From kids to the elderly. Kids make noise, and the elderly sit quietly. I suppose the old folks think back over their lives and remember all sorts of things, just like I'm doing now, and I'm not so old. Can you imagine the memories you must have when you get old?"

"Yes," Alice said, adjusting the blue fluttering scarf over her head and re-tying it at her neck. "It's a pretty place, though."

"Do you know what Charlie used to say when I talked about growing up here? He'd say, 'Tom, you were lucky to have so many brothers and sisters.'"

Tom settled his eyes on Alice, and she looked back at him, not shyly. "Do you know what, Alice... I *was* lucky. The people here were good to me. They always made summer fun and Christmas special, with plenty of little presents for all of us, and a Christmas tree, and lots of candy. Yeah, I was lucky."

Alice could feel what he was really thinking. It was as though she could hear his true voice under the forced one. "But you missed your family, didn't you, Tom?"

He looked at her for a long moment, turning over the question. "Yeah, I did. Am I that easy to read?"

She shrugged. "I know because I went through it, too. First, my father leaving when I was nine, and then my mother dying when I was twelve. Aunt Sally and Uncle Fred did the best they could, and so did my cousins, John and Ruth-Ann, but I always felt different, like an outsider. I felt beholding to them in some way."

They began walking again. Tom said, "Are you looking forward to seeing your father again?"

"I don't know. It's been so long."

"But you remember him, don't you?"

"Some... Even when he was with us, he wasn't around so much. My memories of him are kind of fuzzy. And then Sally has told me stories about him... not very good stories. To be honest, she despises him. Sally's not one to hide things. She tells it as she sees it."

Tom searched for the right thing to say. "Time and war change a person, Alice. And now you're a woman and not a girl."

Alice felt the cold seep into her bones, bringing an impatient restlessness. She wanted to climb back into Tom's car and keep on going for as long and as far as she could. She had been living with her life on hold for so long, waiting for Charles to ask her to marry him; waiting to start a family; waiting for Charles to survive the war and come back to her. And then, Charles was dead, and so were all her dreams. She'd shrunk back into herself— out of the will to go on, out of fight, and out of her right mind.

Alice looked at Tom from an interior distance, assessing him, assessing her emotions. She shivered a little, an inner shiver, not from the cold, but from being close to him.

He felt her eyes on him, and he responded, looking back at her. And so their eyes held, not moving.

"Tom, you never said why you were driving so fast in that snowstorm, when you crashed into the tree."

He didn't answer. They started back to the car and were only a few feet from the parking lot when he stopped, and so did she.

As he considered his answer, he also considered Alice and, as he did so, there was an unwinding in him, an extra beat in his heart that drummed with new life. There was girl and there was woman all about Alice, and they sang together in perfect harmony. There was mystery in her eyes, and there was despair, and there was more. What was it? Desire?

"The truth? I blacked out, Alice. That's what happened. I remember I was close to the house... it was just as Charlie had described it. He described the entire street and the house, and the meadow and the pond behind the house. He told me that his house was two streets over. You have to understand that I'd seen your photo so many times. I told you how he used to show your photo around. I looked at that photo so often that I felt like I knew you... Well, a little anyway."

His gaze was direct for a minute and then it drifted away. "I didn't want to come. I didn't want to see you standing there in front of me, the real Alice. No, not that way."

Tom breathed in a calming breath and blew it out. "So, what happened? I blacked out, and I didn't know where the hell I was until I saw you standing there at the car window, looking in on me. I thought I was dreaming. But that's not all of it. The doctors said I should rest over the Christmas holidays, but I had to see you. I had to do what Charlie had sworn me to do, and it had already been too long."

Alice saw the anguish on his face. "I'm grateful you came."

He looked skyward, lifting a hand. He was about to say something else, but he stopped, pocketing both hands and rolling his shoulders. "Hey, it's cold out here. Are you hungry? The sandwiches were good, but maybe we should find a coffee shop or something and warm up. What do you think?"

Alice was skittishly aware of her growing attraction to Tom and it unnerved her; it brought the rise of heat in her chest. It was impossible. They'd just met, and wasn't she still in love with Charles?

She'd heard about this kind of thing. She'd read about it in magazines. It had something to do with needing a shoulder to cry on. Needing the warmth of another human being. *Beware of Love on the Rebound* was the title of one such magazine article she'd read only recently. It told of grieving wives and girlfriends who'd lost their man in the war.

Alice looked away. "Yes, I'm cold."

Twenty minutes later, Alice and Tom sat at a table in the Bus Stop Luncheonette on the outskirts of town, near the railroad tracks. Outside the wide, plate-glass window were three gas pumps and a Greyhound Bus with a line of passengers ready to board, many of them soldiers toting duffle bags, leaving for the war, or returning for a Christmas furlough. There was a juke-box in the corner playing Bing Crosby's *White Christmas,* and a cigarette-burned counter, displaying a chocolate cake and an apple pie under large plastic covers.

There were two Coca-Cola calendars on the walls, one featuring a panting black dog crouched next to a Coca-Cola bottle, and the other showcasing sun-kissed babes in sweaters with sharp breasts and glitzy grins, tossing a red and white beach ball.

A wide-hipped, middle-aged woman, wearing a gray and white uniform, stood behind the counter, pouring coffee for two sad-sack regulars, in blue overalls and train engineer caps. They smoked and spoke in hushed, grumbling tones.

Alice stared down at her coffee. "When did you say you have to report to your base?"

"January third, at Camp Pendleton. It's not far from San Diego. I suppose I shouldn't tell you that... Loose lips sink ships, so they say."

"I won't tell," Alice said, and then she raised her eyes. "Are you physically ready to return to war?"

Tom leaned back, his eyes blinking, as if he wanted to erase the thought. "It depends on what the docs say."

"Do you want to go back?"

He gave her a bending smile, a smile calculated to hide fear. "I told you, I have never run from my duty, and I'm not going to start now. If they pass me, I'm going. We have to end this war and we have to win it."

Tom swiveled around toward the juke-box. "Do you want to hear anything?"

"I don't know. No. Nothing."

"Are you sure you don't want some cake or pie?"

"No, thanks."

"Then maybe we should start for Cincinnati. We don't want to get there too late. Do you need to call your father?"

"No... He knows I'll get there after dark."

Alice leveled her eyes on him. "Tom... Will you do me a favor?"

"Of course."

"Will you wait for me after I go into my father's house?"

He smiled warmly. "Yeah... sure, I'll wait. I'll go in with you if you want."

Alice watched the Greyhound bus roll out of the station and onto the two-lane road, a stream of white smoke puffing from its exhaust pipe.

"I'd like that. I'd like that very much," Alice said.

CHAPTER 17

December 2016

"Hello, my name is Alice Landis. Is this Judy Barker?"

Alice was alone in her office, standing by the desk, phone in hand.

"Yes, this is Judy Barker. Who did you say you are?" a thin, tentative, female voice said.

"Alice Landis. Is this a good time to talk for a few minutes?"

"What is this about?"

"It's about Sally Long."

"Sally Long? Sally's been dead for many years."

"Yes, I know. I'm trying to find a young woman who lived with Sally and Fred Long in 1944. Her name was Alice Ferrell. I found something of hers and I want to return it."

"Oh... Well, I wouldn't know anything about that. That's long before I was born. I never even met Sally and I've never heard of Alice Ferrell."

Alice strained her mind, trying to come up with the right questions. "Judy, didn't Sally move in with your grandmother after Fred died?"

"Yes. They were sisters. You said you found something of Alice's? That's a long time ago."

"I'm sorry. Let me explain. My husband and I currently live in the house that Sally and Fred owned in the 1940s. We found an old diary written by Alice, and we want to return it."

"A diary? How interesting. It's not Sally's diary?"

"No, it belongs to Alice, who lived with Sally in 1944. That's why I'm trying to find out what happened to her."

After a brief silence, Judy said, "I could call my mother and ask if she knows anything about it, or about Alice Ferrell. There's an off-chance she might remember something. Mom was a teenager when Aunt Sally lived with them, at least that's what I remember."

"I would appreciate that. It's a fun project for me, and it's possible that Alice Ferrell is still alive, although she would be in her nineties."

Judy said, "Wouldn't that be something. Please give me your number and I'll call Mom and then get back to you."

"Thank you, Judy, thank you very much."

After the call, Alice dropped down into her swivel desk chair, feeling a heaviness in her chest. After dinner, Jack had called Kristie, but she hadn't picked up. Worried and frustrated, he'd texted her, with a warning. *As long as you still live under my roof, then you MUST abide by my rules. Running off with some boy I have never met, without even telling me, is unacceptable. You need to return home, NOW.*

Alice wished Jack hadn't been so forceful, not that his words were wrong. Kristie and Jack had never had an easy relationship. He was conservative and often fixed in his opinions, while Kristie was a free spirit, who was always testing his love, pushing his buttons, and pushing boundaries.

She and Alice had always gotten along, but it had come at a cost. There were times Jack felt that Alice was too lenient with Kristie and that she spoiled her. Perhaps Jack was right. She was Kristie's stepmother, and she had to admit that she sought Kristie's and Andrew's approval and affection.

Jack felt the weight of guilt and responsibility for his kids; for the fact that Darla, their mother, had left them for another man and another life. Alice knew that sometimes Jack had difficulty forgiving himself for the broken marriage, and for Darla's death in a fire.

Alice reached for her glass of merlot and sipped at it. Being married and in love was not always an easy affair, like in the movies. Sometimes it was an ordeal, although she knew that her marriage to Jack and the kids was also life-building and nourishing, that it enriched her life immeasurably.

Alice set her glass down, distressed. She needed to speak with her mother. Even though she had died of cancer some years before, whenever Alice was caught in a thicket of confusion and emotion, she would often hear her mother's voice in her head, and have an imaginary conversation with her.

There were times when that "imaginary" conversation seemed real, as if her mother were in Alice's office sitting on the leather sofa, dressed in her favorite green silk tunic, with her legs tucked beneath her. She'd remove her glasses, place one arm of the frame in her mouth, narrow her eyes on Alice and say, "Okay. Go ahead. Let's hear it."

They discussed things; sometimes argued; sometimes laughed. When their little talk was over, Alice always felt better.

This was one of those times when Alice needed her mother's guidance. She leaned back, snuggled down into the chair, closed her eyes, and took a few deep breaths to relax. Her breathing slowed, her shoulders settled, and the tension drained from her body as she drifted into a mellow trance.

It often took a minute or so before Alice could hear her mother's whispery voice.

"Hey, Mom," Alice said, quietly. "Are you there?"

It was a delicate voice, like the fluttering of a hummingbird's wings. "Yes, I'm here, just like I was all those years ago when you were a teenager and you had a crush on that terror of a boy named... Now what was his name?"

"Steve," Alice said, guiltily. "I don't remember his last name, and I don't want to remember it."

"You weren't quite as impulsive and rebellious as Kristie, but you had your moments. I thought you were going to get pregnant."

Alice was chilled by the word "pregnant." It was a conversation she'd wanted to avoid, and yet, it had been on her mind for the last couple of days. "Mom, I want to give Jack a baby. He wants another. He wants *our* child. We've been trying on and off for nearly three years."

"Why on and off? What does that mean?"

"It means we try, and then I get nervous and scared, and then we stop. I mean, I'm thirty-four years old and Jack's pushing forty. We already have Kristie and Andrew. Shouldn't that be enough?"

"I don't know. You tell me."

Alice ignored her mother's request. "Do you know what he said to me the other night as we lay close, our noses pressed together, our breath soft on each other?"

"SOoo romantic you are, daughter of mine," her mother said, in a playfully mocking tone. "Okay, so, I feel how stressed and restless you are. Tell your mother everything."

"Jack said, 'It's okay if you can't, or don't want to, have a baby. We'll be just fine. It's not as if we don't already have two kids who always seem to be on the verge of driving me crazy.'"

"That broke my heart, Mom. Jack is so good and kind, and I know he's disappointed, and I know he loves his kids more than his own life. Do you know what Polycystic Ovarian Syndrome is? According to Dr. Steinmetz, my ob/gyn, that's what I have. She said it's one of the most common causes of female infertility and it affects about five million women. I'm not ovulating regularly. That's a problem."

"Maybe you're trying too hard, Alice. Maybe you're all wound up. Are you eating regularly? You know how you sometimes skip meals because you get so caught up in things. Are you all caught up in things?"

Alice sighed out the word, "Yes..."

"I cautioned you about that years ago. Well, anyway, can this condition be treated?"

"Yes. I'm taking fertility drugs. I'm eating a bigger breakfast and smaller dinners. I'm including more protein and greens and whole grains and beans."

"Well then, dear Alice, things will work out. Most of it's mental, I think. You think too much, and you always did."

Alice sighed again. "Mom, do you know that you were often critical of me?"

"Was I?"

"Yes, you were. I sometimes find myself thinking about my marriage and I think, am I doing this right? Am I thinking about that the right way? Am I a good wife and stepmother? Am I thinking the way Mom, the psychologist, would want me to think? Sometimes I feel like my thoughts are strangling me."

"Alice, dear, you were always so dramatic. But don't you remember? Who are you blaming for all that staticky thinking? Me? Have you forgotten one of the first things I taught you, when you were old enough to know the difference between right and wrong? I said, it's not important what *I* think, it's only important what *you* think. I also recommended that you sit quietly with your eyes closed for at least twenty minutes a day, to let your thoughts settle. In that gathering peace, solutions arise, and sometimes, miracles happen."

Alice smiled, and the silence stretched out. "Mom... I always miss you at Christmas. You always made Christmas the best day of the year, but I have to tell you, I never liked those fruit cakes you baked, with all those little red and green artificial gummy things in them."

"No? Well, you never complained."

"To Dad I complained. We still laugh about it."

"Speaking of your father, have you been to see him lately?"

"No, not lately. I call him."

"You should go see him. He gets lonely."

"No, he's not lonely. He's dating another woman, about eight years younger and, from what he tells me, she's got some gypsy in her."

"And so did I."

"No, you didn't."

"In the right mood and in the right place, Alice, I had the sass, flair and passion of a gypsy. Have you invited your father for Christmas?"

"Yes, and he accepted, and he's bringing the gypsy, although I doubt that she is a gypsy or will look like a gypsy. You know Dad. He likes to shock."

"Good, I'm glad you'll be together. He always loved being with you at Christmas. He loves you with all his crazy heart and big mouth."

Alice sat up, feeling the energy begin to fade. "You're leaving, aren't you?"

"Yes… It's time. Alice, listen to your mother. When you make love to Jack, don't try so hard to make everything perfect. You were always trying to control things and make everything and everyone's life perfect, at least as you saw it. Falling in love with Jack as you did, right out of the blue, was one of the best things that ever happened to you. So now, just relax a little. Let your body speak to you and let it lead the way."

Alice grew defensive. "Mother, I'm thirty-four years old. I think I know how to make love to my husband."

Alice heard her mother's naughty little laugh. "Just sayin', Alice, my love. Think about it. Bye for now. Oh… and I love you and miss you. Kisses."

Minutes later, Alice stood at the windows, her arms folded, staring out into the night. Was the elderly Alice out there somewhere, still alive? Alice turned, returned to the desk and opened the diary randomly, and read an entry.

We didn't make it to my father's house. The car broke down. Tom said it was because of the damage done when it hit that tree. Obviously, the mechanics at the repair shop hadn't found everything.

We're in a motor lodge, in separate rooms, mine away from Tom's on the far end of the parking lot. I insisted on paying for my own room, but Tom wouldn't hear of it. He said it was the least he could do after all the trouble he'd caused me.

Trouble? Tom hasn't been any trouble. He's really been swell. He's more serious than Charles was, and he doesn't smile so much, but when he does, I feel the warmth of it. Sometimes when he looks at me, I don't know what he's thinking, but I like his eyes. They have hurt in them, but kindness too. I don't know why some girl hasn't captured his heart. He really is quite handsome.

I'm sitting up in bed, staring at these knotty pine walls, feeling a drowsy peace. It's been a long day, but a good day. I feel renewed. I feel I can breathe better, deeper. I feel relaxed for the first time in months. I'm glad I left that house— that sad house, where John will never return, where Charles will never return, where Ruth-Ann will probably never return; and where Sally and Fred have lost all their happiness.

I called my father, but nobody picked up. I tried twice. He should have been there. I'll try again in the morning. I'm worried.

There's a garage about two blocks away. The mechanic said he didn't know how long it might take to make the repairs. He's an older man, with white hair and shaking hands. He said all the young mechanics went to war. After he looked the engine over, he told Tom the problem, but I didn't really understand. Something about the engine block, where the crankshaft spins.

What will tomorrow bring? I don't care. Whatever it is, I will face it.

CHAPTER 18

December 1944

The next morning, the car still wasn't ready. Tom had knocked lightly on Alice's door and, when she'd opened it a few inches, he'd said, "I'm sorry, Alice. The man at the garage says it may take him the better part of the day before the car's ready to go."

Later, in the motor lodge lobby, where a big Christmas wreath hung in the front window, Alice called her father again. This time a woman answered, and her voice was tart and unpleasant.

"He's not here. They took him to the hospital."

Alice's voice rose in concern. "The hospital? Is he all right? What happened?"

"Who is this?"

Alice stammered. "Well, you... you see..." It took three tries before she finally managed to utter, "I'm his daughter."

The woman's voice was strident. "If you want to know the truth, he's out of his head. He screams out and wakes me up, and he owes me for two months' rent. I won't let him back into that room unless he, or somebody else, pays me."

Tom was close by, waiting, overhearing. When he saw the anxiety on Alice's face, he sensed she needed privacy. The balding clerk behind the lobby desk was lost in his adding machine, a cigarette dangling from his fat lips.

Tom pushed the glass door open and stepped outside, lighting up a Lucky Strike, his shoulders hunched against the cold as he smoked.

When Alice emerged, her chin down, her expression solemn, Tom flicked his cigarette away and went to her.

"Is everything all right?"

She shook her head. "No, I don't think so. He's at the VA Hospital. That's all the woman knew."

"I'm sorry, Alice. I'm sorry my damned car isn't ready."

She gazed up into the gray, cloudy day. Snow flurries fluttered by, and she heard the moan of a train whistle in the distance. She turned toward the sound. "Maybe I should catch a train or a bus or something and get down there."

"Did you call the VA Hospital?"

She passed him an uneasy glance. "No... I should have, shouldn't I?"

"You still can."

She shook her head and closed her eyes. "No... I... I'm scared. I don't know him. Nothing about him."

Alice stared at Tom, wanting him to understand and not judge her. "He scared me. I remember that. And I remember he brought me one of those big suckers you see at the traveling circus. I didn't want to take it because Mom said I shouldn't. Then they started shouting at each other."

Alice reached into her purse, found her pack of cigarettes, and shook one out. Her hand trembled as she lifted the black veil from her hat, a feathered homburg. She placed the cigarette between her lips and leaned forward as Tom produced his lighter and lit it for her.

Smoking distractedly, she toed at the ground, watching cars pass on the highway. She was worried that Tom was perceiving her as a silly girl who didn't know her own mind.

"We danced once, my father and me. I remember that. We danced to some bouncy tune. He took both my hands and whirled me around the room until I was laughing and dizzy. That was fun."

A minute later, she dropped the cigarette and crushed it out with the toe of her shoe. "Tom... I've always felt like a kind of orphan... like a stranger everyone had to be nice to. Of course, Sally was harsh sometimes, and maybe she even slapped me a few times, but I never held it against her."

"She shouldn't have slapped you, Alice. Nobody should do that."

"Maybe I wasn't so easy to be around. I missed my mother."

"That's no excuse for the woman to hit you."

Alice stared apprehensively at him, feeling the need to share things that had once been private, and yet she was scared to do so. "Tom... I've never said this before, but sometimes I thought that Charles felt sorry for me, too. Sometimes he called me 'his little lost waif' and..." she stopped, unsure if she should continue. "Sometimes he called me Little Orphan Annie. It made me feel... Well, like a lost kid who didn't belong anywhere."

Tom pocketed his hands and stayed silent.

"I didn't like him pitying me like that. It made me feel like an outsider, not part of the Long family, and a little detached from him."

Tom gave her a transient grin. "You know how Charlie could be. Joking around. I'm sure he didn't mean anything by it."

Alice shifted her mood, forcing a smile. "No, of course he didn't. Of course you're right. I say silly things sometimes. They don't really mean anything."

"We all do that, don't we?" Tom said, restlessly, not knowing what else to say.

Alice gave him a quick, narrow look. "What will I say to him? To my father? What if he's dead? That woman on the phone... She runs that boarding house. She said he owes her two months' rent."

"Yeah, I heard that."

And then, as if she were speaking to herself, Alice said. "I'll pay that. Of course I'll pay it. And I'll pay for the next month, too. And then, when I get settled, I'll send him some money every week."

Tom noticed she was shivering. "Alice, it's cold out here. Why don't we get some breakfast? I saw a diner across the road near the gas station. We'll talk about all this."

Alice's eyes shifted from Tom, to the highway, to the office. "I don't want to take the train, Tom, or the bus. Can I wait with you until the car is repaired?"

"Of course. That was our plan. It shouldn't take much longer. We're not so far away from Cincinnati. Once we're underway, we should get there in a little over an hour."

Nearly eight hours later, as darkness was closing in, they drove into the Cincinnati VA Hospital parking lot. Tom found a parking space near the front entrance, and when he shut off the engine, Alice sat stiffly, eyes blinking, hands folded tightly in her lap.

"I don't have a gift. It's almost Christmas and, anyway, shouldn't I bring him a gift or flowers or something? What kind of daughter am I?"

Tom looked left. "I saw a stationery store about a block away. Want to try it?"

She nodded. "Yes. Thanks, Tom, for being so patient with me."

He looked at her and thought, *she's terribly pretty*. In a steady, calm voice he said, "He's your father, Alice. And, he's a veteran. It's no trouble."

A half hour later they entered the hospital, with Alice carrying a bouquet of flowers. She hadn't found anything at the stationery store and, since she didn't know anything about him, she decided flowers were best. It was a simple mixed bouquet of red roses and white carnations.

At the hospital welcome desk, Alice stood tensely, waiting, as a male clerk used his index finger to trace several pages on a clip board until he found her father's room. As he lifted his somber eyes, he cleared his throat.

"Sergeant Clifford Ferrell is fighting an infection... and he has other serious issues. He's not supposed to have visitors. You say you're his daughter?"

"Yes... He wanted me to see him. He sent me a letter."

The clerk tapped the desk with a finger. "All right, but I'll have to have a nurse accompany you. He's in the neuropsychiatric ward. He's going to be transferred to a neuropsychiatric hospital in Columbus, Ohio, in a day or two."

Alice's eyes went wide. "I... didn't know. I haven't seen him in... well, in a long time."

Maggie Dennis was a thin, poised, middle-aged nurse, dressed in a white uniform and starched nurses' cap. Her eyes held kindness, her jaw was determined, and her voice was controlled.

She took Alice and Tom to a private lounge and spoke to them in hushed tones. "I understand you haven't seen your father for some time. Is that right, Miss Ferrell?"

"Yes... He wrote me a letter about a month ago. I didn't contact him right away. I know I should have but, you see, I haven't seen him since I was a girl."

Maggie nodded. "Alice, last April, your father was in Italy. The jeep he was traveling in struck a roadside mine. There were four men in the jeep, and he was the only survivor. His wounds were not so severe, but a week or so after the incident, he had a mental breakdown."

Alice felt a pinching in her chest. She inhaled a quick breath. "Mental...?"

"Yes. Since then, he's been in and out of hospitals. He's had insulin shock therapy, and it seemed to work for a time."

"What is that... insulin shock therapy?"

"The patient receives large doses of insulin over a period of weeks. It causes daily comas, but it helps to shock the patient's system out of mental illness."

Maggie let that sink in and then continued. "Your father is struggling right now, but we are helping him as best we can."

They left the elevator on the sixth floor and walked down a gray-tiled hallway. They passed men in wheelchairs, leafing through magazines, and open rooms with visitors hovering near beds. A priest passed, head down, a *Bible* clutched in his hand. Two nurses left a room, whispering, their eyes filled with purpose as they walked briskly to the nurses' station.

Alice hesitated at the door of 16-R, while Tom and Nurse Dennis stood by. The door was open, and Alice glanced at Tom for support. He nodded, and she adjusted her shoulders in preparation. With her purse swung over a shoulder, cradling the bouquet, she entered, her pulse thudding in her throat.

CHAPTER 19

December 2016

On Monday, December 12, Alice entered the small town of Woodland, Pennsylvania, followed her GPS' directions and turned right onto Pine Street. The house she was looking for was about two miles away, in a pleasant area, near an elementary school. Alice found it easily and parked in front of the modest, blue and white two-story home. It had a tidy lawn and hedges, a front bay window and a generous porch.

The house belonged to Mary Franklin, Judy Barker's mother. After speaking with Alice, Judy had immediately phoned her mother and asked if she remembered Sally and Fred. She repeated everything Alice had said about their house and the diary. Once Mary started remembering the couple, she realized she had some old letters in the attic that she hadn't looked at in years.

Excited to discuss old times, Mary Franklin called Alice Landis and invited her over so they could talk about Sally and peruse the letters together.

"I know I have some old letters from Aunt Sally, but all I remember is that they were like sermons," Mary had said on the phone, with a small laugh. "I don't think I liked Sally much, but then again, I'm eighty-two years old, and my memory isn't always clear. Maybe the letters will remind me of a few things." She paused. "I don't recall the name Alice Ferrell, but I have a kind of vague notion that Sally talked about a young girl she'd taken in, somebody who lived with her and Fred before and during the war."

Mary met Alice at the front door with a welcoming smile and an offer to take her coat. After the coat was stored in the closet and the introductions and small talk about the cold weather had run out, an enthusiastic Mary led Alice into the square living room, a welcoming room, with soft tones of blue, tan and gold. An artificial Christmas tree twinkled white lights, and green and red bulbs added a festive charm. The mantel held a miniature manger scene and two porcelain, golden-haired angels, their pious faces lifted to the heavens, their high arching wings painted a glittery gold.

Mary was slightly stooped, cheerful and demur, with lively eyes. Her white hair was styled in a short pixie cut, which Alice thought suited her perfectly.

Mary pointed to the coffee table where a stack of letters sat waiting, bound by a rubber band.

"I asked my son to climb up into the attic and fetch them for me," Mary said, with a chuckle. "You should have heard him whine and complain about the dust and the low beams. He lives just a little ways down the street so it's no trouble for him, except, between you and me, he's just plain lazy. He wants to sit around and do his wood working all day. His wife is a saint, if you ask me."

Alice accepted the offer of a mug of hot cider and Mary left for the kitchen. Alice sat on the sofa, her eyes locked on the letters, her fingers itching to open them.

Minutes later, Mary returned with two mugs of steaming cider and, after she'd handed one off to Alice, she joined her on the sofa, sitting heavily, with a sighing effort. "I need to get my right knee replaced, but I keep putting it off. I guess I'll have to do it after the first of the year."

Mary turned her gaze on Alice and appraised her. "You're a pretty woman, Alice."

Alice smiled modestly. "Thank you, Mrs. Franklin."

"Oh, for pity's sake, Alice, call me Mary. I haven't been called Mrs. Franklin since my husband, Burt, died three years ago. He'd call me Mrs. Franklin just for spite, and if he really wanted to get my goat, he called me Ben," she said chuckling again, high in her throat. "But he was a good man. He owned and ran the local hardware store in town for longer than I can remember. I did the books for him because I was always good with numbers."

It soon became obvious to Alice that Mary was lonely and loved to talk, so Alice indulged her, despite growing impatience to get her hands on those letters.

"I find it so fascinating that you have the same name as the woman who wrote that diary," Mary said, with a little shake of her head. "That's what Judy told me. Is it true?"

"Yes... my maiden name is Ferrell."

"If that isn't the limit. It's baffling, isn't it, Alice?"

"Yes, it is." Alice took a careful drink of the cider. "This is good. Perfect on a cold day."

"The apples are local," Mary said, sipping hers as well.

"Mary, what was Sally like?"

With a squint of reflection, Mary said, "Aunt Sally Long was a strong, direct woman. When she talked, she made all the words count, as if she were being charged by the word. There was no waste in her talk, if you get my meaning, and if you couldn't take the truth as she saw it, well, that was just too bad. She wasn't a mean woman, but she wasn't one to show much of her feelings either. She was good to Fred, and he was devoted to her, and she was never the same after he died, at least that's what my mother told me."

"And what about Sally and Fred's daughter, Ruth-Ann?"

"From what I remember, Ruth-Ann and her mother never got along, which is why Sally came to live with us after Fred died, and didn't go live with her daughter. My mother thought they were too much alike; both spoke their minds, and neither could take the sharp tongue of the other. Mom said they fought like angry hens, and after the war, Ruth-Ann moved out west somewhere, but I don't know what happened to her."

"Did you know your cousin John well?"

"He was fifteen years older than me and was killed in the war when I was just seven or eight. But Mother liked him. She said he was soft-spoken and shy, and he didn't seem all that comfortable being around people. He was more like Fred that way. More than once, Mom said he was one of the gentle people, and that it was a sin for him to have died in that war."

"So do you remember when Sally moved in with your family?"

"I think sometime in 1950. I'm pretty sure that Fred died in the fall of 1949; I remember because it was around my fifteenth birthday and everybody was wondering what would happen to Sally. It took her a while to admit she didn't want to live alone or move in with Ruth-Ann, but she finally sold the house. Sally lived with us for a good five years before I moved out and got my own apartment with a girlfriend." She laughed. "Sally and I had a few good run-ins. It made my mother angry, but I wasn't about to be bossed around by that woman. Whenever I played songs by Frankie Laine or Eddie Fisher, stern impatience would flash in her eyes and she'd tell me to shut off the radio. I don't know what she had against Eddie Fisher."

Mary pointed at the letters. "But Aunt Sally liked to write letters, and she wrote one to somebody nearly every day. Letters to the editors of the newspapers, to the mayor, to the chief of police, to me, to Ruth-Ann, to people she went to high school with. I remember thinking she was a better letter writer than she was a talker in person."

"Why did she write you? Didn't you live close by?"

"Like I said, I moved out. I wanted to live my own life. I'd met Burt, and everyone expected us to get married, but I wanted to date other boys. I was just twenty-one, and I wasn't ready for marriage. Well, Aunt Sally took it upon herself to tell me what I should do. To preach at me, and since I didn't go to my parents' house all that much, Sally wrote me letters. Needless to say, I never took the time to answer her."

Mary threw up her hands, dramatically. "And what letters they were. At first, I thought they were funny. Sally lived a straight and narrow life, like a shot arrow, and she was sure she knew how everybody else should live, too; straight and narrow like her. Guess what? I wasn't a straight and narrow girl in those days. I liked Philadelphia and parties, and I liked boys and dancing and, yes, I smoked and drank beer, and I had me a good ole time. Sally disapproved of me, so she wrote me those letters, maybe ten or twelve. She let me know, in no uncertain terms, that if I wasn't careful, I was going to get into trouble, in more ways than one."

Alice leaned back and took a sip of her cider, enjoying Mary's story. There was a playful sparkle in her eyes that suggested she'd still like to have herself a good ole time, if given the chance.

"Now you might ask, why did I keep these irritating letters?" Mary asked, smothering a giggle.

"Yes, why did you, if they were so preachy?"

Mary inclined forward, whispering conspiratorially. "Because I thought they were hilarious. My roommate, Gail, and I would read them out loud and laugh. We were naughty, weren't we? Why did I keep them? To tell you the truth, I didn't remember keeping them until a few years ago, when I was going through some old boxes that ended up in the attic. But in those days, people didn't throw things away so much like they do now."

Alice couldn't hide her eagerness any longer. "I can't wait to see if Alice is mentioned in those letters."

Mary slapped her knee with a hand and said, "Yes, enough about me and my big blabber mouth. Let's take a look at those letters and see if Sally ever mentioned Alice Ferrell."

Alice sat up as Mary leaned and reached for the letters. Her liver-spotted hands released the rubber band, and she peeled four letters off the top and handed them to Alice.

Alice hesitated. "Are you sure you don't mind if I read these?"

"Not at all. There's nothing in there that's all that personal, so let's dig in and see what we find."

Mary slipped on her wire-rimmed glasses, reached for a letter in the remaining pile and grinned. "Here goes."

For a time, Mary and Alice sat motionless, Mary's lips moving over the words in the letter she was reading, Alice's eyes impatiently sliding across the pages of her letter, searching for Alice's name.

Mary finished first, with a shake of her head, and started a second. Halfway through, a smile hung on her lips, as old memories were resurrected. She didn't share the memory with Alice.

Alice was on the third letter when something caught her eye. It was a sentence that jumped out at her.

"*You, young lady, remind me of another young lady who used to live with Fred and me. She was the daughter of Fred's half-sister, Lana. I never talked about Lana because she was a lost soul and, frankly, an embarrassment to the family. She married the very devil of a man and he treated her like dirt. He abandoned her and his daughter, and when Lana died, so very young, Fred and I took 12-year-old Alice in. That was her name, Alice Ferrell.*"

Alice jerked erect, holding up the letter. "I've got it. Alice is in this letter!"

Fluttering with new energy, Mary slid over, and Alice pointed out the entry. With delight, Mary took the page and read. "Well, what do you know? And there's more."

"Read it, Mary. What does it say?"

Mary cleared her voice and held the page up, adjusting the distance and the glasses on her nose. She read each word clearly and excitedly.

"*Alice was a smart and shy girl, a little like John, but, as I was to learn, she was also a willful girl. She ran away from home twice, once when she was only fifteen years old, and Fred had to go find her. The second time, she was sixteen. The police picked her up by the side of the road, near Davenport, Iowa. When she got home, all she said to me was, 'I'm sorry, Aunt Sally, but I felt trapped in this house.' I tried to help and guide her.*"

When she was 21 years old, she went off half-cocked, af-ter the soldier she was going to marry was killed in the war. I won't tell you how she ended up, but I will say this: what she did, in my mind, was unforgiveable. When Fred and I were out of town, Alice called and told me, without any hesitation, that she was going to run off with a soldier, whom she hardly knew, to go see her despicable father in Ohio. I was livid, and I told her that if she left, she would never be welcomed back. She left, and no one was going to go find her this time. She was old enough to know better.

So, Mary, I hope I have made it clear that you need to stop your madcap ways with boys and drink, and get ahold of yourself before it's too late. Get your life back on track, and do it now!"

Mary slowly lifted her eyes. "I don't remember ever reading that… but then, it was so many years ago."

Their eyes made contact and Alice said, "This more or less confirms what Alice wrote in the diary, although I didn't know she had run away from home twice before."

The two women finished reading the remaining letters but found nothing else about Alice. They returned them to their envelopes and Mary wrapped them with the rub-ber band, launching into another rapid-fire conversation. Alice cut her off, respectfully saying that she had to get back to the house.

At the front door, Alice took Mary's hand and thanked her.

"Will you keep on trying to find Alice Ferrell?" Mary asked.

"Yes. Especially now. After reading Sally's letter, the historical Alice seems even more alive and even more mysterious. I have to find her or find out what happened to her. I wonder if Sally and Alice ever saw each other again."

Mary made a tsk-tsk sound. "I doubt it. Sally was not an easy woman, or a forgiving one. It's too bad because I think her heart was in the right place. But she was just too critical of everyone. Even my mother, who was a saint compared to the rest of us, got into heated arguments with Sally over her harsh criticisms. More than once, Mom said, 'I don't know how Fred put up with her all those years.' My father just stayed clear of her."

As Alice drove home, a text "dinged" in. It was from Jack. She pulled the car to the curb, reached for her phone and read.

Andrew was in a fight. He's been suspended from school and he's in the hospital. I've just arrived there. You know where it is. Come when you can. Call me.

CHAPTER 20
December 1944

With fear racing through her, Alice stepped into her father's hospital room like a woman entering a dark, unknown cave. She looked right, swallowed, and ventured in further. The privacy curtain had been pulled back to reveal the upper torso and face of a man lying on his back, eyes closed.

Nurse Maggie Dennis followed Alice in and stood by, a quiet shadow.

Alice hesitated, then moved toward the bed. With a catch in her throat, she looked at a hollow-cheeked man she did not know or recognize. He was still, hardly breathing, rail-thin, and he appeared older than forty-six years. His hair was gray; his face, the color of stone, was etched with lines.

As she stared at him, Alice felt nothing. How was that possible? She'd expected to be overcome by pity, grief, or anger—something. After all, this man had helped bring her into the world, and she did recall some fond moments with him: walking down the street together, feeling her little hand enclosed in his. She had a vague memory of sitting on a bench, crying after she had fallen and scraped her knee, and he'd tried to make her laugh, sticking his tongue out and making a funny face. She did laugh, and he'd bought her a strawberry ice cream cone.

Alice lost track of time as she stood there, watching him, reminiscing. Finally, his eyes struggled open. When he sensed a presence and slowly rolled his head toward her, she froze. His eyes were glassy and far away as if he were lost in another world. He blinked, trying to focus on her. Feeling suspended, trembling, she waited, not knowing what to do, or if she should speak.

And then his eyes opened fully on her, accusingly indignant. In a low, scratchy voice, he said, "What are you doing here? Who are you? Are those for me?"

Startled, Alice remembered the flowers and glanced down at them. She cleared her throat, twice. "Yes. Yes, I brought them for you."

His eyes narrowed. "I know who you are. Of course I know."

An icy chill rippled up her spine.

He continued. "I remember the eyes. Your eyes were always so expressive. Even now, with my bad vision, I see fear in them, and let me tell you something, girl, fear is something I know well, and I've had a bellyful of it."

He coughed, a deep, hacking cough that punished his entire body. Nurse Dennis went into action, reaching for a washcloth from a nearby pan of water. She squeezed it and handed it to him; he took it with a quaking hand, his watering eyes finding her, softening on her. "Thank you, Nurse... I don't remember your name. My mind's a dim light bulb, nearly burnt out."

"Maggie."

"Yes, Maggie... How could I forget a good name like that? A damned old man is what I am... Damned before my time."

Cliff Ferrell held the cloth over his mouth while the cough took him again. He jolted up, his face flushed in agony, sweat popping out on his forehead. Maggie moved closer to him, while Alice stepped back.

When the coughing episode was over, Cliff sank back into his pillow, spent and damp with perspiration. Maggie blotted his forehead with a separate cool cloth.

"Shall I call the doctor for you, Sergeant?"

"No... No, Maggie. He'll just tell me another one of his awful jokes," he said, hoarsely, with the hint of a grin, a grin that in his younger days had been sexy and roguish, but now was a grimace from the pain.

"Can't take any more of his jokes... They're killing me."

Cliff's eyes slowly slid back to Alice, and he held them on her, looking her over, his face passing through a range of expressions: pride, worry and melancholy. Alice stood as still and as cold as a block of ice, clutching the flowers tightly in her arm.

"Alice, don't fear me. Not now. Come a little closer. Your old man wants to get a good look at you."

Maggie faded back, allowing Alice to inch toward the bed.

"Pretty flowers. I like the red roses. Christmas roses, huh?"

Alice nodded.

"Pretty flowers and a pretty girl," he said, his voice strained, his eyes grim. He stared at the far wall. "... I didn't do much pretty with my life... But you, Alice, I did that right. Okay, God, give me that one. I did one pretty thing in my life. Yes, my daughter, Alice."

Alice remained still, forcing out the words, "Are... are you in pain?"

"Nah. The morphine fixes me up just fine. Hey, are you married?"

"No."

"No? What's the matter with those boys out there? A pretty girl like you not married?"

She shrugged, her mouth sad, her eyes blinking. She wasn't going to tell him about Charles.

Cliff sighed audibly. "I've been in the Army for almost ten years. Old men like me should get killed. Not those young boys in that jeep. We were two miles from the front when we hit that damned mine. They said it had been set by the Germans months before. But, what the hell. Now the devil's going to have the last laugh. I see him off in the corner at night, standing right over there in the shadows, a big, crooked, happy grin on his face while he watches me. He don't say nothing, that bastard. He just watches, while he puffs away on a big fat Cuban cigar."

Alice didn't want to hear any more about the devil. "When will they let you go... I mean release you?"

His somber eyes found her again. "Alice, listen to me. I need you to listen to me now. I know I don't mean nothin' to you and there's no reason why I should, but I want you to know something."

He coughed again, then cursed, cleared his throat and tried again. "I want you to know that I thought about you... for all those years and, while I was thinking about you, I was sorry for what I did. Leaving you and Lana, your mother, like I did. Not coming to see you when I could have; when I should have. But I have a crazy, restless heart inside me. I couldn't stay in any place for very long. The Army was good for me that way. They took in this junkyard dog and let him roam the world."

He looked away from her, coughed again, and then gave her a side-long glance. "I need you to know that I'm sorry for not being the old man you needed."

Alice struggled to keep her eyes on him. Now, she *was* feeling things: confusion, regret, anger. Their eyes met and held, his full of pleading, "The truth is, and Maggie will back me up on this, I ain't going to make it, Alice. I've got both the grim reaper and the devil fighting over me."

Alice felt the first tremor of emotion. She heard a blur of noise outside. Some man cried out and urgent voices tried to calm him.

Maggie shut the door, then leaned back against it.

Alice stared at him, and his eyes said something grave. "Alice... I want you to do something for me."

She didn't move. She didn't breathe.

"In my room back at the old bitch's boardinghouse, under the bed, you'll find a brown leather satchel, with a good sturdy lock. Inside the satchel, you'll find some money, about five thousand dollars. I've already given the key to Maggie because Maggie is a good soul. It takes a bad soul to recognize a good one. Anyway, she'll give it to you. You go get that satchel before that old battleax breaks in and steals the money. Then I want you to take the money and blow some of it on a grand party in honor of your old, son-of-a-bitchin' father, who never meant no harm to anyone."

Alice smothered a sob.

There was bleak amusement in his eyes. "It's a pretty thing I can do. One last chance at pretty. Will you do that for me, Alice? Will you take the money and go on a bender in my honor? Five thousand ain't no fortune, but it ain't no small amount either. Hell, find some nice guy and go paint the town, and spend that money like it's the end of the world."

To deflect her tears, Alice glanced about, looking for something to put the flowers in. Cliff noticed.

"You keep the flowers, Alice. You deserve them. I've done nothing for you to bring me flowers. Do you know what I was going to do after the war? I was going to buy you lots of pretty dresses and hats and shoes and then come visit you. I was going to spoil you... and then..." The words faded away.

Alice couldn't meet his gaze.

His head and his voice dropped in regret. "Who am I kidding? Hell, the devil's watching and waiting, and I'm dying, and I'm lying through my teeth. I wouldn't have come, Alice. I never would have come to see you. It was only a pipe dream. Truth is, I'd have wandered off to some damn place in Europe or the Far East, and I would have never seen you again. God forgive me for my black, lying soul."

Alice straightened up, trying for dignity, as her wounded eyes spilled heavy tears.

"Put one of them roses in your hair, Alice. Put a rose in your hair, and when you look at yourself in the mirror, forgive your old man for all his goddamned sins."

The room fell into silence. Cliff's eyes closed, his breathing deepened.

Alice tried to say the word, "Father," but the word didn't come. Couldn't come. "Rest now... I'll stay around town. I'll come back and see you."

His eyes popped open, and his face was taut, eyes hard. "No, Alice. I'm a dead man. You do what I told you to do. Take the money and go. Get out. Please do that and go. Thanks for coming, but now, you and me are finished. We've seen each other, and it's done. I don't want to see you again, do you understand?"

His brutal lack of tact struck her like a blow to the heart. Her face broke up, her eyes pinched shut and she sobbed. She whirled around and made for the door. Maggie pulled it open and Alice fled the room, bawling into her hand.

Tom hurried over, and when she saw him, she dropped the flowers and went to him in a rush, burying her face into his wide chest, weeping. He slowly wrapped her in his arms and held her until the emotion faded into a series of jerks.

"Don't worry, Alice," Tom said, soothingly. "It's going to be okay. Everything will be okay."

CHAPTER 21
December 1944

Alice and Tom sat in the High Life Lounge, tucked away in a red booth toward the back of the room. A red globe candle holder sat between them, their faces dappled with flickering light. The bar was lively and cigarette smoke hung in clouds above it, and the music from the juke-box was the Glenn Miller Orchestra playing *Smoke Gets in Your Eyes*.

The lounge area was mostly full, with shadowy couples hovering close, soldiers playing cards, and a couple on the square wood dance floor, swaying to the music.

A Christmas tree glowed colored lights; a tired wreath hung on the front door, and a fat snowman and flying reindeer were stenciled on the plate-glass window. The resident gray tabby cat crept through corner shadows like a beat cop, but few patrons noticed him or his round glowing eyes, alert to every sudden move.

Sashaying through the lounge was a leggy cocktail waitress wearing a red skirt, green top and glossy black hair with bouncy pin curls. Her shifting eyes caught the raised hand, the spilled drink, and the smirks after a risqué comment from a soldier.

Gathered two-deep at the bloated bar were soldiers and laughing girls, as well as locals, stalwart men whose buttocks held fast to the choice barstools despite being nudged and jostled. Grinning with good cheer, the bartender drew down drafts of foaming beer, his red bow tie festive, his black silk arm bands holding up the sleeves of his white shirt.

Alice sat with her elbows on the table, staring down at her tall glass of half-consumed rye and soda. Tom nursed a beer, his pondering eyes focused outside, watching the brash, yellow neon sign blinking out HIGH LIFE LOUNGE—COCKTAILS! DANCING!

Tom pulled his eyes from the garish sign and rested them on Alice. She was slack and dull. "How's your drink?"

"It's okay. I'm not much of a drinker. I think I've only had whiskey once before. Fred poured me some last New Year's Eve."

"Do you want something else?"

"No, thanks."

"Feeling better?"

"A little. That woman at the boarding house wasn't very nice, was she?"

"No, she wasn't. She reminded me of a washer woman back at the orphanage. She used to curse us when we passed; she'd call us lame brains and throwaways."

"What a terrible thing to say to kids."

Tom took a swallow of beer and grinned. "Some of the boys got her back though. Once, they sneaked into the closet where she kept her work shoes and shoved cooked oatmeal up into the toes. Another time when she was eating her lunch in a side room, they tossed in mice. She jumped up and danced around like she was doing an

Irish jig. You could hear her screaming all the way to the next building."

Alice tried to hold the laughter, but she couldn't. It came in fits and starts, then it gushed out and she couldn't stop.

Tom laughed at her laugh. "Good, I got you to laugh."

A minute later, she recovered and wiped her damp eyes. "It's awful what those boys did, but it's funny. Oatmeal of all things."

She leveled her narrowed eyes on him. "I guess you never joined in with the other boys when they pulled their pranks?"

Tom held up his hands in surrender. "Who, me?"

"I see the guilt in your candlelit eyes," Alice said, with another laugh.

Tom was pleased to see her mood shift. "Well, anyway, we got your father's satchel, and you found the money. And that nasty woman got her two months' rent."

Alice dropped her voice. "Tom... I've decided. I'm not going to leave. I'm going to stay and take care of my father."

Tom looked at her, trying to understand. "But you said he told you to go. He said he didn't want to see you."

"I know... but he's sick and medicated. He doesn't know what he's saying. I can't leave him. I'd never forgive myself."

Tom eased back. "All right, Alice, but didn't the nurse, Maggie, say he's going to be transferred to a hospital in Columbus in the next day or two?"

"Yes. I'll go to Columbus and find a place to stay."

Tom looked toward the bar.

"I've got plenty of money. It's *his* money, and I'll use it for him."

"That's a nice thing, Alice. I admire you for it."

Alice shrugged and swept the room with her eyes. "Everybody seems to be in the Christmas spirit."

Tom glanced around, seeing the cocktail waitress standing by a table with three soldiers. They were all laughing. "Yeah... Seems like a friendly place."

Alice took a cautious sip of her drink and winced. "I guess I'll never be a big drinker. I just don't like the taste of it."

"Do you want to go?"

Alice looked at him, earnestly. "Tom, you've been so kind and so good to me. I'll never be able to thank you enough. I don't know what I would have done without you."

"It wasn't so much."

He smiled, and she returned it. "It was to me, and I thank you. Thank you for everything, especially for coming with me to the hospital. I wouldn't have wanted to face my father alone. But now, you don't have to stay with me anymore. I'm going to be fine."

Her smile was timid, nervous.

His eyes darted away.

Alice continued. "I'll find a motel room and stay until I know my father is on his way to Columbus. Then I'll catch a bus. So, you see, everything is working out for both of us. You can start your trip across country and have some fun... before you have to go back... Well, back to..." she stopped, not finishing the sentence.

He stared at her and, in the candlelight, he saw a blank emptiness in her eyes. He folded his hands on the tabletop, released them and then refolded them. "Alice, I can stay. I can take you to Columbus. It's not as if I have to be anyplace, at least not until after the new year."

Alice felt excitement and angst at the same time. "But don't you want to start driving to California?"

Tom drained the beer glass. In a long, hanging moment, Alice sat waiting, while Tom looked above her and around her.

His eyes finally came to hers. "Is it so bad of me, Alice?"

She blinked, waiting. "Bad? I don't know what you mean. Is what bad?"

"Is it so bad that I want to be with you?"

Alice didn't look away. She liked what he'd said, but it scared her.

In a soft, hesitant voice, Tom said, "I could use the excuse that I'm going back to the war and I may never see you again. I could say that, and it would be true. I could also say, you're Charlie's girl and I've got no business wanting to be with you. What kind of friend am I, you might say or think? Yeah, well, maybe I'm thinking it, too. Maybe you think Charlie hasn't been dead long enough, and yeah, you're right about that. It will never be long enough, will it? But I'm not going to say any of those things, Alice. I'm just going to say this. I want to be with you for as long as I can, until we're forced to part. That's the God's truth, and that's as simple as I can say it."

Alice swallowed a breath, turning from him. "Don't say any more, Tom."

She tried to keep her composure, but the trials and emotions of the last few days bubbled up and her face wadded up with despair. "You've got to go, Tom. We can't keep pretending that Charles isn't a ghost, hovering around us. It's not right. It's not right that Charles is dead and we're alive and…" Her voice ran out.

She couldn't look at him. Finally, she slid out of the booth, swinging the strap of her purse over her shoulder. "We should go. I need to go. I need to find a place to stay tonight. Then you must go to California, and I must go to Columbus."

Tom stared in a sorrowful acceptance. A moment later, he flagged down the cocktail waitress and paid the bill.

Outside, it was snowing, a light snow that drifted across the streetlights and dusted the sidewalks and parked cars.

Tom placed the cap on his head, secured it, and then looked left. "I saw a motel not too far from here. I'll drop you off."

Alice shrank a little. "Where will you stay?"

"I won't be staying. I'll leave and drive all night. I like night driving."

Alice opened her mouth to speak, but the words wouldn't come; just white vapor. She had so much to say, but, as in the hospital, the words got trapped in her tight throat.

CHAPTER 22
December 2016

Jack entered the medical center and was quickly cleared by security. He hurried over to the triage nurse but had to wait in line before he could speak to her. Ten minutes later, an impatient Jack walked briskly down a long, blue-tiled corridor, finally locating his son's room at the end of the hall.

Andrew was sitting on an examination table, wearing a blue hospital gown, with the back open. A young, female doctor was busy suturing the knife wound on the left side of his back, finishing off with an overhand knot. She cut the excess thread, ready to move a quarter-inch down the wound to repeat the process, but stopped and glanced up when she heard a light knock on the door.

Jack stood in the doorway, looking on with concern. "I'm Andrew's father, Jack Landis."

The doctor straightened. "Come in, Mr. Landis. I'm Doctor Tullock. I'm just finishing up."

Andrew squinted his nervous eyes on his father, a Band-Aid covering part of his right cheek.

Jack took a few steps into the room. "How is he, Doctor Tullock?"

"He'll be fine. Andrew doesn't have any life-threatening injuries."

"I heard there was a knife involved."

Andrew glanced away.

Dr. Tullock wore blue scrubs. She was a short, thin, energetic woman in her early thirties, with straw-colored blonde hair tied back into a ponytail. Her intelligent, pale blue eyes looked at Jack with a calm, direct friendliness. "Andrew can tell you all about it. The cut was about three inches long and a quarter of an inch deep, so I sutured the wound to lower the risk of infection and scarring. Two fingers on his right hand were also injured. They've been cleaned, disinfected and, as you can see, bandaged. The abrasion on Andrew's face isn't deep or serious, and the x-rays don't reveal broken ribs or any other internal injuries. There's bruising around his right eye; also bruising on his left upper torso and upper arm. Luckily, there was no damage to either eye."

Jack nodded, wishing Andrew would look at him. "Thank you, Doctor."

"Andrew should be ready to go in about fifteen minutes. I'll send him home with a prescription for pain relief and an antibiotic."

"How are you, son?" Jack asked.

Andrew glanced over. "Fine. I'm okay."

"We'll talk when you're released," Jack said, in a low tone.

Andrew nodded. "Sure."

"All right. I'll wait for you in the lounge. Thanks again, Dr. Tullock."

As he entered the ER waiting room, Jack saw two cops, one female and one male. He was sure they'd come to question Andrew. The male cop spoke to the triage nurse, mentioning Andrew's name, while the female cop spoke on her phone. Jack approached the male cop and introduced himself.

Officer Griffin was in his early 30s. He spoke in a low tenor voice, obviously wanting to project serious authority and mature confidence. He led Jack toward the entrance doors, away from the lounge and waiting room, where they could speak in private.

"Who did Andrew fight with?" Jack asked.

"A boy named Mike Turner."

"Who had the knife?"

"Mike Turner."

"Isn't it against the law to carry a knife to school?"

"It was a pocket knife."

Jack waited for an explanation.

"It's not against the law to bring a pocket knife with a blade less than two-and-a-half inches long, but it's against the school's policy, so Mike Turner will be suspended, maybe expelled."

"What was the fight about?" Jack asked.

Officer Griffin was broad, with an angelic face that didn't fit the job or the uniform. Jack thought he resembled a priest or a guidance counselor. His expression was kind, and there was patience and concern in his voice. "We don't have all the facts yet, but it appears the fight was over computer code."

Jack narrowed his eyes. "Computer code? I don't understand."

"Like I said, we're still trying to gather all the facts. So far, we've learned that your son accused Mike Turner of stealing his app idea and the computer code. It is alleged that Mr. Turner submitted the app code and idea to an interested tech company and they purchased it. All this occurred a little over a week ago. It is also alleged that this company paid Mr. Turner an undisclosed amount of money for the idea and code. Again, according to your son, Mike Turner met with Andrew several times, got access to the code, and then stole it. He didn't tell Andrew anything about what he'd done. Your son, Andrew, learned of the events from a girl who attends the same school, Brianna Martin. Do you know her?"

"No… I don't."

Officer Griffin continued, "According to Ms. Martin, after she told Andrew what Mr. Turner had done, he flew into a rage, ran downstairs to the cafeteria and accosted Mr. Turner, who was eating lunch with two friends. In a statement from one of the friends, Andrew asked Mr. Turner if he had sold Andrew's app idea and code to a company. Mr. Turner replied, 'Yes, I did. So what?' Mr. Turner said it had been his idea and code all along. He said Andrew was taking credit for something that was never his. That's when Andrew threw the first punch. A fight between the two boys followed."

Jack gathered a breath. "Where is Mike Turner?"

"He's being examined in a separate medical facility in Cranston. He was arrested because he used a knife on your son."

"Will Andrew be charged with anything?"

The policeman cleared his throat. "Technically, Mr. Turner could file charges against your son for assault, attempting to cause injury, threatening him, verbally or nonverbally, and putting him in fear of imminent harm."

Jack's jaw tightened. "Officer, Mike used a knife on my son. I've seen the injuries. What happens next?"

The policeman's radio crackled, but he ignored it. "There'll be a hearing and, at that time, the charges will be presented."

"In Juvenile Court? Andrew's only sixteen."

"Yes, Mr. Landis. Children under eighteen who are

charged with crimes are usually handled through the juvenile justice system. Proceedings are often informal, and the case could be disposed of without official charges ever being filed."

"What then?" Jack asked, lifting his hands. "What's the punishment?"

"That's up to the court. Usually, the judge decides on rehabilitation rather than punishment, but that depends on the particular juveniles and the situation. Usually, for a first offense, they're treated leniently; they're often given a sentence of community service."

Officer Griffin concluded by saying that the school administrators would probably hand out their own punishment. If the boys fought again, an expulsion hearing would most likely be held.

Jack gave Officer Griffin a frank look. "With all due respect, I don't want my son talking to you unless he's with a lawyer."

Officer Griffin didn't seem offended. Minutes later, both cops climbed into their patrol car and drove away.

Jack returned to the waiting area, joining a white-haired elderly man who sat slumped, his staring eyes somber. Across from him, a young, haggard woman was grappling to control her rambunctious little girl while she talked on her cell phone, her voice agitated, her nerves frayed.

Jack paced for a time then sat uncomfortably in one of the orange plastic chairs, his hands moving in his pockets, his head frequently swiveling toward the entrance, his searching eyes hoping to see Alice.

Jack grappled with the fact that his son had gotten into a fight at school, and that the police had been called. He'd thought Andrew and Mike were friends. Did people often steal computer code? He had no idea.

Jack heard the "bing" of a text, and he glanced at his phone. It was from Andrew. *I'll be out in a few more minutes.*

Jack sat lost in the privacy of his thoughts, feeling the rise of the old, stinging guilt. Had he been a good father to Kristie and Andrew? Would they have been more stable and grounded if their mother hadn't abandoned them and died in that terrible fire all those years ago?

In the last year or so, Jack had often sensed Andrew was masking anger and frustration, but he wouldn't talk about it, at least not to him. Both kids seemed to trust Alice more, and that was all right with him; he wasn't jealous but, then again, he had to admit that sometimes he was hurt and confused. He'd tried to be a good father, a caring and loving father. Had he been too strict? How could he do better? Be better?

When Alice arrived, Jack went to her, quickly bringing her up to date. As always, she was calm and reassuring, but perplexed. "Well, this just came from out of the blue."

"Andrew's done nothing like this before," Jack said, as they stood near the soda machine away from the others. They heard doctors being paged, and both looked impatiently down the hallway.

"He worked so hard on that project," Alice said. "He thought about it day and night. He was constantly studying programming languages and trying things. I can't believe his friend would do this to him."

"What kind of friend could he be?" Jack said, with a sigh. "There's more to this story than we know. I hate to say it, but I hear my father's voice in my head. When I was growing up, he used to say, 'Take the lesson and don't whine. Don't be stupid and not learn from it.' He was a harsh man, but often brutally wise."

"Well, don't share that with Andrew just now. I don't think he'd like it. He must be hurt and angry."

Alice noticed her first: a pretty, young woman came through the automatic glass entry doors. She peeled off her blue ski cap, shook out her shoulder-length, jet black hair and glanced about. She was tall and poised, with the high cheekbones and the striking face of a model.

Jack followed Alice's gaze, and they both watched as the young woman stepped up to the plexiglass window and spoke to the triage nurse through the voice speaker.

Jack and Alice leaned a little, listening with interest.

"Hello, can you please tell me if Andrew Landis will soon be released?"

The nurse said she didn't know. The girl would have to wait. Stepping back, the young woman retrieved her cell phone from her purse and started a text, her thumbs gliding over the keypad. When finished, she gazed about, her dreamy eyes falling softly on Alice and Jack. She approached them with a slight smile.

"Hello, are you Mr. and Mrs. Landis?"

Alice said they were.

The young woman extended a graceful hand. "I'm Brianna Martin, a friend of Andrew's."

Jack gave Alice a side glance of surprise as she took Brianna's hand.

"Nice to meet you," Jack said, noting that the name sounded familiar. "You're a student at the high school?"

"Yes."

"I just spoke to a policeman about what happened. Did you tell Andrew that Mike Turner had sold his app idea and code to some company?"

Brianna was soft spoken, but confident. "Yes, I did. The company's name is *LifeTalk*. I didn't know Andrew would get so angry, but I should have known. I'm sorry

163

if I caused the fight, and he got hurt."

"It's not your fault," Alice said. "Do you know for sure that Mike Turner stole Andrew's code?"

Brianna's eyes held strength and intelligence. "Yes. I helped Andrew work on the app. We worked on it together and it was almost there."

Again, Jack was surprised. Andrew had never mentioned Brianna and, for the life of him, he didn't know why. "Didn't Andrew share the code with Mike as well?" Jack asked.

Brianna nodded. "Yes, but I told him not to. Andrew was kind of, well... Mike is popular and he's a senior. I think Andrew sort of looked up to him. Mike is very smart, but he's also..." her voice dropped away as she considered her words. "Well, we used to date, but then I met Andrew."

Now Alice gave Jack a side glance. Andrew had never mentioned Brianna to her either.

"Andrew never told me about you, Brianna," Alice said.

Her smile was private, and then it widened. "Andrew is secretive. I'm a senior and he's a junior. I kid him about it. I say, I'm older and wiser, and he gets a little mad at me."

Alice smiled, having a good feeling about Brianna. She seemed older than her years. "Have you spoken to or texted Mike?"

"Yes... Of course he denies everything. I mean, well, he's jealous of Andrew."

"Why?" Jack asked.

Brianna displayed a girlish pride. "Because I broke it off with Mike and started dating Andrew."

She looked away toward the windows where the sun broke through the clouds and streamed in. "I think the whole thing, I mean the fight, was basically over me. Mike was jealous, and he wanted to get back at me and Andrew. I'm a good programmer and Andrew is great with ideas. We're a good team. Mike is smart, but not good with ideas. He's good at memorizing things. He's good with people and marketing. I'm not surprised he was able to sell the idea to *LifeTalk*."

Jack was fascinated by Brianna's savvy.

"Frankly, Andrew and I should have copyrighted it. In a few months, that app will be in the App Store, with Mike's name attached to it."

"Does this kind of thing happen often?" Jack asked.

Brianna shifted her feet. "No, but..." She shrugged a shoulder. "... It was an excellent idea, and Mike's father is a businessman with connections."

"Should Andrew sue or something?" Alice asked.

Brianna had an answer ready. "My father's an attorney. I asked him about that. He said it would take a long time, and that the legal costs wouldn't be worth it. He was certain that nothing would come of it."

Just then, Andrew walked slowly down the hallway, favoring his left side. He stopped a short distance away, not meeting anyone's eyes.

"How are you, son?" Jack asked.

"Fine."

Andrew stepped forward, kissed Alice on the cheek, turned, and smiled at Brianna. "Hey."

She smiled back with warm flirtation. "Hey, there, Andrew. The Band Aid adds a rugged look. I hear you broke Mike's nose."

Alice and Jack traded startled glances.

Andrew brightened. "Really? Did I?"

"Yeah. Totally. I got a text from his new girlfriend. She called me some names... Not nice."

Andrew grinned with dark satisfaction, but he stayed quiet.

Brianna offered to drive Andrew home in her late model, burgundy Mustang. After the car left the parking lot, edging into the flow of traffic, Alice and Jack stood staring at each other, trying to make sense of it all.

Jack pressed his lips tightly together, locked his hands behind his back and looked up into the sky. He shrugged.

Alice said, "Yeah, I know. I guess there are things about Andrew that we don't know. And, I guess he's growing up."

Jack walked Alice to her car, his mind stuffed with questions. She opened her door and turned to him. "Do you know what I'm going to suggest to Brianna? That she keep a diary."

Jack shook his head. "You and your diaries. They follow you around."

He gave her a peck on the lips. "Let's go home. I'm not in the mood to go back to work. By the way, with all this stuff going on, how's Brenda doing with her expanded duties?"

"Great. She's happy to get the hours… and she's good with the guests."

"Are we making any money on this boarding house gig?"

"Probably not. But it's fun."

"Fun is good. Let's go home and have a beer or something. You can tell me what you learned about the diary."

Alice dropped her voice. "Jack… I heard Andrew tell

Brianna he's going to get even with Mike."

He looked at her, soberly. "I heard that too. I'll have a talk with him."

CHAPTER 23

December 1944

A red globe candle holder sat between them, their faces dappled with flickering light. The bar was lively and cigarette smoke hung in clouds above it, and the music from the juke-box was the Glenn Miller Orchestra playing *Smoke Gets in Your Eyes*.

At a little after 8 a.m., Alice showered, dressed, and called the hospital from her motel room. She wanted to check on her father's condition and learn what time he'd be moved to the neuropsychiatric hospital in Columbus, Ohio.

Alice was asked to hold while the information was gathered. She eased down onto the unmade bed, her thoughts returning to Tom, speculating as to where he might be. As they had parted, he'd said, "I'm going to drive to St. Louis, pick up Route 66, and then take my time driving to San Diego."

Loneliness returned, spreading through her body like a cold liquid. She missed him. She missed him a lot. He'd been kind and thoughtful, and she'd been grateful for his calming presence and support.

Why didn't she let him drive her to Columbus? What was the matter with her? Had she been buried beneath her grief-stricken skin for so long that she didn't know the truth of her own heart? Tom was a good man, and she felt better about herself when she was with him.

So why had she sent him away? "Stupid," she said aloud, switching the phone to her left ear. Standing, she cursed herself, irritated, wondering what she'd been thinking. A flurry of excuses followed: last night, she'd been overly emotional. Everything had seemed confusing and dark; her heart was bursting, her thoughts unpredictable. A good night's sleep had revived and stabilized her, giving her a new perspective.

But now it was too late. Tom was gone, and she'd never see him again.

She stalked back and forth, stopped, stared into the full-length mirror, and made a face of disappointment. And what if he was killed? How would she live with herself? How would she know?

The voice on the phone jerked her back to the present. "Miss Ferrell?"

"Yes?"

The hospital operator hesitated. "I'm going to hand the phone over to Nurse Maggie Dennis. She says you know her."

"Yes, I do. Is everything all right?"

Maggie came on the line, speaking in a soothing voice. "Alice, this is Maggie. There is no easy way to say this. I'm so sorry to tell you that your father died early this morning. He died peacefully. A nurse was with him, so he didn't die alone. You have my deepest condolences."

The words stung, stealing Alice's breath. She turned again toward the full-length mirror and gaped at herself.

She had a ghastly, shattered expression. A chair was close, and she sagged down into it.

"What do I do?" she asked, her voice small with defeat. "I don't know what to do. Where to go..."

"Come to the hospital, Alice. We'll talk... we'll work it all out."

An hour later, Alice sat in quiet sorrow in a snug hospital office, her hands trembling, her eyes staring. Maggie sat beside her, patiently explaining what needed to be done.

"I recommend that you have your father buried at the Ohio State Veterans Cemetery in Sandusky. It's a lovely place and I think you'll like it. I can give you the name of a funeral director. He will be responsible for the arrangements, and the government will cover most of the expenses."

Before they'd gone to Maggie's office, she'd taken Alice to see her father in the morgue, leading the way down a first floor hallway, left along a short entranceway, then down two flights of stairs into the basement, their footsteps echoing in the quiet space.

Inside the morgue—a cold, silver-gray room with harsh light—an orderly had led them past several enclosed refrigeration boxes to her father's body, which lay covered on a refrigerating table. Alice and Maggie had stood on one side, and the orderly on the other. When Maggie nodded, he turned back the sheet, revealing Cliff Ferrell's upper chest and face.

Alice had stared at the strange man impassively, showing no emotion. She had not cried. No tears. No sobs. Oddly, her father's face appeared younger, and he looked serene. With hooded eyes, she made a tight fist, irrationally wanting to pound something, or punch something, or rage at something.

As she climbed the stairs toward the first floor, Alice's true feelings continued to rise, raw emotions that had been buried deep in her gut for years. They erupted into a maelstrom of anger, confusion, love and despair. But she didn't cry, not this time, and she resolved to bury those feelings in the ground along with her father, and she vowed never to think about the man again. He was dead, and her wayward feelings for him were dead. Once he was laid to rest, that would be the end of it.

Alice watched as Maggie wrote down the name and phone number of the funeral director, and then she gazed out the window into the half-gloom of gray, moving clouds and weak sunlight. Maggie left to get them coffee, and Alice laid her head down on the desktop, gripping the edge, until her knuckles were white.

By the time Alice's taxi dropped her off at the motel, a cold, sharp rain was falling. Inside her room, she shed her coat and hat, dropped them on the chair and stared at the little roses wallpaper, feeling drained and lost.

The bed was the perfect escape, so she slumped down, flopped onto her back, and covered her eyes with an arm. Tomorrow morning, she'd attend the simple memorial service in the hospital chapel that Maggie had arranged. Immediately following, she'd travel in a hired car to Sandusky, Ohio, where she'd spend the night in a motel, and travel to the cemetery the following day for the burial.

She would stand by as her father's casket was lowered into the ground and a shovel of dirt tipped in. Finally, she'd be presented with the flag that had draped his casket. She would keep her face composed in order to project an expression of strength, not that there would be anyone else present who knew her father. She'd be alone.

In a dozing dream, she saw a judge dressed in long black robes, seated behind a raised bench. He gave her a stony stare. As his gavel came down hard, he said, "Case closed! You're free to go."

The hammer sound of the gavel awakened her. Outside, she heard the wind and the murmur of passing traffic. Inside, she heard her own breath.

A gentle knock on the door jarred her, and she sat up, gaping. Another knock. "Yes…?"

And then she heard his voice. "Alice, it's Tom."

She sprang out of bed, wearing her long skirt, blue blouse, and ankle socks. She checked herself in the mirror, finger combed her hair and rushed to the door, releasing the chain and yanking the door open.

Tom stood shyly, wearing his Marine greatcoat, gripping his cap in both hands, head lowered. "How are you, Alice? I called the hospital and spoke to the nurse, Maggie. She told me about your father. I'm sorry. Truly sorry."

Alice fought the impulse to leap for joy. Instead, she nodded. "Thank you, Tom. It's for the best. He's not suffering anymore."

"I was going to bring you something, flowers or something, but…"

She cut in. "I thought you'd gone. I mean, you said you were leaving for St. Louis."

The December wind was quick and cold, with a mix of rain and snow that blew in through the open door.

Alice stared with hopeful eyes. "Do you want to come in?"

He glanced about. "Yeah, thanks. It's cold out here."

Alice moved back, and he entered. When she closed the door they stood, awkwardly, as Tom fidgeted with his hat. Finally, he inspected the room and said, "It's like my room, only I have wallpaper with ferns and leaves and a painting of the Ohio River. I thought they'd all look alike. The woman who runs the place has the face and manners of a bulldog, but the place is clean and tidy."

Alice couldn't stop her smile, feeling a delirium of relief that he hadn't gone. "Are you staying here, too?"

"Yes. I... Well, I drove about five miles and then pulled over. I didn't get too far. I mean, how far can you go with the Victory Speed of thirty-five miles an hour? I don't know why I stopped. Well, yes, I do know why."

He hesitated. Their eyes connected. "Alice... I have a question that's burning inside me, and I've got to ask it. Maybe I wouldn't ask it if the war wasn't all around me, and if I had a lot of time. But Charlie has shown me I don't have a lot of time. Do you know what I mean?"

She nodded, still sky-high that he was standing there.

"Alice, do you feel... something for me? Anything? I just have to know. I know last night I said a lot of things and you said some things, but..."

"I didn't mean those things, Tom," she said quickly. "I didn't mean any of those things. It had been a bad day, that's all."

Tom gave her a firm nod and took in a breath. "Okay, then, here goes. I could fall in love with you, Alice. I know it. It's the first time in my life I've felt these things, and I ache. Could you fall in love with me?"

She wasn't going to be coy or hide her feelings. She'd nearly lost him. She smiled into his eyes and said, "Yes, Tom."

Tom's smile started small, then grew.

Alice said, "But I'm scared for both of us."

"Scared?"

Her voice was as soft as silk, with a hint of breath. "Tom, I don't want you to go back to war."

He grinned, relieved. "Oh, that. That's years away— or at least that's how it seems to me now. When I look at you, when I'm with you, the war and the past go away. They just vanish."

Alice was touched. She wanted him to hold her, to kiss her.

Tom's eyes slid down to her smile and her lovely lips, which were slightly parted. He leaned over and gently kissed her, and Alice melted, absorbing a rush of heat and tender desire.

When he drew back, keeping his eyes fixed on hers, he saw her love for him. He saw that she wanted him as he wanted her.

He spoke at an intimate whisper. "Alice... Travel with me. Let's get to know each other. Let's take that road trip across this great country and pretend the war's over, and that our entire lives are before us. What do you say?"

Alice's pulse was high. Her eyes flicked up to meet his. "Yes, Tom. I'd like that. I'd like that very much."

He leaned in for another kiss, and their eyes closed, and their lips brushed and parted, and their tongues explored.

When they broke the kiss, Tom took a retreating step back. "I'd... Well, I'd better go now... We don't want that woman banging on the door."

The wet, noisy weather added intimacy, and neither moved. Alice didn't want him to go—but she knew it was for the best.

After he was gone, Alice paced, feeling new life course through her veins. Her mind was spinning, her emotions conflicted, her heart full. She'd been so low one moment and so happy the next. She had been lost, but now Tom had found her. He'd come from war, from Charles, from a raging snowstorm, and he'd found her.

How could she be falling in love with Tom? How was it possible? But he was so very attractive, and so very kind, and so very masculine. And he'd kissed her with force, love and want. How could she not fall in love with him? She was giddy and silly, wanting more of him, wanting more from life, and wanting that awful war to end.

She stared at herself in the mirror, lost in dreamy imagination.

CHAPTER 24

December 1944

At the Ohio State Veterans Cemetery, the afternoon air came in damp and cold, while a flat, misty rain fell, and clouds hustled across the sky as if restless to find someplace else to go.

They stood at Cliff Ferrell's gravesite, the only people present other than the employees. Tom held a black umbrella over Alice's bowed head, as an Army chaplain read a verse from the Bible and then uttered a prayer.

When two men began lowering the casket, Tom handed the umbrella to Alice. He snapped to attention and saluted. The chaplain's prayer fell into a whisper, and a stout man shoveled a pile of earth and dropped it onto the casket below.

An elderly man in uniform, thin and stooped, approached Alice with careful steps and presented the flag to her, his gaze reverent and solemn, his hat and shoulders damp from the rain. She nodded her thanks as she accepted it, and the chaplain's prayer died away into the moving wind.

When it was time to leave, Alice tried to move, but her feet hesitated on the wet, brown grass. Tom didn't speak, letting her have all the private time and reflection she needed. He hurt for her. He wished he could utter something wise that would comfort her, but he'd never been good with words.

The night before, they'd booked separate rooms at a motel near the cemetery, and eaten dinner at Alice's Restaurant, having a good laugh about the name. As they'd studied a map of Route 66 and shared ideas, pointing and planning, Tom had frequently seen something dark pass across Alice's face, and he knew her thoughts were preoccupied with her father's burial. He'd expected it, despite her brave demeanor. He knew about that kind of thing. After he'd lost his parents in the car accident, he'd been haunted by childhood memories of them, and they'd often appeared in his thoughts and dreams.

As Alice and Tom started back to the car, gusts of wind rippled their coats, and Alice clamped a hand onto her hat to keep it from sailing away. They stepped around puddles and sticky mud, not talking, not hurrying, but frequently glancing up into the other's face with a warm smile.

Alice was in a cloud of vague memories and shadowy forms. From out of the blowing wind that wheezed across the cemetery, she heard the ghostly cries of her mother's angry voice. "Your father's a no-good bum, Alice. You remember that, if you ever see him again. He's a rat and a bum, and I curse the day I married him. But he charmed me with his crooked, wise guy smile, and that's what men do, you know. They charm you until they get what they want and then they leave you flat, with nothing. No kisses, no self-respect and no money."

Tom held the car door open for Alice and she climbed inside, chilled and shivering. Once Tom was behind the wheel, he cranked the engine and boosted the heater.

"You'll be warm soon. Do you want to stop some-where and warm up?"

Alice's eyes were locked ahead. Her mother's scornful words lingered, and she wanted to press her hands to her ears to shut them out, desperate to flee the cemetery. "No, let's go. Let's get away from here as fast as we can."

Driving along a curving road that led out of the ceme-tery, Alice said, "Six people... Only six people stood by watching a man be put into the ground. Six people stood witness to an entire life, and none of us really knew him at all. How sad that is. How sad not to have any love in your life; no one to care if you live or die."

After a long minute, Alice continued. "My father was as much a stranger to me as any man I pass on any street. I didn't know him and didn't remember much about him. So why did I come to bury him? Was it out of pity? Was it relief that he's finally gone from my life? But he was gone a long time ago, wasn't he?"

Tom wanted her to talk, to get it all out. He was pleased to be the listener; her only listener. It brought him closer to her. Wasn't it simple moments like these that knocked down walls of fear and suspicion, and helped build the foundation for a true relationship?

Tom pointed the car toward Chicago, his windshield wipers slapping away rain. Maybe they'd spend the night at a motel and then pick up Route 66 the next morning.

As rain pelted down, he tossed an occasional glance at Alice, who sat in a gloomy mood. It made him uneasy. Was she having second thoughts about the trip?

"Alice... Are you warm enough?"

That's not what he'd intended to say. He was going to say, "Alice, have you changed your mind? Do you want me to take you back to Pennsylvania?" But he was too scared of the answer, and he couldn't force himself to ask.

"Yes, Tom. I'm much warmer. My feet are damp, but they'll dry soon."

"That's good. Just keep your feet near the heater."

They drove for a time in silence. Finally, Tom spoke up, unable to take the nervous quiet any longer. "I got the idea to travel Route 66 when I heard that troops and supplies are being moved between military bases using Route 66. A friend told me that near Fort Leonard Wood in Missouri, part of the route is divided into a highway to handle the military traffic. And I read in the paper the other day that people looking for jobs in defense plants are using Route 66, heading for California, Oregon and Washington."

Alice's ears perked up when she heard him say defense plants. She knew there were defense plants in Michigan where she could get work; that's where Sally Ann was. Maybe she should go there and get a job. She was a top-notch secretary, and she was sure the law firm would give her a good reference.

For several urgent moments she thought of asking Tom to drop her at the next bus station. She heard Sally's hurtful words in one ear, saying, *"If you go off with that strange man to see your nothing of a father, Alice, then you will never be welcome in my house again. Do you understand me?"*

Doubts began to crack the walls of her resolve. What had she done? She'd agreed to travel across the United States with a man she hardly knew, to a strange place she knew absolutely nothing about. Wasn't her harebrained decision immoral and wrong? She'd let her heart hold her reason hostage.

Alice turned to tell Tom to stop the car, but then he looked at her with the most tender and beguiling smile she'd ever seen and it melted her. His eyes were a gorgeous blue—and penetrated with a warm invitation. She stared into them and she couldn't speak.

"We're on our way, Alice, and it will be the adventure of a lifetime. When I was in the Pacific, I read *The Grapes of Wrath,* by John Steinbeck. Do you know what he called Route 66? He said, 'it's the mother road, the road of flight.' He said, and now I'm paraphrasing because I don't have it memorized, but he said that it goes over red lands and gray lands and up into the mountains, and then it drops down into the desert, goes back up into the mountains, and finally, into the beautiful California valleys. So that's what we're going to do, Alice, you and me are going to explore the red lands, the mountains, the deserts, and the valleys."

By the time he'd finished, Alice's doubts had vanished, and her adventurous, romantic spirit had returned. "It sounds wonderful, Tom. I love what Steinbeck said, I mean about the road of flight. Yes, I love that. Do you know, I've only been out of Pennsylvania twice in my entire life, once to Ohio and once to Chicago."

"I put a new map of Route 66 in the glove compartment," Tom said. "It's better than the one we looked at back in Sandusky. You can follow it and mark where you want to stop and look around. Go ahead, take a look."

Alice did so, removing the map and eagerly unfolding it, swept up, forgetting about catching a bus to Michigan. With a finger, she followed Route 66 southwest through quaint towns in Illinois, until her finger stopped on Springfield. "Oh, look at this. We'll pass through Springfield, where Abraham Lincoln was born."

Tom grinned. "Yeah, and there's more."

She continued. "And in Stanton, Missouri, there are the Meramec Caverns. Oh, look, on the back of the map it says that long ago, local Indian tribes used the Caverns for shelter. Later, Jesse James is said to have used them as a hiding place."

Alice studied the map, her face alive with possibility. "And out west in Arizona is the Petrified Forest. It says here that the trees are millions of years old, and they've turned to stone in strange shapes."

At a red light, Tom braked and glanced over, an affectionate smile on his face. "So what do you think about Route 66?"

Alice looked at him and her sparkling smile said it all. "Excited."

"And there's a lot more, Alice. With any luck, we'll spend Christmas in sunny and warm California."

Outside Chicago, the rain stopped and Tom flipped off the wipers. Inside his chest, he felt an electric, pulsing joy that took him over. "Hey, do you know what, Alice? We can go dancing in the desert under moonlight."

"In the desert?"

"Sure, why not in the desert? And in California, we'll swim in the ocean and pick fresh oranges right off the trees."

His good mood was contagious, and Alice sat up, ready for anything. "I can't wait to do it all."

She pointed at the map, her attention grabbed by yet another attraction. "And look at this. In the Black Mountains in Arizona, there's an old gold-mining town. We'll search for gold and, when we find it, we'll run off and hide somewhere high in the mountains and you'll never have to go back to war."

Tom felt a pleasure so sharp that it made him want to jump out of his skin. And without a thought, he heard himself say aloud, "And we'll find a preacher up there in those mountains and he'll marry us."

Alice stared and smiled, thinking of Charles and what he might say, looking down at them from heaven. What would he say? Maybe he'd say what he'd said to her a few days before he'd left for war, as they'd stood near the duck pond behind the house.

"The world is filled with awful things and wonderful things, Alice. If you find yourself thinking about the awful, then be fair and give equal time to the wonderful."

Tom shrank back, realizing he'd been impulsive. "Pardon me, Alice. I guess I got a little carried away."

Alice stayed silent, privately aroused by the thought of sharing a bed with Tom. And just like that, her head filled with images of a house on a hill, with a baby tucked in her arm and clothes flapping on a clothesline in a warm, yellow wind. She turned her face aside so Tom couldn't read it, because she was sure, even though he'd only known her for such a short time, that he could read her thoughts.

Tom slowed the car and glanced outside the window at the moving, bare-limbed trees. "There's a good kite wind out there," he said. "I used to love flying kites. Me and the other boys made our own and flew them in storms."

Suddenly, for no apparent reason she could understand, Tom's face turned a sickly white. His voice grew deep, hoarse and frightened. "But those storms in the Pacific… they came in fierce and roaring. And then there were the ships and the guns… the guns never stopped… The guns and the Japs coming at us in the storm… coming at us."

His hands on the top of the steering wheel began to shake; beads of sweat popped out on his upper lip and on his forehead.

Concerned, Alice faced him. "Tom... Tom, are you all right?"

His lips twisted up as if he were in pain; his mouth twitched. "I've got to pull over. Got to... Feeling too much... It's too much. Got to pull over."

"Tom?"

Car horns blared as Tom whipped the car right and bounced into a gasoline station lot, turning sharply. She saw they were going to smash into a wooden fence and she braced for impact.

"Tom! Look out!"

Tom slammed on the brakes as the front bumper struck the fence. It shuddered, but held. He threw the column shift into neutral and pulled the emergency brake. In shock, Alice watched him gasp for air, his eyes round and wild; his breath coming fast, mouth-breathing.

His voice was low and terrified. "Shells, coming in... Can't get out. Coming in!"

Terrified, Alice glanced about. "Wait here, Tom. I'll go get help."

"No!" he yelled. "No, Alice. Japs coming at us... coming, firing. Get down! Get your head down!"

CHAPTER 25

December 2016

"I can't believe it's already December thirteenth," Jack said.

"This year just whizzed by," Alice said, sipping coffee at the kitchen island. "I'm behind on everything. Aren't you going to be late for work?"

Jack was standing at the back kitchen window at nine in the morning, staring out onto the upper meadow. Two men, wearing parkas and baseball caps, had set up a tripod and were walking around the area, pointing and talking. Jack knew who they were—surveyors from Morningside Developers, already trying to determine precisely where the property lines were.

"They're at it again," Jack said.

"Yes, I saw them when I came down. It makes me so sad that Lou and Mable Baxter are about to sign the papers to sell their house. I don't think they'll be happy in Florida."

"Mable will be, but not Lou. He's not a fisherman or golfer, and he likes the seasons, like me. I'll miss him."

"Aren't you going to be late for work?"

"Are you trying to get rid of me?"

"You're always so punctual. It makes me nervous when you go off schedule."

"I have a meeting at ten. I already called the guys working the two sites. Everything is fine, at least for now. Of course, that could all change in five minutes."

He glanced at his phone. "I just got a text from Kristie."

Alice turned to him, steadying herself. "And...?"

"Has she texted you lately?"

"Not since yesterday. I showed it to you. I wish she would call."

"That's too much to ask," Jack said, sarcastically. He set his coffee mug on the windowsill ledge and read the text aloud. *Hope you're not mad at me. I'm going to call you tonight. Went skiing this morning. Awesome. Fresh blanket of snow. Good snowpack further down the mountain... I'm fine, Dad, so don't worry, okay? I love you. Give Alice a kiss and don't nasty-talk me! Lol.*

Alice tried to come up with something positive. "She'll be nineteen next month."

Jack didn't seem to hear her. "Tell me something... when it comes to Kristie, do I have eyes that don't see and ears that don't hear?"

"What do you mean?"

"She's always been as restless as a March wind; since she was a tiny thing, running around like a little hurricane. I'd sit her down on the porch swing, she'd swing a couple of times, then wiggle down and run off. I'd take her shopping, she'd ramble off, and I'd find her somewhere wandering around. Once I found her four aisles over, munching on some M&Ms she'd snatched from a little boy who was crying his eyes out. I'd give her a job to do, and when I returned a few minutes later, she'd be gone.

And we know what she did when she was fifteen. Hitch-hiking to see some low-life boy. Thank God you were there. Thank God you saved her life."

Alice ran a hand through her hair, still wet from a recent shower, and drummed her fingers on the counter. "Kristie may be one of those people who has to learn things…"

Jack cut in. "… the hard way?"

"I was going to say, through experience."

"You don't have to be diplomatic, Alice. We both know there's a hard streak of recklessness in her and, for the life of me, I don't know what to do about it. I've talked to her and I've punished her. She even talked to that counselor, as you suggested, but that hasn't helped… Nothing seems to work. Nothing seems to stick."

Alice decided to change the subject. "Did you talk to Andrew about Mike Turner?"

"No," Jack said, slipping his phone into his pocket. He reached for his coffee mug, crossed to her and stopped. He set his mug on the counter and put an arm around her waist. She nestled in closer to him, as his gaze traveled from her damp, scented hair, down to her waiting, soft mouth. He leaned and kissed her, a warm, exploring kiss.

When he drew back, staring lovingly, she smiled up at him, blinking, aroused. "Well, now… Nice and wow, Mr. Landis. Why?"

"Why? You have to ask?"

"Yes," she said, keeping her grin. "You know I'm the curious type."

"Okay… for being here. For loving me. For loving us. All of us. For changing the subject away from Kristie, and for looking so pretty."

"Again, sir, wow. But now, just like that, you're about

to run off to work, leaving me with that spectacular kiss stuck to my soon-to-be-lonely lips. I'll miss you."

"It's nice to be missed."

"And it's nice to be kissed," she said, leaving his arms, batting her eyes and grinning coquettishly, placing a hand to a hip. "I just might keep you around."

He looked at her with a sudden change of expression. "I sometimes wonder if you have second thoughts about signing on with me and this crazy, ready-made family."

She dropped her flirtation and lowered her hand, giving him a searching, quizzical stare. "What a thing to say. How could I ever regret marrying you and living with, and loving, Kristie and Andrew? This family is the best thing that has ever happened to me. I have never regretted marrying you, not for a second, and I have never regretted being Kristie's and Andrew's stepmother. I love them with all my heart, as if they were my own."

He stroked her cheek. "Thanks for that. But sometimes I do wonder... I mean, Kristie isn't easy, and Andrew is secretive, and caught somewhere between boy and man."

"Boy? Really? You saw Brianna. She is one mature girl for seventeen years old, both in body and mind. She has as much poise and self-confidence as any young woman I've ever met. I wish I'd had some of that confidence when I was her age."

Jack nodded. "True. Did you see the way she looked at him?"

"And the way he looked at her. They both lit up like Roman candles when their eyes met. I could feel the attraction sizzle between them."

"So what are you saying?" Jack asked. "Do you think they're going to run off and get married?"

"No, no, nothing like that. She's much too sensible.

But it wouldn't surprise me if they go steady past high school and into college, and maybe beyond. I saw a deep attraction in Brianna's eyes and a kind of surprised fascination in Andrew's, like he's not sure what hit him."

Jack slanted her a look. "Surprised fascination? Well, aren't you the romantic? I think that diary has stirred up something in you."

"Jack, let me talk to Brianna. I think she'll have more influence on Andrew than either of us ever could."

"Great idea," Jack said. "Very good idea. And speaking of the diary, how goes it with the search?"

Alice shrugged loosely, reaching for her coffee mug and sitting on a stool. "I'm not finding anything. Alice probably died years ago, maybe before the internet took off. What gets me is that her diary ends abruptly, with the two of them in Chicago about to travel across country. Tom had a kind of breakdown, which is no doubt post-traumatic stress disorder, although they didn't call it that in 1944."

"You've known this for days."

"I know, I know, but it's getting to me. I mean, Alice filled every page in the diary, and her writing is so emotional and revealing. I can't believe she stopped writing, even if they separated and she ended up working at some war plant in Michigan. She must have continued writing in a second diary. So I wonder if that diary has been lost, or if it wasn't sent back to this house, for whatever reason. Are you sure you've searched everywhere in the room? There must be a second diary."

Jack glanced at his watch. "I've searched every corner of that room, Alice, and there's no second diary."

"Well, I'm going to search down there again."

"Where else could you look?"

"I don't know. There's got to be some thread, some

small clue somewhere."

Jack set his empty coffee mug down. "Well, I've got to get going or I *will* be late."

He bent and gave Alice another peck on the lips and then started for the side door that led to the garage. An idea struck, and he turned back. "You said that Alice and Tom were on their way to California?"

"Yes… But who knows if they ever got there."

"It just occurred to me. Just for fun, why don't you do a census search, starting in 1950 and work up from there. I did a search once for my father's family all the way back to the 1920s. The National Archives has the census on microfilm available from the late 1700s. You should be able to search online."

Alice brightened. "Good idea! What do I have to lose? I could search for Ferrell *and* Lawson."

She sprang off the stool and went to him, planting a big, wet kiss on his lips. "Thanks."

"Happy to be of service."

She lowered her voice. "By the way, I loved last night. You were very hot."

Jack looked down and away.

"Have I made you blush?"

"Yes… Goodbye."

After he was gone, Alice returned to her laptop and began her search with new, inspired energy.

CHAPTER 26
December 1944

At the Windy Motor Court outside Chicago, Alice registered her and Tom in separate cabins. When she signed the register first as Alice Ferrell and then as Tom Lawson, the desk clerk/owner looked on with a stern lack of interest. He had fish lips; his stomach lapped over his belt, and his cheeks were full and florid, suggesting a love of liquor.

"How many nights?" he asked, in a bored tone.

Still shaken from Tom's disturbing episode, she hesitated, throwing a glance back over her shoulder toward the waiting car. When she'd left him, Tom was lost in a stupor of agony, his forehead resting on the top rim of the steering wheel. They'd barely made it to the motel.

During his breakdown, Tom had jerked the car back onto the road as if trying to escape a battle. Alice had been terrified as he fought the steering wheel, his bug-eyes staring, the car often swerving over the yellow line. While he'd mumbled gibberish, and while other drivers laid on their horns, she'd shouted at him, trying to make a connection. It had been a miracle that a cop hadn't pulled them over.

"I'm not sure. My... well, my friend is not feeling well."

The man lifted his frosty eyes. "Is he drunk?"

Alice took offense. "No, he's not drunk. He's a soldier who fought in the Pacific. He's just... well, like I said, he's not feeling well."

A radio blared, and Alice couldn't help but hear the news. The British Eighth Army in Italy had crossed the Lamone, and the American destroyer USS Reid was sunk off Leyte by Japanese kamikaze aircraft. Hearing about the war in the Pacific made her nauseated, and she asked the clerk if he'd switch the thing off.

With superior blandness, he said, "My place. My radio. It stays on."

Alice swallowed her anxiety while the heavy man turned toward the key board and reached for two betasseled metal keys. He placed them on the counter and gave Alice a business look: narrowed eyes that held a hollow promise. "I'll give you a ten percent discount if you book the rooms for three nights. You and the soldier will be happy here."

Alice blinked, not impressed with the man and not sure what he was implying. "I... I just don't know."

He presented a forced enthusiasm, sure he could get the young woman to stay another night or two, if he worked it just right. "It's a darn good price. You won't get a better deal from here to Chicago. And this place fills up fast. It's popular. Damn popular. Lots of salesmen come through, and soldiers on leave. You really should think about it."

Alice didn't like the man. She didn't like his stale, boozy breath, the rank body odor wafting from his dingy white shirt, or his patronizing manner. And she didn't trust him. She wouldn't have booked the rooms if it weren't for Tom's poor condition.

"I'm not… That is, I don't think we'll be staying after tonight."

The man shrugged his narrow shoulders. "Don't think about it too long, sister. I'll give you an hour to decide. I don't have to give the discount, you know. Like I said, we're popular."

It was clear to Alice that the man had a weary contempt for his customers, and probably for himself as well. Though she had limited life experience, she'd seen a lot during the time she'd worked at the law firm, and she'd met all types there, the conniving, the honest and the desperate.

When she returned to the car, sliding in and closing the door, Tom was sitting up, his head leaned back, his eyes closed.

"Are you feeling better?" she asked, twisting her hands.

He rolled his head toward her, managing a tight smile, his eyes glazed with fatigue. "I think so."

"What happened? I don't understand. Has this happened before?"

He looked at her for a long time. "The day I came to see you, in that snowstorm. That's why I slammed into the tree. I blacked out for a moment and lost control of the car."

Alice was worried. "Shouldn't you see a doctor?"

"No more doctors, Alice. I've had it up to my eyeballs with doctors. What I have… They call it combat stress reaction and battle fatigue. I didn't want you to know. But now you know, so I might as well spill it… All of it. So here's the deal. Sometimes I shout in my sleep and try to climb out of windows. For a while, I took a swig regularly from a flask. I've stopped that now. I don't like the feeling of being dull and doped. I wake up with wet sheets and I want to run away, but I don't know where to run to."

Tom shut his eyes and sighed. "Sometimes I think Charlie's the lucky one."

Alice turned from him, staring ahead into the gliding snow flurries. "Don't say that. You just need some rest, Tom. We'll rest here tonight and by tomorrow you'll feel better."

He opened his eyes and looked at her with a weary, entranced expression. "I always feel better when I'm with you, Alice. I know I just had a breakdown, but it wasn't as bad as most and I feel better in my head—in my mind, I mean. It's not easy to explain these things."

Alice tried to smile but failed, her feelings ranging from compassion to apprehension to anxiety. "All right, Tom, let's get you inside and put you to bed. You should sleep the rest of the day and all night. I'm sure you'll feel better by morning."

He brought one eye to bear, the other half closed. "You are very pretty, Alice. The prettiest nurse I ever saw."

The words made her timid and silent. She was on the shakiest ground with Tom, and she needed to be alone to absorb it. His peculiar incident in the car was clouding her thoughts. While he slept, she'd have time to think about what she should do. If she stayed with him and crossed the country with him, what would happen in California when they parted? And, of course, they'd have to part. Then what?

She'd be alone and Tom would leave for war. If she truly were falling in love, wouldn't she be waiting and worrying all over again, just as she had with Charles? Did she really want that? Could she survive the endless, punishing waiting again? Could she survive the possibility of his being killed?

As soon as Alice got Tom safely in his room, he dropped onto the bed and fell asleep. Alice closed and locked the door quietly and found her own room down the hall. After quickly getting herself settled, she found an outside vending machine and bought a bottle of 7up. She took a long, rambling walk on the motel grounds and parking lot while she drank it. Should she stay with Tom or leave for Michigan? It was time she made a decision once and for all.

At noon the next day, Tom's Oldsmobile went roaring and bumping over a gravel road, a detour that skirted a one-mile stretch of Route 66 that was under repair.

"... And it's been under repair for six months," the string-bean-thin, agitated gas pump jockey had said, two miles back at the Texaco station.

As he filled the gas tank, Tom and Alice drank Coca Colas, grinning, enjoying the man's banter. "Somebody's getting rich off that road work, but it sure ain't me. And it hurts our business. It's times like these that I wish I'd been sent off to war. But I've got a bad ear and flat feet. Wouldn't take me. You said you fought in the Pacific?"

Tom said he did.

"I heard the Japs are fierce fighters. That true?"

"Yes..."

When they left the rutty detour road and rolled back onto Route 66, the afternoon sun broke through scattered clouds. The sun cheered Alice. She sat up straight and grand, again happy to be back on the road. She tossed a glance to Tom, and he seemed fine and contented, showing none of the tight stress lines he'd shown the day before after his breakdown.

"I'm so glad you slept well," Alice said.

"Better than I have in years, and that's saying something. That lumpy, squeaky bed must be left over from the 1920s. My cot back in that mosquito-infested, Jap-infested island was more comfortable."

"You really had me worried."

"Don't worry about me, Alice. I'm just fine. I woke up this morning feeling better than I have since... Well, I don't know when. I feel like a kid at Christmas. I feel like a million bucks. We have our whole trip ahead of us."

Alice opened the map again, her eyes falling on the lower left side. "The map says that Route 66 is Two thousand four hundred miles, cuts through eight states and passes through three hundred towns. How long will it take to get to California?"

"I figure about two weeks," Tom said, "including some stops and not following the speed limit. We could probably drive it in eight or nine days, but why? We've got plenty of time."

They visited Abraham Lincoln's home in Springfield and left late that afternoon. As the sun was about to set, they drove across the Old Chain of Rocks Bridge in Collinsville, Illinois. Alice gazed out at the wide Mississippi River in childlike wonder, amazed by its size and grandeur. "I never would have believed it was so vast."

Tom cranked down his window and inhaled the river breeze. "It makes you feel as free as a bird, doesn't it, Alice?"

Alice couldn't pull her big, round eyes from the mighty river. "Yes... And we're about to enter Missouri."

On the other side of the bridge, the car rounded a turn

and rolled off west. The whole world seemed to open up before them like a blessing. The sun slid behind clouds, turning the horizon into a banked fire, and Alice let out a soft sigh. "It's the end to a perfect day."

Tom stared, enchanted by the lovely scene. "You said it, Alice, and we have a lot more perfect days ahead of us."

They enjoyed days of driving along the winding road, and the straight road, and the climbing road, passing farms and lakes, moving through busy towns and bustling cities. They stopped at motels for the night, always booking separate rooms, and they ate in cafés and diners with candy-coated neon signs.

One afternoon, they lingered in Big Buck's narrow shop, crowded with Route 66 banners pinned to the walls, and souvenirs stuffed in wooden bins and on wooden shelves. They stood at the squeaky, rotating postcard display, picking through postcards that featured maps, diners and open roads. Their eyes met and they smiled, ruefully.

"Who would I send a postcard to?" Tom asked. "Maybe a buddy or two from the orphanage. But who knows where they are? It seems a shame not to send one to somebody."

Alice nodded, replacing one she'd been considering. "Yeah. Sally and Fred would probably throw it away. I guess I could send one to the law firm." She shrugged, as if to say, "But why bother."

Their eyes met and, in that yearning moment, they suddenly realized they had only each other, and no one else. They were alone together in the world. Their hearts beat the same rhythm and their thoughts were synchronized, and they both grasped a truth they would recall for the rest of their lives: Time is fragile… each moment is fleeting… when love presents itself, you have to take a risk. That long, private moment yielded a tenderness that drew them closer.

Tom's eyes became anxious and he felt a gnawing in his gut. His loneliness was so acute that he turned his mind to the past. "When I was at the orphanage, we used to plant vegetables in the spring: beets, corn, carrots, peas and turnips. We learned how to set the rows straight, and we used string and seed packets to identify what was growing in each row."

Tom picked up another postcard and stared at it, without seeing it. "I felt a part of something when we did that planting, and yet I still felt outside as well, like I was on the outer rim of a circle looking in. Those boys and girls weren't really my family, were they? They were tossed into that place just like I was. Some of us got close, but then, when we left, well, I haven't kept in touch. It's like I don't want to remember or something."

Alice's eyes were clear and searching. He had captured her feelings precisely, but she'd never been able to articulate them.

Tom replaced the postcard and looked around. "Where are we, anyway?"

"Oklahoma…" Alice said. "Some little town. Vinita."

Tom considered his words, shifting his weight from his right foot to his left. "Alice, do you like kids?"

Alice stared into his eyes, her mind exploring. The sunlight streaming in from the window lit him up. He was a man she liked to look at, and think about, and dream about. She allowed herself to believe that they could have a life and family together.

"Yes, Tom… I like kids."

They fell into silence, Tom standing on one side of the card display and Alice on the other. Each chose a post-card, glanced at it, and replaced it. Then Tom chose another, pretending to consider it. "I want a nice house, not too big, with a white fence and a green, clipped lawn. That's not so much to ask, is it?"

CHAPTER 27
December 2016

Alice didn't have time to search for Alice Ferrell Lawson. There was much work to do in the house and Brenda needed time off for Christmas shopping. She also had a cold.

On Wednesday, December 14, three new guests had checked in. Martin and Meg Benton were both retired, he having managed a string of Midwest grocery stores and she having worked as an accountant. They were fit, polite and quiet, and their plans included walking tours, shopping, and sampling local restaurants. Meg told Alice that she would spend evenings near the parlor fireplace and Christmas tree, reading and napping.

Beatrice Ralston, a widow in her 70s, was nicknamed Sunshine. She had traveled from Denver, after finding the Landis' house online and falling in love with the history, the ambiance, and the good reviews. True to her name, Sunshine was outgoing and friendly, and she had paid through Christmas.

"My daughter, son and grandkids are not happy with me," Sunshine said, "but I told them that, just this once, I wanted to experience something different for the holidays and I wanted to do it alone, so I could meet new people and do anything I wanted to do. So I chose your lovely Bed and Breakfast," she said, with a big smile. With a sweep of a hand indicating toward her rose-colored bedroom, she added, "And I can tell you, I'm not disappointed."

"Let me know if you need anything," Alice said.

"You provide breakfast, right?"

"Yes, we do. You'll receive a menu under your door each evening. If you have any special requests or allergies, let us know when you choose your breakfast, then hang the menu on the doorknob before you go to bed. You can also text us. The number is on the menu."

"And dinner?"

"We don't provide dinner, but there are plenty of restaurants around, and nearly all are available for takeout. There's a notebook on the desk that contains frequently asked questions, things to do in town, and menus and directions to restaurants close by."

Sunshine rubbed her palms together. "I hope we get snow."

"We usually do around Christmas, so I'll keep my fingers crossed," Alice said. "And don't forget our evening complimentary wine with cheese, and tea with cookies."

Sunshine's smile was contagious. "Well, I'll skip the tea and reach for the wine, won't I? I love your Christmas decorations. I already feel as though I've been transported to Christmas land. I'm going to take lots of photos and send them to my kids and grandkids. That will make them jealous. As kids today put at the end of their texts, Lol."

In the midst of her hectic day, Alice found Andrew standing at the kitchen island, making a peanut butter and jelly sandwich.

"We have leftover chicken," Alice said. "Do you want me to make you a sandwich?"

He shrugged. "No, this is okay. Can I have chicken for dinner?"

"Sure. How are you feeling? How's your back?"

"Fine. It doesn't hurt that much, but that pain pill makes me feel a little weird. I don't think I'm going to take any more of them. The cut wasn't that deep. I think that doctor was just being careful."

"It was deep enough. It makes me shiver to think about it."

Andrew still had the Band Aid on his right cheek and a bruise under his left eye. He'd been suspended from school and he'd mostly stayed in his room since returning home. He said he didn't want to scare the guests, and Jack agreed.

"I don't want them to think I beat you up," Jack had said, trying for humor.

Andrew hadn't smiled.

Since his teachers had emailed him assignments, Andrew had school work to do, and he and Brianna often had video chats.

On Tuesday, he'd joined Alice and his father for dinner, but he quickly made it clear he wasn't ready to talk about what had happened. Jack had tried to press him, to Alice's regret, but Andrew remained silent.

Alice stood watching Andrew spread grape jelly over the peanut butter. A thought had been circling in her head and she decided to toss it out.

"How's Brianna?"

"Fine... Good. You know."

"She's very pretty."

"Yeah."

"How long have you known her?"

"I don't know. You know, months, I guess."

"And you've been out together?"

"Yeah… we've been out. She likes to drive, so sometimes after school we just drive places, get some pizza, or drive to Belview Lake. We like it over there."

"What do you do?"

Andrew gave her a look that said, "Give me a break already." But he said, "We sit, walk, talk and study."

"You didn't tell me about her."

Andrew slapped the two slices of bread together and pressed them down. "I would have… I mean, I was going to."

Alice softened her voice. "I like Brianna. She seems smart, and she obviously likes you."

He stared at the sandwich. "Yeah, she's cool."

Alice wanted to keep Andrew talking. "Has she selected a college?"

"Penn State, I guess."

Andrew took a bite of his sandwich, and Alice was pleased when he eased down on a stool and didn't leave.

"What does she want to major in?"

"Law, I think."

"Her father's a lawyer, isn't he?"

"Yeah… But she wants to help people and not just make a lot of money. She doesn't want to go into corporate law. She says the world is all messed up… you know, the environment and all the social stuff… everything. She wants to be one of those who help fix it."

"And what do you want to do, Andrew?"

He looked at her speculatively, aware she was up to something. "Speaking of law, you're asking a lot of questions. I feel like I'm on the witness stand here," he said, lightly, with a hint of humor.

"I'm sorry. I've just been worried about you. We

used to talk more."

He took another bite of the sandwich, chewing thoughtfully. His expression darkened. "I wanted to kill him... Can you believe that? I did... I mean, I really wanted to kill him."

Alice folded her arms, exhaling a little breath. "I guess you're talking about Mike Turner?"

"Yeah, that's who I'm talking about. Nobody does what he did. People don't steal other people's code like that and then sell it. What the hell was that? He did it because of Brianna. She dumped him for me. He's this big senior... smart-ass. A lot of the girls go after him and they think he's like some hot guy. Brianna saw through him, and she dumped his sorry ass."

"Andrew... You'll come up with more ideas. You're talented and smart."

He bored into her with his hot eyes. "I wanted it for Brianna. I wanted to develop it into more than just some stupid shopping app for women. And Brianna had so many good ideas of how we could expand it. Mike is just so, I don't know, smart in one way and so stupid in another."

Andrew turned away. "And then he denied the code was even mine. That's why I punched him. And his father's like connected to all these tech companies, so of course he found a way to sell it, just so he can show everybody how cool he is. That's why I wanted to smash his face in."

Alice needed to change the subject, to calm his anger. Andrew had ocean-deep emotions and an intense approach to life, and that worried her.

"Andrew, I could use your help."

His eyes flipped up. "What kind of help?"

"I need help finding the woman who wrote the diary—the other Alice Ferrell. I'm just so busy. I was thinking maybe you and Brianna could do some searching. Your father suggested searching the U.S. Census, but I found out that the U.S. government won't release personally identifiable information about an individual to any other individual or agency until seventy-two years after it was collected."

Andrew thought about it. "I can ask Brianna. Her father has a lot of connections. He might help."

Alice sat down. "In the diary, she describes how she and a soldier, a Marine named Tom Lawson, are taking a road trip across the country from east to west on Route 66. He has to return to the war in January 1945. It's possible he survived the war and they got married."

The name Route 66 sparked Andrew's interest. "Route 66? Wow. That's cool. About a year ago, Dad said he wanted to take that trip, remember?"

"Yes. I'd still love to do it. Anyway, it also occurred to me that there might be a veteran's data base where Tom Lawson is listed."

"Yeah, I'm sure there is."

"Do you have the time to do some searching?"

His dark mood had lifted, and his eyes held new interest. He bit into the sandwich and chewed, wincing in pain.

"Are you all right?" Alice asked.

"Yeah, my jaw's still sore. One of Mike's friends punched me—when I wasn't looking, of course. Okay, anyway, yeah, sure I'll check out Alice. I like doing research, and Brianna is an ace at it. If anybody can find anybody, it's Brianna. Between the two of us, we should be able to find your Alice Ferrell. And when she gets back, I'll put Kristie on it, too. It won't hurt."

Alice was glad Andrew mentioned Kristie. "Andrew,

have you talked to her?"

"She texted a couple of times, but she didn't really say anything. She just said the skiing and snowboarding are good."

"Did you know she was planning a trip to Colorado?"

"No. No way. She wouldn't tell me. You know how she is, and she's not going to change. I don't see it, anyway. You know how she likes to shock everybody and get attention. I texted her that, and she got all pissed off at me. Just before she left, she told me that when she and Taylor get to Penn State, they plan to live together."

Alice stared, not moving.

"Okay, so I probably shouldn't have told you that," Andrew said.

Alice lifted a hand and let it fall. "She obviously wants to make her own choices. I'll leave that up to her and her father."

"That won't be pretty," Andrew said. "She and Dad just don't get each other, and they never have."

Alice let that go by.

"Don't worry about her. Kristie can take care of herself... Well, most of the time. Anyway, give me all the information about Alice and the soldier and I'll start searching."

Back in her office, Alice booted up her laptop and did a search for Colorado weather. What she saw made her uneasy. She leaned toward the screen and read:

There have been fifty avalanches in Colorado over a span of three days, according to the Colorado Avalanche Information Center. As of Monday, the CAIC has reported 344 natural, human-triggered and/or controlled avalanches in December alone, including 48 from Friday the 9th through Monday the 12th.

Several storms—each dumping multiple feet of snow—have hammered the central and northern mountains this month, and dangerous avalanches persist in the central and northern mountains, the CAIC said in a Tuesday report. Further complicating the state's current avalanche danger is what the CAIC calls "tricky" conditions. These avalanches are difficult to predict and you might not see obvious signs of instability like cracking or collapsing. The CAIC is suggesting that all skiers, hikers and snowboarders exercise extreme caution.

Alice grabbed her phone and texted Kristie. *How are you? I'm reading about avalanches in Colorado. Are you staying safe?*

CHAPTER 28
December 1944

One exhilarating day blurred into the next as Alice and Tom drove across miles of open road, through lazy small towns, sprawling big towns and shimmering deserts. Neon art was everywhere, with every motel having its own unique signature, and every café a brand-new idea.

In ghost towns, there were ragged, billowing curtains in windows, abandoned bicycles in yards, and stacks of plywood next to red brick piles, all that remained of half-finished, forgotten homes.

Route 66 was an endless ribbon of highway that unraveled under shocking blue skies, infinite horizons with golden blue afterglows, and clay-heavy clouds rolling with thunder and cloud-to-ground bursts of lightning. Pelting rains came sliding down in waves, steel arrows exploding off the road, washing the windshield so that Tom and Alice had to pull over and wait for the storm to pass.

There were breathtaking views of purple mountain majesties, red and orange rock formations, and vast, rolling fields that stopped all thought and brought a healing silence.

It was only when military vehicles passed the Oldsmobile that the hard, cold slap of reality jolted Alice and Tom back to the present. And then they'd have to reset their minds and emotions, shove away thoughts about the past and future, and wrestle mind and body to return to the freedom of the open road.

When they drove through Needles, California, on the western banks of the Colorado River, both could already feel the world beginning to close in on them. On the map, Alice noted that they were in the subregion of the Mojave Desert, near the borders of Arizona and Nevada.

Driving past the little towns of Bagdad, Siberia, and Klondike, Alice used her finger to trace the route and measure the distance to Barstow, California, about sixty miles.

Tom looked over, subdued. "Do you want to keep driving all the way to Pasadena?"

Alice shook her head. "No, I don't think so. I don't think I'm ready for cities yet. Maybe we should stay the night in Barstow. It says it's in the heart of the Mojave Desert."

Tom held his hand out the window, feeling the airflow across it. "I guess that's why it feels like spring at Christmas. Can you imagine how hot this place must get in the summer?"

"I'd prefer snow," Alice said.

It was late afternoon, sunny and seventy degrees when they arrived in Barstow, California and turned into the El Rancho Motel parking lot. Tom stopped the car at the front entrance, switched off the engine, and sat back with a little sigh.

"I guess this place is as good as any other. They're all starting to look the same."

Alice looked the place over. "Yes, it seems okay.

They have a Christmas tree and a wreath in the lobby window. That seems out of place in this weather. What day is it?"

Tom laughed a little. "Alice, you know it's December twenty-fourth. In a few hours it will be Christmas Eve."

She turned to him with a smile. "Yes, I know. I'm just playing pretend, wishing we could jump back to Chicago and take the entire journey again."

They couldn't push the inevitable away any longer. They were only a few hours from Los Angeles, and the world of time and place seemed at arm's reach. The relentless demands of duty and country called; commitment and obligation were closing in.

They sat for long minutes as the exhalation of a warm, dry wind blew in from the open windows and stirred Alice's hair. There were several kinds of silences between them. One was a threat: time was running out and decisions had to be made. Another was fear: what lay before them seemed vast and unimaginable; Alice feeling like a leaf blown carelessly by the wind, and Tom, a hunter about to enter a dark jungle filled with the enemy and possible death.

There was also the silence of desire between them. They'd been nearly inseparable for days, and it had taken enormous acts of will and conscience not to act on their swelling passions, which always lay just below the surface of thought, touch and conversation.

Twice, Tom had left his room and started for Alice's. Both times, he'd stopped, reversed, and returned to his room, pacing like a caged animal.

During several lonely nights, Alice had wished Tom would knock on her door and share her bed. Time, distance and being with Tom had all contributed to a sense of new birth; a new identity. Although Charles remained in her thoughts, she had packed him away in a secret place in her soul, while her pulsing heart had opened and flowered with love for Tom, and she wanted to express that love with her body, mind and emotions.

As they sat inside the car, it began to heat up. Tom turned from her, glancing left across the street at a rickety-looking store, with a sign on its tin roof that read **Desert Trading Post**. When he spoke, it was nearly at a whisper. "Alice... Will you marry me?"

Alice didn't move or react. Her expression was calm and under control. She was recalling what Charles had told her last February when she'd asked him if they were going to be married before he left to go overseas.

He'd grinned and made a little joke. "Do you know, Alice, that only this morning, I read in the newspaper that in 1942 alone, nearly two million weddings took place. The reporter said... now whether you want to believe him or not is up to you... anyway, he said that marriages are up eighty-three percent from ten years before. And now, here's the good part: two-thirds of those brides were marrying men newly enlisted in the military."

Alice had been serious. She didn't care for the article or for Charles' jokey manner or tone of voice.

"I don't care about that, Charles. I only care about us."

Charles went on, as if he hadn't heard her. "And, on Sunday, you heard Reverend Massey. Right from the pulpit, as he swept the faces of the people, many of them soldiers, he said, 'Marriage is a serious business. The hasty marriage, caused by glamor and excitement rather than by genuine affection, is one of the evil products of war.'"

That had made her angry, and she'd turned away from him. "You don't want to marry me, do you, Charles? You don't want to give me a baby, do you? Okay, then stop telling me about what you read in the papers or what the minister said. Just tell me yourself, without the jokes."

It was the first time she'd been so open and direct with him.

He'd taken her arm, gently turning her to face him. She'd stared into his eyes, seeing no humor in them. "Of course I want to marry you, Alice, and yes, I want a baby too. But not like this. I don't want to go off to war and die, leaving you alone with a baby. I can't do it. I can't go off with the possibility of it weighing on my mind. I've got enough to think about, don't I?"

She'd been honest, and she'd been selfish. Still, she'd wanted them to marry and start a family.

As Alice sat in the car with Tom, recalling the past, dredging up the painful feelings, remembering how empty she'd felt after Charles had left, the start of tears surprised her.

"Did I say something wrong, Alice?" Tom said, watching the tears roll down her cheeks.

She turned to him with glistening eyes and a smile, and her words came slowly and tentatively. "Tonight, let's register as Mr. and Mrs. Tom Lawson. Let's be married. There's so little time... Isn't there so little time before you go?"

Alice awoke in the half-light of evening and gently sat up, leaning her back against the wooden headboard, her sleepy eyes focused on Tom. He was still asleep, his breathing easy, his broad chest a swirl of dark hair. Alice had loved the feel of his body, heavy on her, persistent and vital. With pleasure and with closed eyes, she allowed her body to recall his breath on her face, his hands exploring her eager body, his warm mouth on hers, their lips sliding, nibbling.

At first, their love making had been mild and slow, with shy kisses and hands reaching. But then hunger and passion added a tender force that was driven by emotion and urgency. When it was over, Alice had rested in a stupor of contentment, her body alive with love and affection for Tom, who lay next to her, gently caressing her hair, her face and her breasts.

It had been a rapture, a private moment that had exalted them, drawing them together into a fortunate work of art, like sky and sea; like a mystery that would require a lifetime to be daily discovered but never solved.

For dinner, they sat in a plush, two-seater booth in the Route 66 Mojave Diner, where a lopsided Christmas tree blinked erratically, as if it had drunk too much Christmas cheer.

"There must be a short in the thing," Tom said, with an easy laugh.

While Bing Crosby and the Andrew Sisters sang *Jingle Bells* on the juke-box, Alice and Tom were giddy and playful, hands touching, eyes bright. Their conversation was extravagant, freed from the prison of uncertainty and nerves they'd experienced traveling across the country. While they cut into their steaks, they were all ideas and airy chatter, and the world at war seemed as far away as Mars or Jupiter.

Tom waved his fork in the air as he made plans. "We should be able to get a marriage license in L.A. on Monday or Tuesday, after the blood tests."

Alice laughed easily as she produced *The Los Angeles Times,* which she'd purchased at the motel front desk. She held up a section. "I've got to show you this."

Tom looked on with bright interest as she handed him a section she'd circled with a pen. "Read those and you'll have a good laugh."

He held the paper with both hands, his eyes moving across it.

"Read it out loud and then tell me if you'd ever post something like that."

Tom read loud enough so that she could hear him over the juke-box music. "Is it the want ads?"

"No, look at the headline. It's *The Marriage Billboard*, a Los Angeles match-making section."

Tom nosed in, grinning. "Oh, well, this should be fun. **Women Seeking Men**. Okay, here we go.

> "*Looking for a man who is not a soldier. He must have enough income to make a settlement of about $500 and be able to keep me in comfort and perhaps travel after the war. The income does not mean as much to me as happiness and real companionship. But I'll take the money, too.*"

Tom laughed. "Scratch that one. Here's the next. This time it's **Men Seeking Women**.

> '*A girl who has not been used to much money, who would like me and marry me for myself, and not for my income. Her income is not so important, but the larger it is, the better.*'"

Alice and Tom broke into laughter. "I like this guy," Tom said. "Everybody's thinking about money."

"That guy sounds like a jerk to me," Alice said. "Go ahead, keep reading. They get better."

"Okay, okay... Let's see. Here's a good one. Back to

Women Seeking Men.

> *'Only tender-hearted. Man of character. I do not mind if he is a war wreck. Tolerant outlook towards other people and their affairs. Patient. Not more selfish than most men.'"*

Tom leaned back, shaking with laughter. "I'm going to call this woman right now," he joked.

"Don't you dare!" Alice said, enjoying herself, her laughter rising. "Go on, read another."

"Okay, moving on, back to **Men Seeking Women**. Here's the last one.

> *'She must have knowledge of building repair, fruit growing and poultry. Able to manage income tax papers etc., but not too clever. Prefer a woman who can darn my socks and doesn't complain about washing clothes.'"*

Tom looked at Alice from over the top of the newspaper, and she was shaking her head. "Oh, brother. To that man I'll only say: Good luck, whoever you are."

After dinner, Alice and Tom strolled arm-in-arm through the quiet town in the dry, warm night. They'd grown quiet and pensive.

"Tom… When you're away, I'm going to get a job."

"You have plenty of money, thanks to your father. We'll put that money in the bank and you can draw interest on it. You won't have to work."

"But I want to. I have to work. With you being gone, I won't be able to stand it if I'm not doing something. That's why I bought that paper, so I could look for work in Los Angeles and San Diego. There are a number of defense plants and aircraft companies. I saw one that's looking for secretaries."

"Which one?"

"Consolidated-Vultee Aircraft, in San Diego. You'll be stationed in San Diego, or close by, so I'm hoping we'll be able to be together when you get a pass, until you're sent overseas."

Tom pulled her to a stop, took her by the shoulders and drew her into his arms. "God, I love you, Alice. I think I fell in love with you from that first moment I saw you standing outside my car window in that snowstorm. God help me, maybe I fell in love with you the first time Charlie showed me your photograph."

She lifted her chin and offered him her lips. "I love you, Tom, with all my heart."

After the kiss, she touched his lips with a finger. "I want your baby, Tom. Please give me a baby."

Looking at her, Tom felt all the darkness in him—the darkness of his past and the darkness of the war—be released; he felt it leave him, and fly away into the desert wind. He knew his shakes were gone, feeling it in the depths of his heart. He'd been healed by Alice's love.

CHAPTER 29

December 2016

On Friday afternoon, December 16, Alice was in the parlor tidying up, plumping the pillows, changing the water in the flower vases, and removing two empty coffee mugs left from breakfast. The three guests were out exploring the town and Christmas shopping, and Andrew was in the basement, doing some simple, home repair projects.

Alice stepped to the Christmas tree, inhaling its sweet scent, running a branch through her hand. Thankfully, only a few needles fell off. On her knees, she smoothed out the tree skirt, embroidered with sprigs of holly and ivy, and checked the water basin. It was nearly full. As she stood, she replayed the conversation she'd had with Jack and Andrew that morning.

Over breakfast, as the three of them sat in the private dining room next to the kitchen, Andrew had asked his father what he could do in the basement room they were remodeling. Jack had told him to rest, but Andrew had insisted he was feeling fine; he was tired of sitting at his computer. All his friends were in school and Brianna had two tests and couldn't talk until evening.

"I'll be okay," Andrew said. "I can use a screwdriver to probe for rot and insect damage in the floor joists and along the wood-framed windows. It's no big deal."

Jack blew the steam from his coffee mug. "You shouldn't be working with those stitches in your back. Take it easy for a few days. The doctor said not to do anything strenuous."

"I'll be careful. If it hurts, I'll stop. I'll seal those cracks and gaps around the pipes. Maybe I'll insulate them. That won't hurt anything, and they need it."

Jack slid his empty plate aside and stared at his son with stern appraisal. "Are you feeling better... I mean about Mike Turner?"

"Honest?"

"Yes."

"No."

"What are you going to do about it?"

He shrugged.

"What's that mean?"

"It means, I don't know. I'd like to catch him alone, without his friends, and..." He didn't finish the sentence.

Alice sat quietly, eyes lowered. She'd wanted to talk to Brianna about it, but she hadn't found the time and then she'd thought better of it, not wanting to intrude where she didn't belong. That was always her dilemma with the kids and Jack. When to interfere and when not to.

"Sometimes it's best to walk away," Jack said.

Andrew looked his father directly in the eye, his half-eaten bowl of cereal pushed away. "Is that what you would do, just walk away, if somebody did to you what Mike did to me?" Andrew's voice was tight and restrained. "I don't think so."

Jack studied his son. "It's a fair question, Andrew."

Jack sat up, giving his son a sharp, searching look. "I

had a man work for me once, about ten years ago. He was a good worker and a quiet one. He always showed up on time, and he always went the extra mile. I was fond of him, and I thought we'd become friends. He borrowed five hundred dollars from me, saying he had a sick daughter. That was the only time he talked about his family. Then, every week, he asked for an advance until payday. I gave it to him three times, refusing a fourth. And then he didn't show up for work. I called him. He didn't answer. I had let him drive one of my old pickups back and forth to work because I trusted him, and he said his car had broken down and he didn't have the money to fix it. That pickup held tools; good, expensive tools."

Jack folded his hands on the table, his eyes intensely serious, not pulling them from his son. "The police found the truck a couple of days later, about a hundred miles away, but the tools were gone. I had trusted him, and it hurt. Turns out, he wasn't married, and he didn't have a daughter."

Andrew wiped his mouth with a napkin, then leaned back. "Did you look for him? I mean, come on, Dad, you must have gone looking for him. You have connections everywhere. And I know you wouldn't let that go."

Alice waited, her eyes fixed on Jack. She'd never heard the story.

"Yes... I went looking for him and I found him. It took me a while, two months."

Alice and Andrew exchanged a quick glance.

Jack continued. "I found him in a smelly, dark bar, slumped over a flat, half-drunk beer. I sat down next to him. I stared at him. He finally, slowly, turned his head. It took a few moments before the booze-vision cleared from his eyes, and then they went wide with recognition. He drew back, fear all about him. He shook all over like he was going to break into pieces. Then he stumbled off his stool and clumsily backed away, his hands held up, expecting me to attack. The place was loud and crowded, and no one paid us any attention. It was that kind of place, where nobody cared if you lived or died. A hellhole of a place. Anyway, I was going to punch him in the face. I had driven over fifty miles to punch him. Then, like a trapped and scared animal, he snarled at me. He said, 'Go ahead. Hit me.' He wriggled his fingers at me and taunted me. He waited, and I waited. The longer I stood there looking at him, the more I felt the anger drain out of me, and I just felt pity for him. I thought, he's got to live with himself every day of his life, and the living fact that he's here in this stinking, hellish place means that, inside, he's living in hell. I walked away, and I never regretted walking away."

Andrew turned his face aside and scratched the side of his nose.

Jack stood up. "Son, all of us have to live inside ourselves. Do you really want to carry all that anger and bitterness inside? I don't know, maybe you do. But it's toxic, and it's a kind of sickness that will eat away at you. Why don't you channel your energy toward writing more code for something else? This time protect it. You've learned a valuable lesson. So, show Mike and the world that you can do it again and again. From what Brianna said about him, he doesn't have the skill or the talent. You do. So use it."

After Jack had left for work, Andrew turned to Alice. He was remote and subdued. "Brianna and I are going to work on finding your Alice Ferrell tomorrow. Is that soon enough?"

Alice nodded. "Sure."

Andrew rose, placed his dishes into the dishwasher

and left for the basement.

In the parlor that afternoon, Alice was hanging two more Victorian ornaments on the Christmas tree when her phone buzzed. She retrieved it from her back jeans pocket—Kristie was calling.

The night before, she'd texted to say she and Taylor had decided to stay Friday and Saturday and take a flight home on Sunday. Jack had texted her back, ordering her to return immediately. She didn't respond. Neither Jack nor Alice had slept well, and she'd been walking on pins and needles all morning.

Alice took the call. "Kristie."

Kristie's voice was tight with barely contained panic. "Alice... I need your help."

Alice raised and settled her shoulders. "What is it?"

"Taylor's been in an accident. A really bad accident."

"What kind of accident?"

"We were skiing... It was so perfect. A perfect morning. I just don't..."

Alice eased down on the sofa and swallowed. "Tell me, Kristie. What's happened to Taylor?"

"We were skiing down an advanced course... He veered away from me—showing off. He was weaving and doing stupid stunts. Stupid. Stupid! Why? He... oh my God, Alice. He was going so fast. He was wearing a helmet, but he was going too fast and he hit a tree."

Alice shot up. "Oh, God. Kristie, how is he? Where is he?"

Kristie choked back sobs. "Ski patrollers came. His face was all bloody. It was awful. They said he was alive, but he didn't wake up. He didn't open his eyes. I kept yelling at him to wake up."

"Kristie, where is he?"

Alice knew Kristie was about to come apart. She

heard it in her voice. "Kristie, are you all right?"

She was crying. "Yes... Yes." She struggled to go on. "I... well... They took him down to the resort's medical clinic, but then right away, they transferred him to a hospital."

"Where are you?"

Kristie wept into the phone, making little hiccupping sounds. "Some hospital... I don't know where the hell I am. Some hospital, and somebody said they'd called Taylor's mother. Dammit, Alice, I'm at the hospital and this doctor came out and said something like, Taylor had blunt-force trauma to the head. Oh, God, Alice. Oh, my God, Alice, please help me. The doctor said Taylor's in a coma."

Alice heard Kristie break down, her voice raspy with stress and grief. "I don't know what to do, Alice. I don't know... Why was he showing off like that? Why? Can you come? Please, don't tell Dad, and please come."

Alice sat still, her breathing coming fast as she worked to process the terrible news.

"Alice, are you there?"

"Yes, I'm here."

"Please come, Alice. I need you. Please. Don't tell Dad. Please come and don't tell Daddy."

"All right. I'll come. Do you have friends there with you?"

"No, no... They all left today. We were supposed to... but..."

"All right. Okay. Tell me where you're staying. Go back there."

"I don't want to be alone, Alice. I can't be alone now. What if Taylor dies? What if he never wakes up? I don't know what to do. Don't tell Dad. Please don't."

"I know it's hard, but try to calm down a little. Do

you have a car?"

"A car... No, it's back at the hotel. I came here with somebody... I don't know who. Maybe a cop or somebody that works at the hotel. I can't think. I'm a mess. Come."

"Can you call for an Uber or a cab?"

"Yeah, I guess so."

"Okay. Do it. Now, give me all the information. I'll book a flight and meet you at your hotel. Then we'll come home together."

"Don't tell Dad, Alice."

Alice breathed in, bracing herself. She lowered her voice, speaking with calm authority. "I have to tell your father, Kristie. I'm not going to keep this from him. He has to know."

Kristie's voice rose with anger and raw emotion. "No, he doesn't. Don't do this to me, okay!"

Alice stood up, her voice firm. "I'm going to tell him, Kristie. He's your father, and he has to know."

"Dammit!"

"Text me everything. As soon as I have a flight and time, I'll get in touch. Okay?"

There was a pause, and then Alice heard Kristie's deep sobs.

"Kristie?"

"Yes... Yes. Okay. Whatever. Come as fast as you can. I don't want to be alone."

After Alice hung up, she sagged back down onto the sofa, feeling drained. Her head dropped forward, and her shoulders bowed under the weight. She'd have to call Connie, Taylor's mother. She'd have to call Jack. She'd have to book her flight.

Her heart ached for Connie and for Taylor. Her mind

was whirling and wild. *Taylor is so young and so full of life, and he's Connie's only son. Her only child. He was just doing what all boys do; showing off for his girlfriend. Surely he'll survive.*

CHAPTER 30

December 2016

Alice sat in the window seat of the 727, gazing out as a wing dipped, allowing her to view a snowy, expanding landscape rising to distant, shadowy mountains. She turned her gaze down and saw the airport parking lot, with cars winking in bright morning sunlight. The plane was making its final approach into the Denver International Airport, after a little over four hours in the air.

The pitch change of the jet engines and the metallic sound of the lowering landing flaps made her anxious, not just because she'd never been entirely comfortable flying, but they also triggered thoughts of Kristie and her unstable, agitated state of mind; they triggered worried thoughts about Taylor. Was he still alive? Would he survive?

Alice and Kristie had spoken a little after 5 a.m., just before Alice boarded the airplane in Philadelphia. Kristie had sounded fragile and weepy.

"I haven't heard anything from the hospital. I don't know how Taylor is and it's driving me crazy. I can't come home," she'd said. "I can't face Dad. No way.

Not now and I don't know… I don't know when. I may just move out somewhere. I've got two girlfriends."

Alice kept her voice calm and steady. "Don't think so much right now, Kristie. Did you sleep?"

"Maybe a couple of hours. I was so exhausted and I couldn't shut my mind off. I just don't know what to do or think. I keep seeing Taylor laying there, looking dead, covered with blood. I tried to scream, but nothing came out. I couldn't get any sound out."

"Okay, listen. My flight lands in Denver around ten…"

Kristie cut in. "… We were having so much fun. We just wanted to get away and have fun. Was that so wrong? Was that so bad?"

Alice said, "We'll talk later."

"I'll pick you up," Kristie said. "I have our rental, so I might as well use it. There's a surcharge of twenty-five dollars a day because Taylor was only twenty and I…"

Alice interrupted. "… No, Kristie. Stay there. You're in no condition to drive. I'll get a cab. It's only about forty minutes to the resort from the airport. I'll call you when I get to Denver. Try to sleep."

Inside the airport terminal, Alice walked briskly, tugging her roller wheel suitcase, searching for the taxi stand. Her mind was still playing back yesterday's events and her conversations with Jack.

Alice had called Brenda, and she'd agreed to come over and look after things. Andrew said he'd pitch in and do whatever needed to be done, and then he'd texted Brianna and she said she'd drive over and help out.

Alice called Jack at work and delivered Kristie's news, keeping the emotion and fear from her voice. After uttering a few exasperated words, he'd hung up and started for home.

Meanwhile, Alice called Connie Barnes, a call she'd dreaded. As expected, the woman was shattered, unable to say more than a few words between cries of anxiety and grief. Alice asked if she wanted company, but she declined saying, "My sister and ex are coming. We're flying to Denver as soon as we can get a flight. My friend's here now."

When Jack arrived, he and Alice faced off in the kitchen, with the doors closed and an uncomfortable space between them. Alice's thoughts stalled, and Jack's anger was silent, but she saw it in the hard metal of his eyes. He pondered, and stewed, and fretted, allowing his mind to work on every aspect of the issue, his usual method.

Finally, he said, "Did you make the airplane reservations?"

Alice held him in her nervous eyes. "Yes... Just for me."

"Why just for you?"

"Jack, Kristie is a mess. She doesn't want to come home because she's scared to death of you."

"And she should be."

Alice sighed. "Jack, come on. Not now. I need a little time alone with her."

Jack's jaw tightened as he mulled over her words and pushed down his anger. "Look, it's an awful thing. I can't imagine what Taylor's mother must be going through, but Kristie needs to come home now. She also needs to take responsibility for her actions and that means facing me. I want her to tell me why she thinks it's okay for her to run off with some boy I have never met, without asking my permission, when she is still only eighteen years old and living under our roof."

Alice tried to detach from the turmoil. She nodded. "I agree with you, Jack. I do. But can it wait a few days until she's recovered a little from the shock of Taylor's accident? I mean... she did see the boy almost die, and he still might die. He's in a coma. That's not something she'll forget for the rest of her life."

Jack did a slow neck roll, and then massaged his forehead. "I have a God-awful headache," he said, then softened his voice. "I'm sorry for the kid, Taylor. Sorry for him and for his mother."

They let the silence linger, allowing some of the emotion to drain away, each seeking another approach to the conversation.

Jack stared beyond Alice, at the wall. "I've never known what to say to Kristie because she's so unlike me. Is it me, or does she always want to fight something, or rebel against something? She's careless and irresponsible. She wants independence, except she doesn't know what that means."

He shook his head. "The truth is, I've never known how to love her, and it just... It just beats me up inside."

Alice went to him, tenderness in her eyes. "Jack... Kristie is trying to find her way. I don't like the way she's doing it, but I understand. When I found your diary in that B&B and read it, I felt something begin to unravel inside and it scared me. I wanted to run from it. Everything I'd believed about myself, everything I'd thought I was, came crashing down and I was never the same."

Alice moved closer. "But here I am, Jack Landis. I could be wrong, but I think that's what just happened to Kristie. Things are crashing down, and I don't think she'll ever be the same."

Jack felt the magnetic pull of Alice, and he gave her a wide, loving grin. "You, my pretty wife, make me fumble my thoughts. Yes, here you are, and thank God you're here and that you found my diary."

His grin slowly faded. "But about Kristie, I hope you're right. I hope she finds herself or just grows up a little bit. I guess we'll just have to see."

They waited, searching each other's faces. Jack finally yielded to the reality. "All right, Alice, you go ahead alone, and I'll hang around here and make sure Andrew doesn't do anything crazy. So far, this Christmas season has not been very peaceful, and not so very merry."

Alice lifted on tiptoes and kissed him. "Don't give up. We have nine days. A lot can happen in nine days."

Her hair was fragrant, her skin soft, her face beautiful. Jack drew her into an embrace, holding her close. "Work your magic on Kristie, Alice. You always seem to have the right touch with her."

Alice's taxi turned into the snowplowed parking lot of the Snowcrest Ski Resort, and stopped near the two-story condo where Kristie was waiting. Alice paid the driver and stepped out into the crisp air and dazzling sunshine. The area was tucked away from the main lodge, nestled in a thick grove of snow-heavy trees, climbing hills and a sun-bright lake in the distance.

Alice whispered a little prayer and advanced, just as Kristie burst from the first-floor condo door and rushed into Alice's waiting arms.

"I'm so glad you're here," Kristie said, pressing her face into Alice's shoulder.

Inside, Kristie led Alice across the spacious living room into a well-appointed bedroom. She stood by as Alice parked her suitcase and shed her hat, gloves and coat.

"It's a beautiful place," Alice said, noticing Kristie's swollen, sad eyes. She wore stylish jeans with holes in both knees, and a burgundy sweatshirt that had SNOWCREST printed across the chest in bold, white letters.

Kristie folded her arms. "Taylor's things are still here. I talked to his mother last night and this morning. She's real bad. She tries to talk, and I try to talk, and neither one of us says much."

"Has Taylor's condition improved?"

Kristie shook her head. "No, he's the same."

Alice released a sigh. "Okay, do you have any coffee? I'm desperate."

Kristie dropped her arms. "Yeah, I can make some. It's easy. Are you hungry? We've got some things. Bread and cheese and oatmeal. Taylor likes oatmeal, go figure. Instant."

They sat at a round table with a spectacular view of the sky and snow-rich mountains. Alice ate sliced cheese and toast, and sipped the hot coffee. The food helped revive her flagging energy. She hadn't slept well the night before.

Kristie sat slumped in the chair, drained and depressed, with her head down. "How's Dad? I mean, what did he say... You know, I thought he would come anyway, because... well, because he gets all, I don't know, all freaked out."

"He is freaked out," Alice said. "He was going to come, but I talked him out of it."

Kristie looked up, trying to read Alice's mood. "You blame me for all this, don't you?"

"Blame you for what? For Taylor's accident because he was showing off? Of course I don't blame you. I do think you were selfish and thoughtless for not asking us before you left with him, but..." Alice let the rest of the sentence drop.

Kristie swung off the chair and stood beside it, her breathing staggered, her hands on her hips. "Don't do that, okay? I can't hear this right now. What do you want me to say? I'm sorry? Well, I am sorry, but don't punish me with your bullshit words."

"Okay, then don't ask me questions you don't want to hear the answers to."

A slow burn formed in Kristie's eyes. "I thought you were here to be my friend."

"I'm here because I love you and I want to help you through this. And I'm also here because you and I have always been honest and open with each other. I'm not your real mother and I never will be, but I love you with all my heart, as if you were my daughter, and I want you to learn from this. I want you to think long and hard about how your decisions affect other people."

Alice rose and went to Kristie, who was staring down at the floor. "Kristie… your father and I love you deeply." Alice's voice held compassion. "Yes, you're nearly all grown up, but all that means is that now you get the privilege to consider other people's feelings and not just your own. You now get the opportunity to show some responsibility to those who care about you and love you."

Kristie didn't look up.

"Your father hardly slept last night. He's been worried sick about you. He worked in the basement until dawn. When I left for the airport, he told me something. He said that when you were a baby and he first held you in his arms, he thought you were the greatest miracle, the best thing that had ever happened to him. He said you were a beautiful, feisty little thing, and he loved you so much that he ached with it. He still aches with love for you."

Kristie made a gulping sob and leaned her head into Alice's chest. She wept while Alice caressed her hair, while the quiet grew, and the morning lengthened, and the sun bathed them.

After Alice had put Kristie to bed, she leaned and kissed her on the forehead. "You sleep now. We'll stay here as long as you need to stay; until you get your balance back, and then we'll go home. We'll go home and celebrate Christmas."

CHAPTER 31

December 1944

In Los Angeles on Wednesday morning, December 27, Alice and Tom walked briskly through the bustling morning crowds, edging along the sidewalk en route to the courthouse for their civil wedding. It was overcast, and a fine mist made the day humid, vague and out of focus. The traffic was heavy, horns blared and tempers were short.

Tom said, "It's first come, first serve, so hopefully we'll be one of the first couples."

"Do you have our papers?" Alice asked, her high heels clicking across the sidewalk, her eyes moving and nervous.

"Yes... Right here in my coat pocket. I've checked three times."

"And you have the ring?"

Tom dug into his pocket and felt the square jewelry box. "Yes. Got it. I have everything. Like I said yesterday, the City Clerk said we can hire a witness. He said some are always loitering about. They have to sign the marriage license, though. I told you that already, didn't I? I guess I'm a little jumpy."

"But it does seem odd to have a perfect stranger sign our marriage license."

Tom glanced at her, tension making his face hot. "But you still want to go through with it, don't you, Alice?"

"Of course, Tom. Yes."

Tom pointed. "There's the courthouse, just ahead."

He linked her arm into his. "Let's go."

As they approached the flights of ascending stairs, a soiled man in tattered clothes and a crumpled hat glared at them as if they were enemies. With a cigarette cupped in his hand, he watched them mount the stairs with a sullen, feral expression.

"You'll see," the man muttered, gruffly. "You'll see what happens to you. You threw yourself at that soldier, didn't you, sister? Well, let me tell you something… May the gates of hell open wide and swallow you both up. That's what I say to you both."

Tom turned sharply, strafing the man with his eyes. He opened his mouth to yell at him, just as the man cackled like a crazy witch, his eyes wide and filled with madness.

Seeing it was futile, Tom took Alice's arm as he led her up the flight of seemingly never-ending stairs. Panting for breath, they passed the massive columns and entered the soaring marble courthouse lobby, busy with people scurrying about in all directions. Feeling pressure mount, they rushed by a majestic Christmas tree and searched for the elevators.

With a forceful determination, Tom nudged them into a cramped elevator, flashing Alice a reassuring smile. They exited onto the sixth floor, hurried down the corridor and saw a long line.

"That can't be the room, can it, Tom?" Alice asked, worried. "It's a long line."

"No, that's probably for something else."

They hustled ahead past the line and stopped at the open door. They peered inside. The room was spacious, and it was packed full; every chair and bench were occupied. They glanced up at the sign above the door that read **Office of the City Clerk: Marriage Bureau**.

Their eyes expanded on the wide, crowded room, bloated with couples holding hands, or whispering confidences or glancing about anxiously.

Alice's face fell when she realized that the line they saw *was* the marriage line—a long line of waiting couples stretching back thirty-feet, outside into the hallway. More than half of those were impatient soldiers with their fidgety, future brides.

"Holy smoke," Tom said, pushing his cap back off his forehead. "I didn't figure it would be this crowded. Who would have thought that so many people wanted to get married this early in the morning."

"Didn't they give you a waiting number, Tom? Something?"

"No... The man said first-come first-serve, until they close at five p.m."

Alice blew out a breath. "Okay, well, let's get into that line before it gets any longer."

They joined the others, both masking disappointment and worry. Tom tapped a sailor on the shoulder and asked if he was in line to get married. The sailor nodded, sizing him up.

"Marine, huh?"

"Yeah. So are you getting married?" Tom asked.

The sailor's gum-chewing, toothy redheaded girlfriend said, "You betcha, Marine." Then she winked at her sailor. "You got lots of time to wait and sweat it out, right, Davy?" she said, with a laugh, and a sharp elbow to his ribs.

He backed away, grabbing his side, his face pinched in pain. "Hey, watch it, baby. That hurt."

She rolled her eyes. "Oh, brother. *That* hurt? Well, you ain't exactly Popeye, are you?"

"And you ain't no Betty Grable neither, doll."

An argument ensued.

Tom and Alice took a step back and unbuttoned their coats. Alice stood on tiptoes looking ahead, frowning, dispirited by the line that seemed to extend for miles. Her new heels pinched her toes, and she wasn't happy about how her new victory rolls hairdo had wilted in the rain and humidity.

But she'd been thrilled to find a pair of real nylons, a near impossibility because of the war, and even though she'd paid an exorbitant price for them, they were worth every cent, giving her a feeling of sophistication and confidence.

Alice hadn't chosen a white wedding dress. She'd save that for when she and Tom were married in a church. Being close to Hollywood, she'd chosen what she considered to be a Hollywood glamor dress: a muted salmon pink crepe with beaded trim and fox fur cuffs. She'd purchased her black-veiled, elegant and luxurious feather mesh hat at Castelli's Lady's Fashions on Hollywood and Vine.

Tom looked at her lovingly. "You're the prettiest girl in the place."

"And you are the handsomest soldier."

He glanced about apologetically. "Sorry about the long line. I just didn't figure this. Maybe we should have taken that guy's offer at the hotel, to get married at the chapel at Forest Lawn."

"No," Alice said. "I don't want us to get married in a

cemetery... especially not on a cloudy, rainy day like this."

Just then, a man came striding down the hall in a dark, pinstriped suit. He had a brawny build, weathered face, curly hair and an authoritative, resonant voice. "All right now, listen up. Any couple here that don't have all their paperwork can't get married. If you don't have your marriage license in hand, before your ceremony, you will not be married. So don't wait in this line. Go downstairs to the third floor. Make sure you have your blood test results, proof of citizenship, proof of former marriages, annulments, divorces, etc. Finally, if for some reason you decide to leave and not get married today, take note that in Los Angeles county, your marriage license expires after ninety days. Soldiers shipping out, keep that in mind."

Alice and Tom exchanged nervous glances.

"It's not exactly what I thought it would be," Tom said.

Alice kept up a brave, smiling front. "It's not so bad. It won't take long." She lowered her chin and inhaled the sweet scent of her pink orchid corsage. "Thanks again for this, Tom. I love it."

The line crawled, the hallway became sweltering from steam heat and cigarette smoke, and everyone was growing irritable and impatient.

An eternity later, when they were inside the main room and only a few couples away from the private, enclosed chapel where the ceremonies were conducted, Tom nodded Alice a smile. "It won't be long now."

Alice glanced about. A soldier, three couples up, smoked fretfully, while the round-faced girl beside him wept into a hankie.

Suddenly, from inside the chapel, they heard a cry of anguish. Bursting from the door came a young woman sobbing audibly, rushing across the room and out into the hallway in blundering, embarrassed flight. Seconds later, a sailor appeared, distressed. He ran after her, shouting her name. "Betsy! Come back, Betsy."

The entire line shrank back toward the wall, some making sarcastic remarks, some laughing to break the tension.

"Gee... I wonder what happened," Alice said, troubled, adjusting her corsage.

Tom kept his eyes ahead, willing the line to move. "Cold feet, I guess."

Minutes later, a blonde goddess left the chapel, her arm linked in the arm of a tall Army captain. His head was thrown back proudly, his white, pearly teeth showing. She was beaming, walking with a slow, floaty assurance.

Still the line dragged with mumbling complaints, whispering arguments and a lot of head-scratching and cursing.

Just when the shine was going out of the day, a plain woman in her middle thirties left the chapel, holding the hand of a cute, pudgy girl of about eight. The little girl held the strings of two balloons that floated behind her, one red, the other white. A timid, older man, gray at the temples, walked behind, his expression frosty and introverted. As the mother strolled by, the little girl lifted her eyes up to Alice. She stopped, halting her mother.

"Hello..." the little girl said.

Alice leaned over, smiling. "Hello."

The man stopped short, looking confused.

The little girl reached out and handed Alice the white balloon string. "I like your hat. I like the veil and the feathers."

"Thank you," Alice said, touched. "But I can't take your balloon."

The little girl frowned. "Why not? I have one. Take it."

Alice did so, reluctantly, with a tender smile. "Thank you. Thank you very much."

The little girl's mother glanced back with a fleeting, tired grin. "Come on, Mary, we have to go now."

When it was finally their turn, Alice and Tom were waved into the room with stout authority and a dismissive glance from a no-nonsense matron.

The little chapel displayed a hanging cross, a stained-glass window, and a trellis featuring climbing fake roses. The witness was an elderly woman with a kindly smile, a flat black hat, and a long, black dress in the style of the early 1900s. But she stood beside the couple, holding the string of the white balloon, with an expression of professional pride and solemn reverence.

The presiding Justice of the Peace wore a dark suit, dingy white shirt, and crooked, black string tie. He was balding, pale and thin, and he conducted the ceremony with the abrupt efficiency of a tired expert.

Alice's legs felt rubbery and her insides trembled. Her voice broke and her eyes turned moist when she said, "... For richer, for poorer, in sickness and in health, to love and to cherish, till death us do part, according to God's holy law, and this is my solemn vow."

Tom kept his worshipful eyes on Alice, ignoring the uninspired ceremony and the bored faces. When he slipped the ring onto Alice's finger, he whispered, "I love you."

When it was over, Alice noticed that a certain tension left Tom's face and posture. He leaned toward her ear and whispered, so only she could hear, "I'm sorry for all this. When I get back, we're going to have a real wedding, in a church, with a real minister and not an undertaker."

Alice giggled in her hand, squeezing his arm. Happiness rose from the bottom of her soul and floated up, blushing her cheeks, generating a vivid, blissful smile. "I don't care, Tom. I love you. I'm your wife now."

Before this day, Tom's many past sorrows had lodged in his heart. They'd made him rigid, lonely and somber; they'd been a kept secret, maybe even a proud secret. But now he was married to Alice, the love of his life. As he held her in his arms, inhaling the sweet scent of her, thankful for her goodness and for her love of him, there was a thawing of those sorrows, like ice being melted by the sun. There was a lightness in his head and heart that he'd never known, and he was changed, and he was set free and he was, finally, happy.

The Justice of the Peace said, flatly. "You may kiss the bride. And Merry Christmas..." He cleared his throat and corrected his error. "Excuse me, I mean Happy New Year."

Their kiss was long and sweet. They seemed to glide from the chapel and float down the hallway to the elevators, through the vast lobby and out into the world, a new world, filled with mist and fog, but with the bright, sunny promise of a glorious life together.

CHAPTER 32

December 1944

Alice and Tom spent their honeymoon at a two-bedroom beach bungalow near the ocean in Santa Barbara. It was painted a cheerful white and yellow and had plenty of windows, with romantic views of the sea and rolling dunes.

Their lazy, laughing days were spent sleeping late, swimming, sunbathing, or setting sail in a blue and white sailing dinghy Tom had rented from a marina close by. Having learned to sail on a lake near the orphanage, Tom handled the little boat with easy precision, nudging it along the shoreline, the single sail bending into the wind.

Tom was all smiles, filled with a boyish delight as he observed Alice's lovely face upturned to the sun and rushing wind. Her hair caught the breeze, and the glittering spray sparked her newly tanned skin as she gazed out into the lemon-blue magic of the day.

They gave up a day to search for an apartment for Alice. Tom wanted her safely settled before he returned to Camp Pendleton, fifteen miles north of San Diego. It was a cloudy day, and, as it turned out, a day of surprises. It was also a subdued day, on which both avoided any conversation about their looming separation, or Alice's plan to seek employment at Consolidated-Vultee Aircraft in San Diego.

Their apartment search was a bust. Wartime San Diego was a boomtown and existing housing was filled to capacity. Many families slept in their cars or in all-night cinemas, garages, barracks, or tents. Some families were even forced to sleep in abandoned streetcars. Three and four people lived in one-room apartments, and most were government workers, or those who worked in restaurants, nightclubs, and bars.

Alice and Tom eventually found themselves in Horton Plaza, at Fourth and Broadway, the busy center of the lively, hustling Navy town. Due to gas rationing, there were few automobiles, but the streetcar and bus lines from throughout the city all converged at the Plaza.

After speaking to soldiers and plant defense workers, they learned that the Plaza was always busy, as people on swing shifts, graveyard shifts, and day shifts came and went at all hours. But, more importantly, people touched base there, met there and said goodbye there. As one soldier from New York City said, "It's like a sunny, cleaner Grand Central Station."

Alice noticed that the dress code was more rigid. Women's dresses were hemmed well below the knee, girls wore bobby sox, and women war workers were dressed in unfamiliar work pants. Alice also noted the hairstyles: the pompadour and curled bangs, two of the more popular coiffures she'd seen in Chicago.

It was toward late afternoon, when their spirits were low and energy flagging, that they got a break. A well-dressed woman in her late 20s, wearing baggy stockings, had overheard them talking to a man about finding a place to live. Alice spotted the baggy stockings right away. It was a wartime inconvenience when only rayon hosiery was available, and once it stretched out, it stayed stretched.

The woman drifted over. She was tall and willowy, with luscious blonde hair and curled bangs. Her face portrayed a soft dignity, her lips were full and red, her body all curves, her eyes accented and large.

"Excuse me," she said in a small voice. "I couldn't help overhearing. Are you looking for a place to stay?"

Tom looked the woman over, not with hungry eyes, but with the suspicious eyes of a man not wanting to be swindled. He observed a smooth sophistication, but a sad, world-weariness, similar to the expressions of war widows he'd seen when he was in the hospital.

Alice observed the woman with mild apprehension. Dressed as she was in a stylish winter coat, dazzling earrings and new high-heeled shoes, it was obvious she didn't work in a war plant.

"Yes... I'm looking for a place," Alice answered, tentatively.

"For only you, or will it be the two of you?"

"Just me. Tom has to return to his base."

The woman moistened her lips before she spoke, and then she looked skyward. "I detest a cloudy day. It makes me feel blue." And then her melancholy eyes settled on Alice. "I have a room. My... well, my roommate left this morning. She ran off and married a sailor, God help her. Anyway, it's a large room with three windows. You'd have access to the kitchen and the living room, which is also rather spacious. I work nights, so you'd have the place to yourself if you work the day shift."

Alice gave Tom a side-glance.

"What's your name?" Tom asked.

The woman slid her eyes toward him, looking him up

and down, and it wasn't clear what she was thinking. "My brother was a Marine. He was killed at the Battle of Tarawa in November 1943."

Tom and Alice lowered their gazes.

"I'm sorry," Alice said.

"So am I. He was a good brother. We got along well, and I loved him. Anyway, my name is Judith Bain. Would you like the room? If not, I can rent it in a heartbeat. But you probably know that; I can tell you've been looking for hours. That look is common around here."

Alice was conflicted. Tom unsure.

"Where is it?" Tom asked.

"Five blocks from here, on Defender Street. The street is quiet enough and the neighbors are older, and not so friendly, which suits me just fine."

"Could we go see it?"

"No time for that. I have errands to run and then I have to go to work. I'm afraid it's one of those take-it-or-leave-it deals."

Tom gave Judith a dubious glance.

"I'll take it," Alice said.

Early morning on January 3, 1945, Tom packed his duffel bag and loaded it into the trunk of the car, along with Alice's two suitcases. She lingered in the bungalow doorway, passing a final glance at the place before joining Tom, ducking into the passenger seat and closing the door.

Tom drove into town and parked the car near The Bomber Cafe at 849 Fourth Avenue, close to where he would board a troop bus that would take him to Camp Pendleton.

They ate breakfast, mostly in a somber silence. Finally, just to fill the pulsing gap, Alice said, "Have you been to Camp Pendleton?"

"Yes."

"What's it like?"

"Pretty much like any war base, except that it has a long stretch of ocean beach they use for amphibious training. The terrain inland is good for battalion-sized infantry maneuvers, tank maneuvers, and artillery ranges. I'm sure all that sounds boring to you."

Alice couldn't meet his eyes. "The doctors will examine you, won't they? I mean, they won't let you go back to war if you're not ready, will they?"

His smile was mild. "Don't worry, Alice. I'll pass. I'm feeling better than ever, thanks to you."

Alice felt the gloom rise in her. At the next booth, she saw a man snap out a newspaper. She couldn't help but see the headlines, as he'd carefully folded over the front page.

27 MORE AXIS PLANES DOWNED OFF TUNISIA

Below that, heading a second column, was another, smaller headline.

SINGLE MEN FIRST IN NEW DRAFT ORDER

And then the tears came. Alice reached into her purse for a handkerchief and touched the corners of her eyes.

"I'm sorry, Tom, I promised I wouldn't do this. I just hate this war so much."

"It's all right, Alice."

She wiped her eyes while he drained the last of his coffee, then glanced at his watch. "It's almost that time."

Alice dropped into despair, refusing to look at him.

"Hey, cheer up, Alice. Look at me. Smile. You're about to start a new adventure."

She looked at him, but she didn't smile. "An adventure without you."

"I'll be back before you know it. Anyway, good luck with the new apartment... and with Judith. You've got the key, right?"

"Yes, I have it."

"She's a bit mysterious, that one," Tom said. "When you get the chance, maybe you should look around for another place."

"I'll be okay. Don't worry about me. Anyway, I'll be busy. I'm going to apply for that job tomorrow. It's a six-day work week, so if I get it, I won't be spending much time in that apartment."

"And your money is safely in the bank. That's a load off my mind."

"Don't worry so much, Tom."

Tom changed the subject. "With all the gas rationing, you won't be able to drive much. It's just as well. I think we pretty much finished the old girl off on Route 66."

Outside, in glorious sunshine and a salty breeze, she walked him to Horton Plaza where the bus waited. With a tight chest, tight throat and shiny, wet eyes, Alice kissed Tom, and they held the kiss. When they broke, he pressed her close to him.

"Write me every day, and I'll do the same. Don't worry about me. I'm going to make it. I'm going to survive this damned war and come back to you. We're going to have a wonderful life together, Alice. Believe it."

When the bus pulled away, the tears pumped from her, and she stood staring into the blurring distance long after the bus had drifted out of sight. And then, all of Alice's iron gallantry fell away and she let the tears flow.

She drove to her new home, apprehensive, then relieved when she found the place was comfortable-looking and clean. Judith had left a note on the door of her room, along with towels and sheets. The room was sparsely furnished, but it did have a desk and chair where she could write to Tom.

Alice made up her bed and unpacked her suitcase, quickly filling the small closet and the four-drawer bureau. She sat on the bed, trying to decide what to do next. Food. She had to have food, so she forced herself back onto the street and found the nearest grocery store. She bought what she could without a ration book, including eggs, bread, coffee and powdered milk.

That night, she lay in her bed, bleak and suffering. How could she endure the next few months knowing Tom was returning to combat? She heard her heart thrumming, felt it breaking, wanting Tom beside her.

Just before dawn, Judith entered the apartment, but Alice didn't get up. Tears held in her eyes and, finally, at first light, all thought fell away into the hope that she had gotten pregnant. Just before she dropped off to sleep, her whispering prayers filled the room.

"Please… let me be pregnant."

If Tom were killed, at least she'd have his baby.

CHAPTER 33

December 2016

"How is she?" Jack asked, pacing the kitchen, cell phone in hand.

Alice was at the Snowcrest Ski Resort, standing in a pool of afternoon sunlight in the condo living room. She was staring out the window at a vast snow-covered mountain, the ski trails and ski lifts miniature and distant, but visible.

"She's asleep. Finally. I got her to eat some and then we talked for a long time. I may have been a bit hard on her. I wish you were here."

"I'm sure whatever you said was right. You know she loves and admires you."

"Thanks for that. It hasn't been easy. I still wish you were here."

"And I wish you were here. But she's better? I mean, she's feeling better about things, if that's the word?"

"I think so. It will take time. Hopefully, she'll be asleep for a while. Sleep will help."

"When do you think you'll come home?"

"Tomorrow, I hope."

Alice heard Jack sigh into his phone. "Did she say anything about me?"

"Yes, she did."

"I'm afraid to hear it," he said.

"It's something the two of you have to work out. You need to sit down and have a face-to-face talk."

"I want to. She's never around or she... I don't know, she won't talk about things."

"I hate to say it, but she still thinks about her mother, and she misses her. And as we've said before, Kristie's like her, unpredictable, moody and artistic. And I'm going to be frank... She still feels like you helped drive Darla away."

Jack's voice took on an edge. "That's just not true, and she knows it. Darla left *us*. I didn't want her to go. I did everything I could to keep her with us and not run out on the kids. Kristie knows that. We've talked about it."

"Most of her knows. Some of her is still trying to work it out and come to some truth about it. She told me she wants to take a trip; she called it a "journal writing/photography trip," to find where her mother lived. She wants to interview people who knew her, and who knew the man she married. Her husband was a famous painter."

"Yes, I know he was. And I'm sure there's more," Jack said, wearily.

"Yes. She wants to document every memory, emotion and detail about her mother before she forgets, and then she wants to write a book about it, including photos, and then feature parts of her mother's novel, *Improvisations*."

"What did you say?"

"I told her I thought it was a good idea. I told her that when it's finished, if it feels right to her, she should try to publish it. Maybe the same publisher who published Darla's novel would publish it."

"Okay, well, it doesn't surprise me... That, no doubt, will be her next wild adventure. Well, do you know what? Maybe she should. Maybe it would do her good and maybe it would do me good, too."

Alice hesitated.

Again, Jack sighed into the phone. "You're hesitating. There's even more, isn't there?"

"Yes... She wants to find a psychic, a medium, and try to talk to her mother."

"God help me," Jack said, despair in his voice.

"But she loves you, Jack. She told me she loves you, but that you scare her sometimes."

"I scare *her*? She scares *me*! I never know what she's going to do next."

"Like I said, you two have to work it out and have as many heart-to-hearts as it takes to clear the air. I suspect you'll be having these kinds of conversations with her for many years to come, probably even when we're both old and gray and rocking in our chairs out on the back porch."

"All right, look, let's change the subject. How is Taylor? Have you heard from Connie Barnes?"

"No... Kristie said they talked, but it was sad talk with a lot of tears. He's still in intensive care and in a coma."

"Poor woman," Jack said. "It's such a tragic accident, and so pointless. Just a kid showing off."

"I can't imagine what Connie must be going through, especially during Christmas. How are you?"

"I'm fine."

"Did you sleep some?"

"Some."

"And Andrew? How is he?"

"He's been helping out all day, and Brianna came over.

She's quite a young woman. Very mature, and she's good for Andrew, I think. I know he's only sixteen, but, I don't know, they seem well suited to each other. Comfortable, if you know what I mean. Do you know anything about her family?"

"Just what you know. Have you talked to her?"

"Not much. It's been a bit hectic."

"How are the guests?"

"They seem fine. I think we've all managed to keep the hectic energy away from them. They've placed some of their Christmas presents under the tree and they're raving about Brenda's hot chocolate and cookies, especially those sugar cookies with the red sprinkles. They're a real hit and, of course, Brenda is all smiles."

"So, she's feeling okay? No more cold?"

"Nothing wrong with Brenda, and she deserves whatever it is you're paying her."

"Probably not enough, but I'll give her a good Christmas bonus."

After a brief silence, Jack said, "Alice, I reread Alice's diary again last night when I couldn't sleep."

"I thought you were in the basement, working."

"Some of the time, but I couldn't do much. I was afraid I'd wake up the house. Anyway, I found something in the diary that I didn't focus on the first time. To be honest, I kind of skimmed the thing. Anyway, do you remember the part where Charles said his grandfather knew two men who'd fought in the Civil War, and how they're buried on the meadow under the trees?"

"Yeah, I remember."

"I had a thought."

"About?"

"In 1944, Charles said their gravestones were hard to find. That's over... what, about seventy years ago? He also said that most people didn't remember that the graves are there."

"What are you getting at?"

"Just this: if those graves are there, and maybe more... well. In other words, if there is a small Civil War cemetery up there under those trees, I think we have a way of stopping Morningside Development."

Alice's voice rose in excitement. "Are you serious?"

"Very. I put a call into the City Council and I'm waiting to hear back."

"What can they do?"

"They can check the County Genealogical Society records for death records. But here's the other thing. I went up there this morning and poked around with a shovel. After about twenty minutes of digging around, very carefully, I found one broken headstone, but the dates on it were eroded away. I got excited, and I poked around some more, again being very careful not to damage anything. About fifteen minutes later, I found what I'm pretty sure are two sunken graves. I thought, why don't people know these graves are here? How could it be? The answer in my head said, because no one is around any longer who remembers them or cares about them."

"Jack... I am very, very, even crazy excited. Go on."

"Okay, I'm not positive, but I'm eighty percent sure that those graves are from a long time ago. Some animal has recently been nesting in one of them. Professionals from Penn State or some historical society might be able to uncover more graves, which would indicate multiple burials in the same area."

Alice dropped into the nearest chair. "This is unbelievable, Jack. Just unbelievable. Can we really stop those developers?"

"Maybe... If it's an historical site, and if, just if, there's someone buried in that little plot of ground who's famous or, at the very least, locally well-known, then we might have a chance of getting the county to preserve it as an historical cemetery. From there we..."

Alice shot up, interrupting. "... Then we've got them! They won't be able to build anything up there—certainly not a road or a bunch of cheap houses. Jack, you're wonderful. I would have never thought about that."

"I should have thought about it the first time I read that diary. I think I was so surprised by finding it, and then discovering it was written by a woman with your name, that I just wasn't thinking straight. If there are graves up there, then all I have to do is tell the local paper. They'll take it from there. It will hit the internet and that will do it."

Alice paced in an excited circle, switching her cell phone from her right ear to her left. "I can see the headlines, Jack. Are you ready? Civil War Cemetery Lost, Now Found."

"I like it, Alice. I like it a lot."

CHAPTER 34

January 1945

As she had confidently predicted, Mrs. Alice Ferrell Lawson was swiftly hired by Consolidated-Vultee Aircraft as a secretary to two engineers. They were responsible for the continued development of the four-engine bomber, the B-24 Liberator, as well as the PBY, a maritime patrol bomber and search and rescue seaplane.

On her first day of work, Monday, January 22, 1945, Alice joined a line inside a high security fence topped with razor wire, and was cleared by cold-eyed, granite-jawed security officers. She walked with other employees beneath a large camouflage net to Plant Number Two. In a wonder, Alice noticed that camouflage nets also covered Pacific Highway, adjacent to the buildings of Consolidated, and that the entire area of Lindbergh Field, Consolidated Aircraft, and Pacific Highway were camouflage painted so that they appeared to be part of a town, with streets and houses.

Alice was assigned to the first shift, 8 a.m. to 5 p.m., and she quickly found herself inundated by fervent energy, sober faces, and urgent pressure. The work was intense and demanding but ultimately rewarding.

For the first time in her life, Alice was a part of something larger than herself, dedicated to a life-and-death struggle for the very soul and survival of the United States and the world. She was working with a focused and committed family of men and women, all laboring with one goal in mind and a common purpose: to win the war. And to her, the war was personal. She was working to save her husband's life and the lives of other men and women like him.

Alice worked six days a week, often missing lunch, but she was seldom fatigued. Each morning she awakened, resolved and adrenalized to be with her work family, burning with patriotism and enthusiasm.

Judith Bain had been invaluable helping Alice adjust to her new life in a thriving war city. On note paper, Judith had jotted down the names and locations of the best and the cheapest restaurants, and where to shop for clothes and food. She'd also informed Alice where she could obtain ration stamp books and small red and blue cardboard tokens that were used to control the sale of scarce foods such as sugar, cheese, canned fish, meat and fats.

Their conflicting schedules, and Alice's long work hours, had prevented the ladies from getting fully acquainted. They'd only had time for passing polite conversation and the usual war news. Alice didn't know where Judith worked or what she did, and she hadn't volunteered any information.

Alice spent most of her free time washing clothes, shopping, cleaning and writing letters to Tom. One night when she couldn't sleep, she'd taken a walk in a misty rain, talking to Tom as if he were walking beside her. The damp pavement gleamed under the street lamps, and she recalled a rainy night they'd spent in Elk City, Oklahoma, just off Route 66. They'd sauntered happily in a similar light rain, sharing stories about their pasts and dreaming about the future, after the war.

And then Alice had ached for him. A knot of fear in her gut had sent her rushing to a corner church; she hadn't noticed the denomination. It was closed, of course, but she'd stood by the door with a bowed head, whispering a desperate prayer to God that He save Tom from harm and bring him back to her.

One evening in late January, Judith didn't go to work, and when Alice returned home, she found her sitting on the couch staring into space. To Alice's surprise, Judith turned about and said, "Hello, there, roommate, how about I buy us both some dinner?"

During the day, the Overleaf Café was a lunch counter in the lobby of a downtown building. At night, it was transformed into a modest restaurant, filled with soldiers and their girls, with officers on leave and with a few elderly people who sought the comfort of others and the reasonable menu prices.

The café was busy, but as Alice and Judith entered, they swiftly swooped down to a table that had just been vacated by two sailors. The sailors were all smiling delight as they held the chairs for the girls and then lingered, grinning. One asked if they could join them.

With a melting smile, Judith said, "I'm afraid our Captain husbands wouldn't approve. Take care of yourselves out there on the seas, sailors, and come back to your hometown sweethearts."

The sailors trudged away, reluctant and disappointed.

Judith ordered a whiskey and soda. "I need this," she said to the overweight middle-aged waiter. Alice asked for a bottle of Coke with extra ice.

They studied the menus in silence, with the hum of conversation all around them, the sound of clattering dishes and a juke-box playing *So Long Pal* by Al Dexter.

It was obvious that Judith had something to say. Alice had seen her tense expression and empty smile at the apartment, when she'd invited Alice to dinner. Alice hoped she wasn't going to ask her to move out.

The kale soup was ten cents, the tuna sandwich twenty-five cents, the meat loaf and chicken dinners forty cents, and the Spam and turkey sandwiches twenty cents. Coke and coffee were a nickel.

Judith ordered the meat loaf dinner and Alice, chicken. As she sipped her whiskey, Judith's pretty eyes filled with a gentle sadness. She placed her elbows on the table, folded her hands, and rested her chin on them as she peered into Alice's eyes.

"Has he shipped out yet?"

"You mean Tom?"

"Yes, I mean your handsome Marine, Tom."

Alice looked down. "Soon... I got a letter today. When we were on our honeymoon, we established a kind of code, so that I'd know when he was going... You know, so the censors wouldn't mark it out. He's shipping out next week."

"He's quite..." Judith moved her eyes, trying to come up with the right word. "Mysterious, I think is the word."

Alice smiled. "Mysterious?"

"Yes. He has the air of a tragic romantic. Like in my favorite novel, *Women in Love*, by D. H. Lawrence."

"I don't like the sound of that, tragic romantic."

"Have you read it?"

"No... And now, I don't think I will," Alice said.

"Don't worry, Alice. The tragic romantics always survive. Well, most of the time, anyway. By tragic I mean, I can see he's had a lot of sadness in his life, but he doesn't let it get him down. He's a hero, and he's a handsome hero."

Alice didn't want to talk about it. "Yes, I think he's handsome. And, yes, he hasn't had an easy life. I'd give anything if he didn't have to go back to that awful war. He's done enough. Somebody else should have to go."

Judith studied her. "And you're pretty, Alice, and it's easy to see that he adores you, and is protective of you. How nice. How rare. You're suited for each other. I could see that from the first. That's why I stepped over and invited you to take the room. Since I was a little girl, I've had a sort of sixth sense about things... about people. My grandmother thought I was a little witch. Of course, I thought she was a witch, too, so we didn't get along so well."

Judith tried to smile, but her mouth wouldn't hold it. Alice noted a sudden shift in her expression, as if a painful thought slid in. Judith lifted her head, not pulling her now damp eyes from Alice. Her eyes were filling with tears, and when she spoke, there was pain in her voice.

"Okay, so maybe I don't have a sixth sense about men. I'm pregnant, Alice. What a fat-head I am. Happy New Year."

Judith's declaration was so abrupt that Alice froze in her chair. She had reached for her glass of Coke, but her hand stopped, and as she replaced the glass, she swallowed. The words Alice was going to say were all wrong; she was going to say, "Are you married?" By the time she'd discarded those words, trying to form new ones, Judith spoke again.

"I've known for a while. I knew when I met you. I knew I could trust you, Alice. You have a genuine kindness about you. You're one of the gentle folk, I think. Oh, I don't mean you don't have strength, you do, but mostly you let your... shall I say, your good heart and your woman's intuition guide you."

Again, Alice was lost for words. Judith was one of the most elegant and sophisticated women she'd ever met, and one of the most inscrutable.

Judith ran a finger along her lower lip as she fell into thought. "I met him on a dark, blue night, with a timid light dripping from the moon, making a golden path across the ocean. How romantic, isn't it, Alice? That's from a poem my brother wrote a year before he was killed in this... this terrible war. He was a good writer. He was working on a novel. Why does God kill off the good people, Alice, and keep the wretched ones alive, like me?"

"Don't say that, Judith," Alice said, quickly. "Don't put yourself down like that."

Judith didn't lift a finger; it took too much energy. "I'm just feeling sorry for myself, and for my wonderful brother."

Judith presented a wide, meaningless grin. "I didn't really meet the father of my child like that, Alice. I said that to pretty it up, but there's no prettying it up. I'm a dancer at a club called the Cat's Whiskers, a quaint little club near Balboa Park, where sailors gawk, whistle and pant, and toss money. It's a place where older men, not in the military, escape from their wives and drop by for a couple of drinks and a proposition to the leggy sing-er/dancer. Not that my singing is any good. Frankly, I stink as a singer, but I'm a good dancer."

Judith fixed Alice with a hard stare. "I don't believe I told you any of this, did I?"

Alice lowered her chin and shook her head.

"Well, I have good legs, hair that curls all by itself, good cheek bones and a fair body. What else can a girl ask for? But my hips are a bit too wide. I suppose God wanted me to bear children, didn't he? And now I'm going to see how all that goes."

Alice struggled to find good words, but her mind was a muddle. To her disappointment, her first thought had not been, "Oh, Judith, I'm so sorry this happened to you." No, her first thought had been, "Judith, *I'm* the one who should be pregnant. I'm married and we tried. I'm *not* pregnant. It's not fair."

Judith continued. "And to top it off, the man is a lawyer, he's married with two kids, and he's a rat. Hey, do you know what? I could be one of those low-down dames you see in the movies, like Joan Crawford or Barbara Stanwyck or, I don't know. So here I am. Dancer falls for rat, who leaves her flat when he finds out dancer is going to have his baby. Do you know what he said? 'No, baby. I'm not the father and you and I know it. I know I'm not the only man you've been fooling around with.'"

Alice looked on in stunned outrage as the air seemed to go out of Judith. She slumped, looking small and dispirited.

Judith continued, her voice a deep, weary contralto. "I was a good girl, Alice. A good girl from Des Moines, Iowa, who wanted to meet a nice guy, get married and have kids. How did this happen? How did I wind up here like this?"

Compassion compelled Alice to speak. "I can help, Judith."

Judith shook her head. "No, you can't. Nobody can."

Alice leaned forward. "I *can* help, and I *will* help. We'll figure it out together."

Judith glanced up, her eyes bitter. "What you mean to say is you can help me find a doctor who won't butcher me up."

Judith's stinging words shook Alice. "No, Judith. Not that."

"Yes that, and I can do that. I have to. It's either that, or I take a powder and leave this…" she made a sweeping gesture with her hand. "This… crazy world."

And then Judith was on her feet. Without another word, she swung around and marched off, leaving Alice alone in a startled silence.

A minute later, the waiter brought their dinners, and Alice asked for the bill. Perplexed, the waiter started to speak, but stopped when he saw Alice's bold eyes and trembling hands. On a blue notepad, he scribbled out the total, tore off the page and handed it to her. She paid, left a tip, and hurried out of the café.

Outside, she searched left and right. Judith was standing alone in the shadow of the Hollywood Theater, weeping into her hand. Alice hurried over, instinctively wrapping an arm around Judith's shoulders, drawing her in, her voice low with comfort. "We're going to work it out, Judith. You'll see."

Judith struggled to speak through a quivering voice and streaming tears. "See this theater? I was going to go to Hollywood and be a big star. That's where my mother thinks I am. In Hollywood. I told her I'm making pictures, small parts. Daddy said I didn't have what it takes. Damn him, I guess he's right, isn't he? But I'm not a tramp, Alice. I'm not. I shouldn't have fallen for that married rat, and I'm sorry, but I'm not a tramp."

Alice held her close. "Come on, let's go home. Let's go home and have a good cry. Then you'll sleep for as long as you can, and I'll make us a pie or something. My Aunt Sally used to say that the world looks better when you bake a pie. Everything will look better in the morning and then we'll come up with something."

Judith blinked through tears. "I'm supposed to be at work, dancing for the sailors."

"You can take a night off."

"They'll fire me."

"Fine, let them. I'll get you a job at the war plant. They'll love you. Come on, let's go."

They started off, arm in arm, as indifferent crowds flowed around them, as the garish neon lights from bars, restaurants and the movie theater spilled out across the sidewalk, and the heavy-throated sound of a squad of airplanes flew overhead.

Judith looked up and stopped, drying her eyes with a handkerchief. "I wish I could fly away with those airplanes somewhere over that rainbow. I'd never come back."

CHAPTER 35

December 2016

Alice and Kristie arrived home just after dark on Sunday, December 18. A light snow was falling, with the promise of four inches by morning. Inside the house, Kristie was remote and sullen. Alice was tired. She'd texted Jack before their flight and told him they'd take a cab from the airport to the house, adding that she wasn't up for the miles of strained silence between him and Kristie as they drove home in his car.

Jack said he understood, and that he wasn't up to it either. When they arrived home, he was in the basement, working on the "diary room." By the time he emerged to give Alice a welcome home kiss, Kristie had toted her suitcase up the stairs to her room, where she promptly closed and locked the door.

Alice said, "You just missed her."

"Probably for the best, don't you think? She'll need her time. How is she?"

"Suffering, confused and a little angry."

"Angry?"

"At God."

Jack nodded, understanding. "Any word from Connie?"

"She texted Kristie when she got to the hospital, but we haven't heard since. I'm hoping she'll let us know if Taylor comes out of the coma or they decide to bring him home. Where's Andrew?"

Jack jerked his chin toward the stairs. "He and Brianna are in the upstairs living room searching for your Alice."

Alice perked up. "Any luck?"

"Don't know. Why don't you go up and ask them?"

"What time did Brenda leave?"

"About four."

"How are the guests?"

"In the parlor."

"I'll drop in and say hello, then go up and see how the kids are doing on the search. Still no word from the City Council on the graves?"

"No… It's Sunday. I'll call again first thing in the morning. I don't want this to wait until after Christmas."

Alice removed her hat, hung her coat in the hall closet and parked her suitcase at Jack's feet, with a pleading glance and head-nod toward the staircase. Jack hauled it upstairs, while Alice stepped to the round hall mirror. She finger-placed her hair, smoothed the front of her burgundy sweater and started toward the parlor to greet her guests, Martin and Meg Benton and Sunshine. She found them in easy comfort, seated near the glowing Christmas tree, now surrounded by lavishly wrapped presents. The gleaming fireplace warmed the room, and a vase of lovely white and red carnations sat on the coffee table.

Alice cheerfully answered their questions about her trip, bending her answers toward the positive side, focusing on how lovely the ski lodge had been. Because snow was falling, the three guests were all excitement and energy, looking ten years younger. Sunshine asked if there was a hill to go sledding on.

"Oh, yes, and we have two flexible flyer sleds you can use," Alice said.

Sunshine clapped her hands in girlish joy. "You'll come with me, won't you, Alice, to make sure I don't break my neck?"

Alice pushed away thoughts of Taylor and smiled. "Of course. It's not a big hill, but it will do for us. We'll look out for each other."

Upstairs, Alice found Andrew and Brianna in the front living room seated on the couch, each with a laptop open before them.

"Hi, there, you two. How's it going?"

They glanced up, eyes adjusting. Brianna rose with a friendly smile. "Hello, Mrs. Landis. It's nice to see you again."

Alice smiled a greeting. "It's good to see you as well, Brianna. You're always welcome here."

Andrew stood and gave Alice a kiss on the cheek. "Glad you're back. Dad will be happier."

"How are the stitches?" Alice asked, examining his face. "Your color is better. Not so pale."

"I'm fine. The bruises are fading around my eye. See?" he said, tilting his face toward the light.

"Yes, better, but I still see a little yellow there."

"Not so much," Andrew countered.

"I love this house," Brianna said. "I love everything you've done with it. I told Andrew that if I were going to decorate this place, I'd have done exactly the same. It has such a welcoming and homey quality about it."

"Thank you," Alice said. "Kristie helped a lot, and Andrew and Jack did the rebuilding and finishing work.

It truly was a family affair. We had many a pizza party, and a few good arguments."

"I hope you won't sell it," Brianna said. "Andrew told me about the development company wanting to build some housing project."

"No, we won't sell, and I hope Jack has found something that will stop them before they begin. But we'll see."

Alice clasped her hands together. "Now, I can't wait any longer. Have you found anything on Alice Ferrell?"

Brianna smiled. "When Andrew told me about the diary, and that she shared your name, I couldn't believe it. I thought he was joking."

"Yes, I think we all felt that it was a little strange, to say the least," Alice said. "I've been obsessed with trying to find out what happened to her ever since."

Andrew and Brianna exchanged an excited glance.

"And what does that glance mean?" Alice asked, impatiently.

Andrew nodded to Brianna. "We have good news and maybe bad news."

Alice inhaled a little breath, and blew it out. "Okay... Bad news first."

Brianna's hair was tied into a ponytail. She took the end, played with it, then let it go. "We found Corporal Tom Lawson."

Alice's breath stopped.

Andrew said, "He was fairly easy to find on the veteran's site."

"Yes, okay, and?"

"He was killed in February 1944 in the Battle of Eniwetok."

Alice's face sank. She thought, considered and readjusted her stance. "Wait a minute. February 1944? Can't be."

"Why can't be?" Andrew asked.

"Because, according to Alice's diary, she met Tom Lawson in December 1944."

Brianna spoke up. "Okay, so here's the good news. There are three Thomas Lawsons who served in the Marine Corps during World War Two."

Alice's gaze went to Andrew, then swung back to Brianna when she said, "We've found information on two of the Tom Lawsons. The one Andrew told you about was killed in February 1944. The other Tom Lawson served in Europe. During the Normandy invasion, he was a sharpshooter. They used their rifles to detonate floating mines to help clear the way for Navy ships. He survived the war but died in 1974."

Alice shook her head, as if to clear it. "Okay, help me out here. D-Day was in June 1944, right?"

Brianna nodded. "Yes."

"Well then, that can't be our Tom Lawson either, can it? The diary said he fought in the Pacific, not in Europe. So why haven't you found the third Tom Lawson? That must be our guy."

"We're still looking," Andrew said. "It's not so easy. The more we dig, the more information we get, and it gets confusing."

"I'm sorry," Alice said, with a sigh. "I'm tired and way too impatient."

"How's Kristie?" Andrew asked. "And Taylor?"

"There's no news on Taylor. Kristie is okay... Well, not so good. She needs time. Seeing Taylor nearly killed was a shock, and it's still a shock. As far as we know, he's still in a coma."

"It's awful," Brianna said. "I'm so sorry for her and for his family."

Alice nodded. "Thank you both for searching. I do appreciate it. I'm going to get something to eat and call it a day."

As she turned to leave, Andrew said, "Wait a minute. We think we found Alice."

Alice whirled around. "What?"

Brianna smiled extravagantly. "We were saving the best for last."

Alice's eyes went wide as she approached them. "Tell me."

"Andrew told me about the seventy-two-year census rule, so I asked my Dad if he could help. He got in touch with some of his legal and political friends and he pulled some strings. He was awesome, and we got the info we needed. We did a massive and thorough census search, starting at 2010, the last census," Brianna said.

"We figured if Alice was still alive, then that would probably show her most recent residence."

"That was smart," Alice said. "What did you find?"

"There are a number of Alice Ferrells," Brianna added, "but we found only one Alice Ferrell Lawson. The Ferrell spelling is unique."

Alice lit up, pumping her fist, bursting with joy. "YES! Tell me. Where is she... or where was she?"

Andrew grinned. "Everything matches. Her name and age. As of 2010, she was living in Lititz, Pennsylvania."

Alice blinked twice, letting that sink in, sure she'd heard wrong. "Pennsylvania? Do you mean she's living in Pennsylvania? Right here in Pennsylvania?"

Andrew and Brianna nodded.

"As of 2010," Andrew said, proudly.

Brianna said, "We did some social media searches, but we haven't found anything yet... But we did..."

Alice interrupted. "… How far is Lititz from here?" she asked, feeling new life pump through her veins. "Is it close?"

"About forty miles," Andrew said.

"I don't believe it. Are you sure? Only forty miles?"

"We're sure," Andrew said. "But again, that's as of 2010."

"We didn't find her obituary, so maybe…" Brianna shrugged a shoulder. "She'd be in her nineties."

Alice struggled to control her racing thoughts. "I've never heard of Lititz."

"It's a foodie town," Andrew said. "It's known for the Julius Sturgis Pretzel Bakery, and they…"

Brianna cut in. "… they were the first commercial pretzel bakery in the United States."

Alice stared at them, and all the fatigue and stress of the last few days vanished. She was galvanized—ready to jump into her car and drive to Lititz. "All right, what do we do next? Drive to Lititz and ask around? No, that doesn't make sense, does it?"

"Brianna was trying to tell you that we have an address and phone number," Andrew said, softly.

Alice's heart fluttered. "Wow! Did you call?"

"No," Brianna said. "We wanted to leave that to you."

"I'll text you the number," Andrew said.

Alice kissed them both on their cheeks. "Thank you. Thank you both. I can't tell you how excited I am."

CHAPTER 36
March 1945

Alice gradually grew comfortable living in San Diego, even though it was a liberty town for service personnel from ships in the harbor, and a temporary home for the many soldiers stationed at nearby military bases. Despite the energetic crowds, the town had a purposeful, happy atmosphere, and she felt that, with so many dedicated workers and determined soldiers, they'd surely win the war, and soon.

Judith had been fired from her job as a dancer at The Cat's Whiskers. She'd told Alice a little about the place and the owner. "A guy named Rosco Dixon owns the place. He's a big, hard-boned man, with dusty brown eyes that don't trust anybody. I'm glad he fired me. He was an animal who was always pawing at me."

"You'll find better work, Judith. You needed to get out of there, anyway."

About a week later, Rosco called, and Alice picked up the phone to hear a gruff-voiced man.

"Is Judith there?"

When Judith took the phone, he asked her to come back. "I've got some regulars that keep pestering me about you. They're blaming me that you left. I told them you walked out on me, but they don't want to hear it. Look, come back, baby, and I'll give you a little raise. I'll even give you another song. Now, what do you say?"

"I have other plans, Rosco. No deal."

"What do you mean, other plans? I'm offering you a raise, here. What's the matter with you? I'm offering you damn good money, more money than I'm paying any of those other dumb broads."

"No, thanks. Have a good life, Rosco."

He'd slammed down the phone, and Judith grinned with relief and satisfaction. "That felt so good."

Alice was pleased. "Now it's on to your new life, Judith."

Judith's grin slowly faded. She stared, instantly worried. "I haven't prayed since before my brother's death, but I think it's time to dust one off, polish it up and hope the Big Man is in a good mood."

Alice went swiftly into action to find Judith a job before she sank into another depression. Fortunately, Judith's mother had been a high school English teacher who'd forced her daughter to take a typing class her junior year in high school. Alice found a place that rented out typewriters, and she brought one home so that Judith could brush up on her typing. She quickly gained accuracy and speed, and Alice discovered that Judith was not only a good typist, she also had good spelling and grammar skills.

In less than two weeks, Judith went to work at Consolidated Aircraft. She was hired as the secretary to Frank Richards, a young, attractive engineer from New York City, who'd also recently been hired.

On her coffee breaks, Alice often drifted by Judith's desk to check on her. As the weeks passed, she began to observe that Mr. Richards was timid and nervous around Judith, a clear indication that he found her attractive. Judith denied it and wouldn't talk about it.

To Alice's relief, the job helped to boost Judith's self-esteem and distract her from dark thoughts about her baby and the uncertain future.

During the third week of March, Alice received her latest letter from Tom. As usual, he'd used their secret codes to tell her things the censors would have blacked out.

While Judith cooked dinner, Alice took the letter to her room to read in privacy.

Dearest Alice:

It was a long journey to get here. The damn ship rolled and rolled, and a lot of the guys got seasick. Not yours truly. I've never minded being on the water. Hey, maybe I should have enlisted in the Navy.

So now that we're here, where are we? It's the usual lovely tropical vacation spot, filled with nasty mosquitos, broiling sun, heavy rains, mud, and hot beer, with a little combat thrown in for light entertainment.

Don't worry about me, sweetheart. I'm fine. I'm fighting with the best guys in the world and we're going to win this war as fast as we can.

How are you, my lovely wife? Don't worry so much that you're not pregnant. It will happen. That's the way nature is. Whenever you worry too much about something, Mother Nature seems to say, "No, darling, not now." But when you just say "Relax" and then say, "Hey, Mother Nature, when you get around to it, I'd like a baby, but no rush," then that's when it will happen. Of course, I'll have to be in the picture at some point, don't you think? I hope you're laughing. I love your laugh. Do I sound like a guy in love with a girl—the best and the most pretty girl?

So, we'll both have some faith about the baby. Look, Mother Nature put us together, didn't she? Just like that, at the snap of her fingers, she brought us together in a snow-storm and a car crash. So, she won't abandon us.

I hear your voice in my head at night, when the insects are scratching in the dark, and I remember the desert at night when we were driving along Route 66. Remember how we stopped to listen, and to look up into the infinite swirl of stars? How I wanted to kiss you. I wanted to ask you to marry me right there. Well, so many times.

Now when I look up into the night sky so filled with those millions and millions of stars, and I hear the roar of the sea, I miss you so much my chest hurts.

Okay, my love, I've got to go. I want to get this letter post-ed. Please take care of yourself. I'm happy to hear you like your work. Have you been able to get Judith any work yet? I'd love to know. Your letters are often delayed, so, by now, maybe she's working. Anyway, I hope the girl and her baby are all right. What a fix, huh? Poor girl. She seemed nice. She's lucky to have you as a friend.

Love and kisses, Alice. You're in my prayers, and I've never been much of a praying man. I pray for you and for us, every night, and before every battle.

More love to you, and a kiss,

Tom

Over dinner that same night, Judith was quiet and guarded. She picked at her peas and stared off into space.

"Is everything all right?" Alice asked.

"Yes... Fine. How's Tom?" she asked, still not look-ing up.

"He's fine. His last letter was written so long ago. I

wish... I just wish I could talk to him, for just a minute or two. I was checking the papers this morning, trying to learn where he might be, but I don't know, everything is so vague, and the Marines and the Navy are moving so fast."

Judith raised her eyes. "He'll be okay, Alice. He's one of the good guys. The good men."

Alice took a sip of water. "Did you hear about Nancy Clarke? She's the secretary for that General... I forget his name."

Judith's eyes lowered again. "Yes, I heard. How ironic... or maybe just plain sad and just plain tragic, that her husband was killed in a B-24, the same airplane that Consolidated designed."

"She left her job and went back home... Iowa, I think," Alice said, gloomily. "They were only married a year or so. God, that depresses me."

"It's not going to happen to you, Alice."

"How do you know, Judith? You don't. You don't know."

"I feel it, okay? I do."

Alice dropped her head with a sigh. "All right, let's talk about something else."

Judith poured the rest of the beer into her glass and watched it foam. "Frank asked me out," she said, flatly.

Alice sat up, surprised. "He did? What did you say?"

"I didn't know what to say. It's against the rules, you know. He was very discrete about it. He caught up with me when I was leaving the building."

Judith lifted a hand in a vague gesture. "As crazy as this sounds, do you know what immediately shot into my wild, spinning mind? I thought, *Mr. Richards, I think you should know that I'm almost four months pregnant, but you can't see it because I know how to dress to hide it... and it helps that I'm tall.* I didn't say that, of course."

"So what did you say?"

Judith met Alice's eyes. "I said yes. Can you believe it? Just like the stupid girl I am, I looked up into his very nice face, into his very lovely eyes and at his very kissable lips, and I said, yes."

"Judith, that's wonderful."

Judith's face dropped. "How the hell is it wonderful? I'm pregnant. I can't believe it. The first time in my life, a handsome, educated and very nice man wants to take me out, and I'm pregnant with another man's baby."

Judith stood up, standing in place, staring down. She reached for her beer and drained the glass, her color high, her eyes searching.

Alice sat back, folding her hands. "Judith, just go out and have a good time, that's all. You don't have to tell him anything and you don't have to commit to anything. Just get out of here and enjoy yourself. Let things go the way they go."

Judith kept nodding her head. "Yeah... Yes, of course you're right, Alice. I want to go out with him. I like him. I like him a lot and I know he's attracted to me, but you know, he's always been a gentleman. Always. No paws, no lust pitch, no lurid glances. Just nice. I looked up his biography. I know I shouldn't have, but I did anyway. He comes from a wealthy family in New York... Westchester. I don't know where that is exactly, because I've never been to New York."

"When are you going out?"

"Tomorrow night... Saturday, right? I mean, this is Friday. My brain is all jumbled up. I just wish I didn't feel like a dope."

"You're not a dope. Where is he taking you?"

"Dinner, and a movie, I guess."

"It'll be fun."

Judith nodded, and they didn't talk for moments, while the little brown dog next door barked his head off.

"He always barks this time of night," Alice said.

"Feeding time," Judith said, easing back down in her chair. "I called my mother two days ago. I was going to tell her about the baby. I was going to ask her if I could come home and have the baby."

Alice waited.

"I couldn't do it. I didn't tell her. And you know what? Time is just tick-tick-ticking away and my little baby is growing a little bit bigger every day."

"Don't think so much this weekend. Go out on your date and have a ball. Enjoy yourself. Pretend you're going to your high school prom with the most handsome guy on the football team."

Judith's laughter burst out. "I love the way you think, Alice. You have all these champagne romance bubbles going off in your head. I love it. I might even learn to be a romantic if I hang around you long enough, and not the cynical, whining broad that I am."

Alice narrowed her eyes, wisely. "You're about to be a romantic, Judith, so play the part well. Frank Richards may just sweep you off your feet."

Judith gave Alice a sincere smile. "You're a good friend, Alice. The best friend a girl like me could have. If it hadn't been for you, I'd probably be swimming to China by now."

In bed that night, Alice was worried about Judith. She was fragile and unpredictable. In the short time she'd known her, she'd seen the swift mood swings, the trembling hands, the hope, and the anxiety rise and fall, sometimes in only minutes.

Alice rolled onto her back and stared up at the ceiling.

She prayed for Tom, and she prayed that Judith's date with Frank Richards would go well. If it didn't go well, would Judith be able to manage the emotional storm that surely would come?

CHAPTER 37

December 2016

On Tuesday morning, Alice drove the winding, two-lane road through maple and white oak, still glazed with Monday's snowfall. Kristie sat in the passenger seat, alert and watchful, checking the GPS app on her cell phone.

"It's about five more miles," Kristie said.

"I'm so nervous," Alice said, glancing over. "Thanks for coming along. I need the support."

"Are you kidding? I wanted to come. I wouldn't have missed it for anything. And anyway, it gets my mind off Taylor. Thank God he came out of the coma and they're bringing him home. I don't know how I'm going to face Mrs. Barnes when I go see him. I won't know what to say."

"I'm sure she doesn't blame you, Kristie."

"You're still coming with me, aren't you... when I go see him in the hospital?"

"Yes, of course."

Kristie eased back into the seat. "I hope he's okay... I mean his mind and everything."

"He's young and strong, and he'll have good care. I'm

sure he'll make a full recovery, and I'm sure he'll want to see you as soon as he can."

Kristie glanced out the window at the snowy land and sun-bright day. "I don't know about that. Everything feels so weird now. It's scary how fast things can change."

"My mother used to call it trial by existence."

Kristie faced Alice. "Your mother was a psychologist, wasn't she?"

"Yes. She worked in public schools, and she had her own private practice working mostly with women."

"Do you think I'd be a good psychologist?"

"Yes, I do."

"I wish I could have met your mother."

"She would have liked you, and you her. She was direct, honest and fun, and she was a bit of a philosopher."

"Well, a philosopher I'm not."

"You're young, Kristie. Give it a little more time."

Kristie went into thought. "I want to be a writer, but maybe I could do both. I mean, why couldn't I? I took a psych course last semester and I liked it."

"Yes, you could do both."

Kristie turned back to the window. "Do you miss your mother?"

"Every day."

"I'll think about it over Christmas. Maybe I'll ask Taylor what he thinks. It might help break the ice or something, because it's going to be totally awkward when we first see each other."

"Are we still on course?" Alice asked.

Kristie glanced at her phone. "Yeah. Keep going. It's going to be fun meeting Mrs. Lawson, isn't it?"

"Fun and stressful," Alice said, recalling her call to Alice Ferrell Lawson. To her frustration, the number Andrew and Brianna had found on the internet had been disconnected. Undaunted, Alice had started her own search and, two hours later, she discovered the name Oliver Thomas Lawson in an obituary on a site called *Obit-Tree*.

She'd read that he'd recently died, in March 2016, and one of his surviving relatives was a grandmother, Alice Ferrell Lawson. She was still alive at ninety-three years old, living at Forest View Valley Assisted Living and Nursing Home in the small town of Patchett, Pennsylvania.

Alice had leapt up from her chair in triumph, having been so overcome with joy that her eyes had misted over. The Nursing Home's phone number had been easy to find and, with a shaky hand, Alice dialed it and waited while she paced her office.

On the other end of the line, a soft-spoken woman answered. Alice cleared her voice and asked if Alice Lawson was a resident there.

"Yes, Mrs. Alice Lawson resides here."

Alice's mouth snapped shut. She was too emotional to speak. Alice Lawson was alive!

"Hello... Hello, are you there?" the soft voice asked.

"Yes, yes, I'm here. Would it be possible to... Can I speak to Mrs. Lawson?"

"Are you a relative?"

"No... I found something of hers, and I'm sure she'll want it back."

Alice explained how she'd found the diary, leaving out that Mrs. Lawson and Alice shared the same names.

When Alice was transferred to Mrs. Lawson's phone, expectation was high in her throat. There were two, then three rings. On the fourth ring, she heard background noise, as if someone were struggling with the phone. And then she heard a tremulous voice, thin and whispery.

"Hello, this is Alice Lawson. To whom am I speaking?"

Alice steadied her breath. "Mrs. Lawson? Is this Mrs. Alice Ferrell Lawson?"

"Yes... Who is this?"

"Mrs. Lawson, I have something of yours and I think you might want it back."

"I beg your pardon. What did you say? Please speak up, I'm rather hard of hearing and I'm not wearing my hearing aids."

"Mrs. Lawson, I live at 298 Chestnut Street in Meadow Green, Pennsylvania. I found a diary there that you wrote in 1944. As I said, I thought you might want it returned to you."

After a long, agonizing silence, Alice heard Mrs. Lawson say, in an even shakier, emotional voice, "Oh, my... After all these long years, you have found my old diary?"

"Yes... Can I come and see you? I'd love to give it to you."

Kristie guided Alice through a small town, left across some railroad tracks and down a serpentine road near a construction site, where men in hardhats crawled along the roofs of half-built condos. Alice turned right onto a quiet road that led past modest homes and an old white church with a soaring white steeple, to an open area occupied by the Forest View Valley Home.

It was an L-shaped, redbrick, two-story building with plenty of windows and four acres of land. There were snowplowed walkways that led to benches and a grove of trees, and others that led to the rear entrance, to two parked ambulances.

The area was neatly landscaped, with shrubs capped with snow, dormant flower gardens, a cluster of trees for good shade in summer, and more benches that offered pleasant views of rising, distant hills.

Alice parked the car in the parking lot, shut off the engine, and released an anxious sigh.

Kristie looked over. "Are you okay?"

Alice dropped her head in a silent nod. "Yep. Okay, but very tense."

"Mrs. Lawson is probably as nervous as you are."

"I'm sure. She got emotional on the phone. Friendly, but emotional. I can't wait to ask her how that diary ended up in the lost and found bin. According to the diary, she'd left the house and planned never to return."

Kristie grinned broadly. "I am, like, so psyched. That diary is so alive. I almost feel like I know her, or that we've already met."

"We probably shouldn't say too much about it," Alice said. "She might think we imposed on her privacy."

"I won't say anything. I'll just sit and keep my mouth shut."

Alice placed her hands on the top rim of the steering wheel, lifted her chin and blew out the jet of a sigh. "Okay, enough with the sighing. Here goes. Don't forget the flowers."

The lobby of the residence was spacious, clean and airy, with a beautiful, lighted Christmas tree and plenty of cheerful decorations. At the round lobby desk, Kristie stood by while Alice spoke to a young receptionist. She asked for their IDs and then, with a compact camera attached to the desk, she snapped their photos.

"I'll call Mrs. Lawson and let her know you're here," the pleasant receptionist said.

With their security badges clearly displayed, Alice and Kristie were escorted by a young security guard, with tattoos on his arms and neck, down a long, polished hallway, through double doors, then left into another wing.

When they came to the third door on the left, the guard stopped, pointing. "This is Mrs. Lawson's room," he said, waiting, eyes locked ahead.

"Thank you," Alice said.

The brown door was partially open, and Alice heard muted music coming from inside, Christmas carols. She gently knocked. A moment later, the door opened and a thin, stooped woman with soft, white hair, a wan, expectant face and alert, intelligent eyes peered out at Alice. Her manner was reserved, proper and subdued. When she spoke, her voice was small and tentative.

"Are you Mrs. Landis?" she asked.

Alice felt a prickling of the flesh on the back of her hands and neck. "Yes, Mrs. Lawson, I am, and this is my step-daughter, Kristie. I mentioned that she might come."

Mrs. Lawson's eyes opened fully on Kristie; her smile was welcoming. "Kristie..." she repeated. "A very pretty name for a very pretty young woman."

Mrs. Lawson nodded to the security guard, and he rambled off down the hallway. Then she stepped aside. "Please, come in. I have been looking forward to this visit ever since you called."

Inside the room, Alice presented the flower bouquet, featuring roses, white lilies, and red and white carnations.

"Merry Christmas!" Alice and Kristie said, smiling.

Mrs. Lawson's eyes opened wide in delight. "Oh, look at them. They're so beautiful. Thank you."

There was sun brightness shining into the room, highlighting a square end table by the windows, where several framed, black-and-white and color photos were displayed. There were photographs of babies, adults, and teenagers in various outfits: swimming suits, dress suits, graduation caps-and-gowns. There were also sepia tone portraits from the 1940s. Alice's eyes traveled over them, her mind alive with speculation.

Mrs. Lawson's apartment consisted of a living room, a dining room, a small separate kitchen and a back bedroom, with the door slightly ajar.

"I'm very fortunate that, at my age, I can still have some independence," Mrs. Lawson said. "It's a pleasant place, with twenty-four-hour medical services and good security."

It was a cozy apartment, decorated in soft blues and muted gray and yellows, designed with taste and furnished for comfort. Alice was sure the oval coffee table was an antique, and on it was a sweet, decorated, miniature Christmas tree.

Mrs. Lawson followed Alice's eyes. "Charlie, one of my grandkids, sent me that," she said, proudly. "It cheers me up every time I look at it."

The unexpected rolltop desk, tidy with papers, was also surely a relic from the past. It held more framed photos and portraits.

Mrs. Lawson indicated toward the sofa. "Please sit down and I'll put these lovely flowers in a vase. I have made a pot of coffee. Do you drink coffee? My husband and I were never tea drinkers."

"Coffee would be wonderful," Alice said.

To Kristie, Mrs. Lawson said, "Perhaps you would prefer a soda? I have ginger ale."

Alice offered to help, but Mrs. Lawson declined and ambled into the tidy kitchen, pausing to pass her nose over the flowers.

Minutes later Alice and Mrs. Lawson sipped coffee and Kristie a ginger ale. Mrs. Lawson had placed the vase of flowers on the coffee table near the little tree, and they helped to cheer and scent the room.

There was a hesitancy in the room, all three unsure how to begin.

Kristie spoke first. "I'm going to be honest, Mrs. Lawson. I read the entire diary and I loved it."

Alice shot her a look, but Kristie continued. "We didn't know who you were, or if you were still alive. It was so beautifully written. It made me cry sometimes. We were really careful with it, because some of the pages are brittle, but Mom took real good care of it."

Alice glanced up at Mrs. Lawson to gauge her reaction. Surprisingly, the woman had a pleasant smile. "It's nice of you to say so, Kristie. I never thought myself much of a writer."

"But you're a wonderful writer, Mrs. Lawson," Kristie insisted. "I did cry a few times."

Alice masked irritation. Why had Kristie been so blunt, especially after saying she'd keep her mouth shut?

Mrs. Lawson scratched an eyebrow with her little finger and then, in a level voice, she said, "Those things happened so many years ago. I was just a girl, a little older than you are now, Kristie. The diary was written during the war, when we were all so worried and scared for the world."

Kristie sat on the edge of the couch, waiting, watching. Alice didn't move.

Mrs. Lawson placed her hands in her lap. "I think I can say that, back then, most of us were searching for grace. Yes, grace, to make it through those uncertain times. That's the best way I can say it."

Alice placed her coffee mug aside, reached into her gray, carryall bag and slowly drew out the diary, which was carefully preserved in a zipped plastic bag. Mrs. Lawson's eyes expanded on it.

Alice rose and took the diary to Mrs. Lawson, presenting it to her.

With a blue-veined, trembling hand, Mrs. Lawson accepted it, her eyes welling up. "Thank you, Alice. I am so grateful to you for taking the time to find me and return it. As you may imagine, it holds so many old memories."

"There are also a couple of photos in there that we found in the basement," Alice added. "I think they're of you and Charles."

Alice Lawson let that sink in, her mouth trembling. "Charles... I see... I don't think I'll look at them right now. I'll wait until I'm alone."

"Of course," Alice said, then returned to the couch. She and Kristie looked away, after seeing tears rolling down Mrs. Lawson's cheeks. From her longing expression, it was evident that fragments of old faces and memories had resurfaced and touched her.

Moments later, after she'd gently wiped her eyes with a tissue, she said, "So you know my story, don't you? A story that seems to have happened so many lifetimes ago. And yet, I see their faces so clearly, as if they had just walked into the room and sat down."

Alice leaned forward. "Mrs. Lawson, we don't know the entire story. We don't know what happened... Did you and Tom Lawson marry? Your last name suggests that you did. Did he survive the war?"

Mrs. Lawson's eyes drifted away toward the windows, and she stared out, leaving Alice and Kristie to sit quietly with anxious attention.

When Mrs. Lawson spoke, her voice was quiet and private, as if she were speaking more to herself than to them. "I received a letter from Tom, in July of 1945, I think. He said the Army and Marines had taken Okinawa at a heavy cost. I'd heard about it on the radio and read the newspapers but, of course, the information was sketchy, at best. I was so nervous because I hadn't heard from Tom in weeks. In his last letter, he used our own secret codes to tell me that soon they were going to invade Japan. I was worried sick, day and night. And then in August, the United States dropped those atomic bombs on Japan and, within days, the war was over."

Mrs. Lawson moved her eyes back to Alice and Kristie. "I was so happy, and so worried, and so heartsick. It was weeks before I learned what had happened to Tom."

And then Mrs. Lawson finished her story.

CHAPTER 38
December 2016

Mrs. Lawson set the diary aside, struggled to her feet, and moved to the table holding the exhibited photographs. She reached for an "8x11" sepia photo of a young woman and a soldier in uniform, her eyes resting warmly on it as old memories flooded in. She turned to Alice and Kristie.

"This was our wedding photograph, Tom and me. We had it taken in Los Angeles, just a few blocks from the courthouse where we were married."

She crossed to Alice and handed the framed photo to her. Kristie leaned over for a look.

"As you can see, we toasted each other with our eyes. That was Tom's idea; not to look at the camera but to look at each other. I think he was more the romantic than I was."

Mrs. Lawson went back to her chair and lowered herself down.

"It's a wonderful photo," Alice said. "Your husband was a handsome man."

"Yeah, really handsome," Kristie said. "And he has a good face... a trusting kind of face."

Mrs. Lawson smiled, reflectively. "Yes, Kristie, he was a man you could trust."

Alice and Kristie looked up, waiting for more.

"Do you know that it took until April 1946 before Tom returned home from the war to San Diego?"

Alice straightened. "So your husband survived the war and returned home?"

"Yes, Tom survived that terrible war and came back home to me. But it seemed an eternity. As I said, it was the last week of April 1946 before I saw him, many months after the war had ended. There were so many soldiers returning from Europe and the Pacific. Everyone was dizzy with impatience and happiness. Oh, the parties that went on after the Japanese surrendered. It makes my head spin to think of it now. My best friend and roommate at the time, Judith Bain, and I went dancing three nights a week. She was pregnant, and I was married, but it didn't matter. Her fiancé, Frank, danced with us both, and it was so much fun."

"Was Judith's fiancé a soldier, too?" Kristie asked.

"No, he was an engineer who worked at the same war plant that we did. She was his secretary. He said he fell in love with Judith at first sight, and they were married before Tom returned home."

"Wasn't that fast?" Kristie asked.

Mrs. Lawson smiled patiently. "Those were difficult days, Kristie. We were all so young and the war had killed so many men. The war made life seem short and fragile. Anyway, Judith... well, she was, as we used to say in those days, in the family way, but the father of the baby had abandoned her. Frank Richards was a good man. He didn't care. He told Judith that the baby would be their baby, and he would love it as his own. Yes, Frank was a fine man. Their little girl, Sarah, grew up to be a dedicated nurse, who bore two children of her own."

"Did you stay in touch with Judith?" Alice asked.

"Oh, yes. She and Frank moved away to New York in 1946. I missed her so much. We'd become the best of friends... so close during those awful and lonely days and nights. We managed to visit during summer holidays and, occasionally, at Thanksgiving."

"Is she still alive?" Kristie asked.

"No, Judith died in 1998, but she'd had a wonderful life and a loving husband, with three children and many grandchildren. Frank lived until 2005, I think. He always sent me a Christmas card."

Alice handed Mrs. Lawson's wedding photo to Kristie, and she gave it a closer look.

"You must have been so happy to see your husband," Kristie said.

"Oh, yes. I will never forget the day Tom returned from the war. I waited for over three hours at the port where the ships were coming in, all of them overflowing with soldiers. Finally, I saw him, and did I light up. Tom hurried down the gangway, waving at me with his big, broad grin, shouldering his bulky duffle bag. I was all tears and smiles, feeling as though I was about to burst with happiness. The rising, salty mist was cool, and my mind whirled, and my heart sang. It was the happiest day of my life."

"When did you leave California?" Alice asked.

"In 1947, I think. Yes, that's right. Judith and Frank had left months before. Tom and I packed up our car and moved to Cleveland, Ohio. We lived there until Tom finished his Civil Engineering degree, thanks to the GI Bill. By then, we had two children, Mary and Carl. And then Tom got a good job in Philadelphia and we moved to a quiet suburb, and lived there until Tom passed away in 2006."

The softness of fond memories left Mrs. Lawson's eyes and, again, she gazed out the window. "That's when I moved to Lititz, not too far from here."

"Do your children live close by?" Alice asked.

Mrs. Lawson didn't face Alice. "Both my Mary and Carl have passed…"

Kristie lowered the framed photo to her lap. "I'm so sorry."

Mrs. Lawson's voice was breathy and a little sad. "Mary was never very strong. She died at forty-four. Carl died two years ago, but he had a good life."

"Do you have any family nearby?" Alice asked.

"No, not close, but my grandchildren and great-grandchildren call and email. I don't have a cell phone, but I do have a little tablet. They send photos and presents. I'm very blessed."

Alice sought to frame her next question carefully. "Mrs. Lawson, how did your diary end up in the lost and found bin in the basement of our house? Do you know?"

Mrs. Lawson smiled, wistfully. "I have been thinking about it since you called with the news. I have to tell you that I thought my diary had been tossed out years ago. I'm astonished that you found it. The best reason I have for its survival is this. In 1948, I received a call from my Uncle Fred Long, asking me if I'd come to the house to help care for Aunt Sally. He said she was quite ill. I was surprised, because my aunt had written me off, so to speak. I hadn't heard from her more than two or three times since I'd left that house back in 1944."

Mrs. Lawson inclined forward, lowering her voice to a conspiratorial whisper. "She disapproved of me traveling with Tom, Charles' best friend, and she was outraged that I went to see my father, who died soon after. At any rate,

I went to the house, and I did look after Sally, who said little to me when I was there."

Mrs. Lawson shook her head. "Fred told me, in confidence, that Aunt Sally missed me, and I was the only one she wanted around to help nurse her back to health. I was there about a week. When I arrived, I saw the stubble on Fred's face, the lines along his eyes and cheeks, and I smelled whiskey on his breath. He'd aged a lot since I'd last seen him, and he didn't look well.

"Anyway, I thought it would be interesting to reread my old diary while I was there, so I left home with my two diaries, the one you found, which I called my Christmas Diary, and a second, which I have tucked away in my closet in the bedroom. No one else will read that one, at least not until I have moved on from this world. Well, like always, Aunt Sally was busy with knitting, crocheting and her cloudy moods. Her emotions were few and heavy, but we got along all right, with nods and mumbles and the occasional, 'Don't know why you showed up here, Alice. Fred shouldn't have called you.'

"After Aunt Sally's health improved, I left that house with a wave and a goodbye. There was no kiss from Sally, or even a thank you, and that was all right with me. That's the way Sally was. Fred slipped me some money, but I refused it.

"When I returned home, I discovered I'd left my Christmas Diary at their house. Of course I was upset, terrified that Sally or Fred would read it, so I called Uncle Fred immediately."

Mrs. Lawson settled back in her chair, wiping her mouth with her wizened hand. "Aunt Sally kept putting me off, saying she still wasn't feeling so good. Sadly, a little later, Fred caught pneumonia and died. Sally was so distraught that she refused to have a public funeral. She became reclusive for a time, and then she moved away to live with her sister."

"Sally must have found the diary, don't you think?" Alice asked.

"I really don't know. We never spoke about it, and who knows if Fred even told her about it? If she found it, I suppose she thought it was silly—if she thought about it at all."

Alice explained how, in the 1950s, a former neighbor had written and told her that the house had been bought and turned into a boarding house.

"Sally sold it with all the furniture and it's likely the diary was found in some drawer or closet and then tossed into the lost and found bin."

"And at some point," Alice said, "the bin must have been stored in that old, damp, unused room and forgotten."

Mrs. Lawson nodded. "It is a wonder, isn't it? A wonder that you found it all these years later?"

Alice leveled her eyes on Mrs. Lawson. "And there's one more thing that I want to share with you. My maiden name is Ferrell, Alice Ferrell."

Mrs. Lawson's eyes narrowed, as if she couldn't quite process the information. "Did you say your name is Alice Ferrell?"

Alice nodded. "Yes. You can imagine how I felt when I found the diary and learned that you, the author of that diary, shared my name."

Mrs. Lawson stared, bewildered. "I don't understand…"

Kristie spoke up. "I think the diary wanted to be found, and it wanted to be found by Mom, so we could find you. Mom was the conduit that connected us to the diary and then to you, Mrs. Lawson. It was like synchronicity. I wrote a paper on synchronicity for science class a month ago. Synchronicity is the occurrence of events that appear to be significantly related, but they have no obvious underlying connection."

Slowly, the tension left Mrs. Lawson's face, and she smiled. "Perhaps you're right, Kristie, I don't know. When you have lived as long as I have, and you've been humbled many times by life's mysteries, sometimes you just have to throw up your hands and, as Tom used to say, 'Take the gifts from God and simply give thanks.'"

Alice saw fatigue in Mrs. Lawson's eyes. She wanted to talk further, but she sensed it was time to leave, so she rose, and Kristie followed. "I think we'd better go now and let you rest," Alice said.

Mrs. Lawson pushed to her feet and smiled into Alice's eyes. "You both have made me so very happy. I can't tell you how much I appreciate your coming and bringing me my old diary. I will read it tonight, and it will bring back so many good memories. Truly, I have missed it. Thank you."

As Alice and Kristie stepped out into the hallway, with Mrs. Lawson standing by, Kristie had a thought. She turned.

"Mrs. Lawson... Why don't you come and celebrate Christmas with us? I mean, if you're not going to be with your family."

Alice brightened. "Yes, what a great idea. A wonderful idea. Yes, come, Mrs. Lawson. I'll pick you up. You can see the house again; walk through it and remember. You can even stay the night if you want. We have an extra room. In fact, you'll remember it as the back bedroom, the room Tom stayed in, in 1944. It's next to my office. Jack, my husband, finished remodeling it about a month ago, and we haven't used it yet. Yes, please come."

Mrs. Lawson felt a little catch in her throat. "How kind you both are. How very kind, but I…"

"Please come," Kristie pleaded. "Mom and I are going to cook, my brother and his girlfriend will be there, along with three of our house guests, my grandfather, and my father. I know they'd all love it if you came. Say yes. You don't have any other plans, do you?"

Mrs. Lawson looked up shyly, her eyes misty. "Well… They're going to provide a nice Christmas dinner here, in the dining room."

Alice touched Mrs. Lawson's arm, smiling warmly. "I think the two Alice Ferrells should be together at Christmas, don't you?"

Mrs. Lawson returned Alice's smile. A moment later she nodded, her mind made up. "Yes, Alice Ferrell. I do believe you are right about that. So, I would love to come and be a part of your family on Christmas."

CHAPTER 39

December 25, 2016

When Jack entered the dining room, bearing the eighteen-pound, plump, golden-brown turkey on a silver tray, everyone plunged into complimentary conversation. There were "Oohs" and, "Ahhs" and, "Doesn't that smell heavenly?" and, "It's just beautiful," and, "How many pounds is that?"

In the corner, the stately Christmas tree blinked out happiness, and the holly and ivy table arrangement lifted hearts. The eleven people seated around the oval table viewed the Christmas Day spread with eager appetites.

Seated on one side of the table were Andrew and Brianna, Martin and Meg Benton. On the other were Kristie, her grandfather, 65-year-old John Ferrell, and his girlfriend, Margie. Next to Margie was Sunshine, wearing a white sweater with a big embroidered Christmas tree on the front.

Jack sat on one end of the table and Alice on the other, with Alice Lawson seated to her right.

The cranberry sauce shimmered under the chandelier, and the light danced off the crystal glasses of red and white wine. There was a mound of whipped, buttery mashed potatoes, and marshmallow'd sweet potatoes sat next to the green beans. There was a ceramic bowl of creamed peas, the inevitable celery stuffed with cream cheese and olives, and a wooden cutting board heaped with warm slices of thick, crusty bread.

Joyful hearts were light, faces glowed, and all were enjoying the celebration of family, friends, food, life and love.

And then it began—anxious hands reaching—the shifting of bowls; plates filling up; hands gripping things; arms passing things; and elbows getting in the way. The chatter rose, and laughter was easy, and it all somehow harmonized with lilting Christmas tunes coming from a smart speaker.

And then there was Bixby, the calico cat few, other than Jack, ever saw except at feeding time, or when there was the possibility of a feast. Bixby was Jack's cat, because Jack had saved him. Bixby was an expert on feasts, having come from a restaurant called Bixby's, which had closed. Jack had found him there while his company remodeled the space for a new business, and he'd brought him home.

From his preferred position just around the corner from the kitchen, Bixby sat stoical, watchful, and hopeful, his steady, moon-colored eyes not missing the dance of passing bowls or Jack's skillful carving of the turkey.

It was the possible mistake that kept Bixby alert and purring like an outboard motor; that kept him still as a gargoyle. Bixby lived for the shaky hand or distracted motion, when a tilted plate or a dropped plate brought the promise of a delightful, stolen snack.

Bixby knew, from a year of reconnoitering the kitchen and dining room, that if things didn't play out as he wished, there was always his friend, Jack, who'd come to the rescue. Bixby's unblinking eyes would wait for Jack's hand that, at some point, would drift downward. That's when Bixby would spring forward, snatch the prey, and flash off for the safety of a shadowy room.

And so Christmas flowered and bloomed in the Landis house, and the scent of it, the joy and the love of it, sang in the air and enriched every heart.

After the cleanup, everyone retired to the parlor, some sitting, some standing, some with coffee mugs, some with mugs of hot chocolate, some with eggnog.

Kristie strummed her guitar and led them into song. Uninhibited, they broke into loud fa la la's, and *Jingle Bells*, and *Rockin' Around the Christmas Tree,* and few knew the words, so they made them up. Alice's father, John, surprised everyone when he sang *Grandpa Got Run Over by A Beer Truck.*

Sunshine doubled over laughing, Jack grinned, and Alice gave her father a mock frown, followed by a loving smile.

Finally, Alice lowered the lights, and they all joined in to sing *Silent Night.*

Immediately following, Kristie grabbed a red Santa bag, an old pillowcase she'd dyed red, dug inside, and withdrew small, beautifully wrapped gifts she'd purchased for everyone.

As she began passing them out, playing Santa Claus, Jack saw the absolute delight on her face, and it touched him. They'd agreed to have their little heart-to-heart talk sometime during the next couple of days, at Angelo's Pizzeria, her choice. He was well aware that their relationship would always be a work in progress, but as he watched her, softened by her thoughtfulness and generosity, his heart swelled with new love for her.

The gifts ranged from funny socks, wild and weird ties,

and a jacks and ball set, to a soap-on-a-rope, a Christmas t-shirt, a Santa bobble head, and a teddy bear for Mrs. Lawson.

When a pleasant relaxation descended, the group fell into easy conversation and laughter. Brianna and Sunshine sat near Mrs. Lawson, speaking with animation. Martin and Meg Benton told Alice it was one of their best Christmases, and Jack and Andrew moved to the corner of the room for a chat.

"How do you feel about things?" Jack asked.

Andrew had his eyes on Brianna as she, Sunshine, and Mrs. Lawson chatted. "I guess you're referring to Mike Turner?"

"And Brianna."

"Brianna's cool about it all. She said, forget about Mike. He's not worth it. We've already started working on another project."

"Good," Jack said, pleased. "I like her."

Andrew nodded with a hint of a proud smile. "She wants us to go to the same college."

"You still have the rest of this year, and then your senior year."

"Yeah, I know. That's what I told her. She said, start making plans now, because it will go fast. I don't know, maybe she's a little bossy, but I don't mind so much."

Jack wanted to laugh, but he didn't.

And then John Ferrell and Margie drew up. John was broad and compact, with plenty of salt and pepper hair, a heavy jaw and a thick neck. He was a loud man, with strong opinions and moving hands, ready to make a point and drive it home.

"What a Christmas, Jack. What a dinner. I think it's your best party, although last year was good, too."

Margie was a little overweight, with a round face and a

ready smile. She had a cap of gray hair that put her on the cute side. Her voice was small, her laugh a kind of squeak. "I told John that your house is just a dream house. It reminds me of something out of one of those magazines."

John glanced at her, eyes narrowed. "Do you mean like *Home and Garden,* or *Home Beautiful,* or some damn thing like that?"

"Yes, John. Just like that. It's just so homey."

"That's Alice's touch," Jack said. "Interior design is one of her many talents."

John cocked his head to one side. "Alice told me you stopped that development company flat. Sent them packing with their tails between their legs."

"Yes, for the time being, we've stopped them."

"And ain't it something that they actually found Civil War graves?" John said, with a shake of his head.

"Yes, it is," Jack said. "And it was all because of the diary we found in the basement. The diary that Mrs. Alice Lawson wrote in 1944."

Margie lifted her shoulders and shivered, making a "brrrr" sound. "It gives me goose pimples thinking about it."

Jack continued. "The lead investigator of the Greenwood Archaeological Project said his team found grave shafts, based upon what they saw on ground-penetrating radar."

"Amazing," John said.

"Imagine that," Margie said.

Andrew spoke up. "Yeah, and after Christmas, the excavation team is going to continue looking for even more grave shafts. Then they'll start hand excavation. I definitely want to be there for that."

"The best part," Jack said, "is that they found two

hidden gravestones, and they were able to identify one as Rufus Gains Washington, a sort of local hero and a distant cousin of George Washington. That's what stopped Morningside Development. When the news hit the papers and the internet a few days ago, you should have seen the comments. I couldn't be happier."

Jack nodded toward Mrs. Lawson. "And it's all thanks to that diary. Who would have thought."

When Brianna and Sunshine drifted away from Mrs. Lawson, Alice and Kristie went over. Alice sat in a chair next to her, and Kristie kneeled.

"I'm so glad you came, Mrs. Lawson," Kristie said.

Alice Lawson lowered her eyes, smiling. "I have had a wonderful time. The best day in years. Thank you for inviting me."

Alice Landis reached for Alice Lawson's hand. "And, now that we've found each other, we two Alice Ferrells have to stay in touch and stay together."

"For sure," Kristie said, smiling at Mrs. Lawson. "And do you know what would be even better? Why don't you come and live with us?"

Alice Lawson uttered a laugh of surprise. "Live with you?"

Alice nodded. "Yes. It's a great idea! We'd love to have you live here, Mrs. Lawson. Truly."

Mrs. Lawson smiled affectionately. "You are too kind to me. Now I am not going to cry, so don't ask me again, or I *will* cry. But I have my own little place, with all my old and new things that are dear to me. I'll stay there where I won't be a bother."

"You won't be a bother," Kristie said. "Really, you won't."

Mrs. Lawson looked at Kristie. "But you must come and see me. Will you?"

"Of course," Kristie said. "Mom and I will come and, in the spring, we'll bring you here so you can sit in the gardens. In summer, we'll row a boat on the pond, just like you did long ago in the 1940s."

Alice Lawson removed her glasses and turned her head to hide the tears in her eyes. "Now, *that* I will do, or at least I will watch you two. My legs don't balance the way they used to."

Kristie continued, her voice filled with enthusiasm. "And we'll have picnics and we'll go for walks and celebrate all the holidays together."

Mrs. Lawson rested her eyes tenderly on Kristie. "What a lovely girl you are, Kristie. You have a good heart, a kind heart."

Mrs. Lawson turned to Alice. "And you, Alice... I'm not going to get all sentimental, but I want to say that you have brought me joy and happiness I never thought I'd find again. The truth is, I've been lonely, and I didn't know it until I met you and your wonderful family."

Alice Landis gently squeezed Alice Lawson's hand. "Think about it, Mrs. Lawson... Alice. Think about moving in with us. It's the same house. It's just the same as it was when you wrote your diary, back in 1944."

Mrs. Lawson considered Alice's words, slowly casting her eyes about the room. For a moment, she stared out into remoteness as if she'd traveled to a different time and place. When she spoke, her voice was soft and introspective. "Oh, no, it isn't the same house, Alice. This house is very special. It breathes love, and it holds love within its walls."

Kristie rose and kissed Mrs. Lawson on the cheek.

"Just think about it… Think about living with us."

"You wouldn't be any trouble, cousin," Alice said, smiling.

Mrs. Lawson turned to Alice with surprise. "Cousin?"

"Yes. It seems that Andrew and Brianna did some ancestry research and they learned that you and I are distant cousins."

Kristie clapped her hands together. "That's awesome. We're family."

Alice Lawson chuckled. "Well, what do you know about that? Cousins. How wonderful. Even at my age, life can still keep on surprising me."

Mrs. Lawson pointed toward the Christmas tree. "And speaking of surprises, Kristie, there is a present from me to you. Under the tree, the red one with a white bow. I think you should open it now."

Kristie glanced over.

"Go ahead, you can open it. I have one for your mother and father and brother, too, but let's start with yours first."

Excited, Kristie rushed to the tree, stooped, found the gift and retrieved it. Back at Alice Lawson's chair, Kristie kneeled, holding the present up and shaking it.

"It's not breakable," Mrs. Lawson said. "I think you might like it."

Kristie slipped off the lavish white bow and energetically removed the wrapping. She studied the white box, her eyes opening in anticipation as she sat back on her heels.

Mrs. Lawson nodded and made a gesture with her hand. "Go ahead. Open the box."

Kristie pried off the lid and stared, her eyes expanding with wonder. "Oh, wow!"

Kristie removed it and held it up. It was a handmade,

red leather diary, with a lock and key and a black silk ribbon bookmark. Entranced, Kristie used the key to open it, carefully flipping through the blank pages that featured two kinds of paper, lined white and blank white.

"I love it... I just love it," Kristie said.

Mrs. Lawson folded her hands, pleased. "I thought it appropriate that you begin a brand-new Christmas diary tonight, in the same house where I started mine in December 1944."

The two Alices and Kristie exchanged glances.

"I'm sure you have a lot to write about, don't you, Kristie?" Alice asked.

Kristie's thoughts turned to Taylor. She'd seen him in the hospital the day before and he was recovering quickly, already cracking jokes. She thought of Alice, and Alice Lawson. She thought of her own mother and their time together; she wanted to record all those memories before they faded like a dream. And then there was her father. Writing about him could easily take up half the diary.

Kristie nodded, with an expression of introspective fascination. "Yes... I have a lot I want to write about."

Kristie set the diary aside, sprang up and hugged Alice Lawson's neck. "Thank you. I'll fill every page, just like you did."

When Jack glanced over to see Kristie hugging Mrs. Lawson, he gave Alice a quizzical look, as if to say, "What's that all about?"

Alice reached for Kristie's new diary and held it up for him to see. He nodded with some surprise and a lifted eyebrow. Then he lowered his warm, loving gaze on her as he mouthed the words, "Merry Christmas. I love you."

Alice took in the richly decorated room, filled with

guests, friends and family. All were relaxed and cheerful, and they were having such a good time. She wandered the room under a Christmas spell, filled with gratitude and joy. It was one of those perfectly balanced moments of peace and good will, when all was right with the world. It was the best Christmas of her life.

Thank You!

Thank you for taking the time to read *The Christmas Diary Lost and Found*. If you enjoyed it, please consider telling your friends or posting a short review. Word of mouth is an author's best friend, and it is much appreciated.

Thank you,
Elyse Douglas

Other Novels You Might Enjoy

The Christmas Diary Book 1
Christmas for Juliet
The Christmas Bridge
The Date Before Christmas
The Christmas Women
Christmas Ever After
The Summer Diary
The Summer Letters
The Other Side of Summer
Wanting Rita

Time Travel Novels

The Christmas Eve Letter (A Time Travel Novel) Book 1

The Christmas Eve Daughter (A Time Travel Novel) Book 2

The Christmas Eve Secret (A Time Travel Novel) Book 3

The Christmas Eve Promise (A Time Travel Novel) Book 4

Time Shutter (A Time Travel Romance)
The Lost Mata Hari Ring (A Time Travel Novel)
The Christmas Town (A Time Travel Novel)
Time Change (A Time Travel Novel)
Time Sensitive (A Time Travel Novel)

Romantic Suspense Novels

Daring Summer
Frantic
Betrayed

www.elysedouglas.com

Editorial Reviews

THE LOST MATA HARI RING – A Time Travel Novel by Elyse Douglas

"This book is hard to put down! It is pitch-perfect and hits all the right notes. It is the best book I have read in a while!"

5 Stars!
--Bound4Escape Blog and Reviews

"The characters are well defined, and the scenes easily visualized. It is a poignant, bitter-sweet emotionally charged read."
5-Stars!
--Rockin' Book Reviews

"This book captivated me to the end!"
--StoryBook Reviews

"A captivating adventure..."
--Community Bookstop

"...Putting *The Lost Mata Hari Ring* down for any length of time proved to be impossible."
--Lisa's Writopia

"I found myself drawn into the story and holding my breath to see what would happen next..."
--Blog: A Room Without Books is Empty

Editorial Reviews

THE CHRISTMAS TOWN – A Time Travel Novel
by Elyse Douglas

"The Christmas Town is a beautifully written story. It draws you in from the first page, and fully engages you up until the very last. The story is funny, happy, and magical. The characters are all likable and very well-rounded. This is a great book to read during the holiday season, and a delightful read during any time of the year."
--Bauman Book Reviews

"I would love to see this book become another one of those beloved Christmas film traditions, to be treasured over the years! The characters are loveable; the settings vivid. Period details are believable. A delightful read at any time of year! Don't miss this novel!"
--A Night's Dream of Books

THE SUMMER LETTERS – A Novel
by Elyse Douglas

"A perfect summer read!"
--Fiction Addiction

"In Elyse Douglas' novel THE SUMMER LETTERS, the characters' emotions, their drives, passions and memories are all so expertly woven; we get a taste of what life was like for veterans, women, small town folk, and all those people we think have lived too long to remember (but they never really forget, do they?).
I couldn't stop reading, not for a moment. Such an amazing read. Flawless."
5 Stars!
--Anteria Writes Blog - To Dream, To Write, To Live

"A wonderful, beautiful love story that I absolutely enjoyed reading."
5 Stars!
--Books, Dreams, Life - Blog

"*The Summer Letters* is a fabulous choice for the beach or cottage this year, so you can live and breathe the same feelings and smells as the characters in this wonderful story."
--Reads & Reels Blog